Laurence Sterne

A SENTIMENTAL JOURNEY
AND OTHER WRITINGS

Edited by
TOM KEYMER
Royal Holloway and Bedford New College
University of London

EVERYMAN
J. M. DENT · LONDON
CHARLES E. TUTTLE
VERMONT

Introduction, chronology and critical apparatus © J. M. Dent 1994

A Sentimental Journey through France and Italy first included
in Everyman's Library in 1927

A Sentimental Journey and Other Writings first published
in Everyman in 1994

J. M. Dent
Orion Publishing Group
Orion House, 5 Upper St Martin's Lane,
London WC2H 9EA
and
Charles E. Tuttle Co. Inc.
28 South Main Street,
Rutland, Vermont 05701, USA

Typeset in Sabon by Cambridge Composing (UK)
Printed in Great Britain by
The Guernsey Press Co. Ltd, Guernsey, C.I.

British Library Cataloguing-in-Publication Data
is available upon request.

ISBN 0 460 87336 9

CONTENTS

NOTE ON THE AUTHOR

LAURENCE STERNE was born on 24 November 1713 in Clonmel, Co. Tipperary, where his father's regiment had been posted. He spent an itinerant boyhood in Ireland and England before being sent to Hipperholme School near Halifax in 1723, going on to Jesus College, Cambridge, in 1733. He then embarked on a clerical career in Yorkshire, becoming vicar of Sutton-on-the-Forest in 1738, a prebendary of York Minster in 1741, and vicar of Stillington in 1744. Early publications include *Query upon Query* (1741), two sermons (1747 and 1750), and an unknown quantity of Whiggish polemical writing. In March 1741 he married Elizabeth Lumley, and in 1758 he wrote most of his unpublished *Memoirs* for their sole surviving child Lydia. *A Political Romance* was printed in York but withdrawn from sale in January 1759, and Sterne then began work on a rejected early version of *Tristram Shandy*, probably including the *Fragment*. The first two volumes of his masterpiece *The Life and Opinions of Tristram Shandy, Gentleman* appeared late in 1759, the remaining seven being published at irregular intervals between 1761 and 1767. In 1760 Sterne settled at 'Shandy Hall' as parson of Coxwold, publishing *The Sermons of Mr. Yorick* (1760–6) and juggling his clerical vocation with sentimental liaisons (with Kitty Fourmantel, 1759–60; with Eliza Draper, 1767) and continental tours (to France, 1762–4; to France and Italy, 1765–6). These provided material for *A Sentimental Journey through France and Italy*, published only weeks before the illnesses with which Sterne had struggled for years at last killed him on 18 March 1768. His body was buried at St George's Hanover Square, stolen two nights later, recognised in the anatomy schools at Cambridge, reburied, exhumed during redevelopment of the site two centuries later, and reburied in the churchyard at Coxwold on 8 June 1969.

NOTE ON THE EDITOR

TOM KEYMER read English at Gonville & Caius College, Cambridge, and was later Research Fellow and Quatercentenary Visiting Fellow at Emmanuel College, Cambridge. He is now Lecturer in English at Royal Holloway & Bedford New College, University of London. His recent and forthcoming publications include essays on Fielding, Pope, Smart, and Sterne, and he is the author of *Richardson's 'Clarissa' and the Eighteenth-Century Reader* (Cambridge University Press, 1992).

CHRONOLOGY OF STERNE'S LIFE

Year	Age	Life
1713		Born Clonmel, Ireland (24 Nov.)
1723	9	Sent to school near Halifax
1733	19	Enters Jesus College, Cambridge
1737	23	B.A.; assistant curate of St Ives, Hunts.
1738	24	Assistant curate of Catton, Yorks.; ordination; vicar of Sutton-on-the-Forest
1740	26	M.A.
1741	27	Prebend of Givendale in York Minster; marries Elizabeth Lumley; *Query upon Query* published
1742	28	Prebend of North Newbald
1744	30	Vicar of Stillington
1745	31	Birth and death of first daughter Lydia
1747	33–4	*The Case of Elijah* preached and published; birth of surviving daughter Lydia
1750	36	*The Abuses of Conscience* preached and published
1751	37	Appointed Commissary of the Peculiar Court of Pickering and Pocklington
1756	42	Gains lands from Sutton Enclosure Act
1759	45–6	*Political Romance* printed and withdrawn (Jan.); liaison with Kitty Fourmantel; *Tristram Shandy*, I–II (Dec.)
1760	46	Preferred to curacy of Coxwold; *The Sermons of Mr. Yorick*, I–II
1761	47–8	*Tristram Shandy*, III–IV (Jan.) and V–VI (Dec.)
1762	48	Travels to Paris (Jan.)

CHRONOLOGY OF HIS TIMES

Year	Literary Context	Historical Events
1713	Addison, *Cato*; Pope, *Windsor Forest*	Treaty of Utrecht ends War of Spanish Succession
1723	Mandeville, *Fable of the Bees*, 2nd edn	Black Act; Atterbury exiled
1733	Pope, *Essay on Man* (−1734)	Excise crisis
1737	Fielding, *Historical Register*; Havard, *King Charles the First*	Stage Licensing Act
1738	Johnson, *London*	Third Treaty of Vienna; Herculaneum excavated
1740	Richardson, *Pamela*	War of Austrian Succession breaks out
1741	Fielding, *Shamela*; Hume, *Essays Moral and Political* (−1742)	Cartagena expedition
1742	Fielding, *Joseph Andrews*; Pope, *New Dunciad*	Walpole resigns
1744	S. Fielding, *David Simple* (−1753)	Broad-Bottom ministry; invasion scares
1745	Fielding, *True Patriot* (−1746)	Jacobite rising
1747	Richardson, *Clarissa* (−1748)	Execution of Lord Lovat
1750	Johnson, *Rambler* (−1752)	London earthquake
1751	Fielding, *Amelia*; Richardson, *Clarissa* (revised edn)	Diderot and d'Alembert begin publishing *Encyclopédie* (−1780)
1756	Burke, *Vindication of Natural Society*; Home, *Douglas*	Seven Years War breaks out; 'Black Hole of Calcutta'
1759	Johnson, *Rasselas*; Smith, *Theory of Moral Sentiments*	'Year of Victories' (Guadeloupe, Minden, Quebec, etc.); British Museum opens
1760	Smollett, *Sir Launcelot Greaves* (−1761)	Accession of George III
1761	F. Sheridan, *Sidney Bidulph*	Bridgewater Canal completed
1762	Macpherson, *Fingal*	Bute ministry

Year	Age	Life
1763	49–50	In Toulouse and Montpellier with wife and daughter
1764	50	Returns to England (May)
1765	51	*Tristram Shandy*, VII–VIII (Jan.); travels to France and Italy (Oct.)
1766	52	*The Sermons of Mr. Yorick*, III–IV (Jan.); returns to England (June)
1767	53	*Tristram Shandy*, IX (Jan.); liaison with Eliza Draper
1768	54	*Sentimental Journey*, I–II (Feb.); death (18 March)
1769		*Sermons by the Late Rev. Mr. Sterne*, V–VI
1773		*Letters from Yorick to Eliza*; death of Elizabeth Sterne
1775		*Letters of the Late Rev. Mr. Laurence Sterne* (including *Memoirs, Impromptu, Fragment*)

Year	Literary Context	Historical Events
1763	Smart, *Song to David*; Wilkes, *North Briton* No. 45	Treaty of Paris ends Seven Years War
1764	Walpole, *Castle of Otranto*	Wilkes expelled from Commons
1765	Percy, *Reliques of Ancient English Poetry*	Rockingham ministry; Stamp Act
1766	Brooke, *Fool of Quality* (–1770); Goldsmith, *Vicar of Wakefield*; Smollett, *Travels through France and Italy*	Bread riots; death of James III; work begins on Grand Trunk Canal
1767	Ferguson, *History of Civil Society*	Townshend duties on tea, etc.
1768	Goldsmith, *Good-Natur'd Man*	Royal Academy founded
1769	Shakespeare Jubilee at Stratford	Wedgwood's Etruria factory opens
1773	Goldsmith, *She Stoops To Conquer*	'Boston Tea Party'
1775	R. B. Sheridan, *The Rivals*; Johnson, *Journey to the Western Islands, Taxation No Tyranny*	Battles of Lexington, Concord, Bunker Hill

INTRODUCTION

I

'*Sentimental*! what is that? It is not English; he might as well say *Continental*.' Thus John Wesley, leading Methodist and dismissive reader of *A Sentimental Journey*, in 1772. To Wesley's mind, 'no determinate idea' was conveyed by 'this nonsensical word'. He meant no compliment when he added: 'However, the book agrees full well with the title, for one is as queer as the other.'

So what is it, or what was it, to be sentimental? The word is first recorded less than twenty years before the publication of Sterne's novel, and only then in a reference to its indeterminate meaning. Writing in 1749, Lady Bradshaigh asks the novelist Samuel Richardson:

> what, in your opinion, is the meaning of the word *sentimental*, so much in vogue amongst the polite, both in town and country? I have asked several who make use of it, and have generally received for answer, it is – it is – *sentimental*. Every thing clever and agreeable is comprehended in that word . . . I am frequently astonished to hear such a one is a *sentimental* man; we were a *sentimental* party; I have been taking a *sentimental* walk.

Richardson's reply is lost, but it is clear that for him the word was more than a voguish inanity. It meant more, too, than simply 'exhibiting refined and elevated feeling' or the more pejorative 'addicted to indulgence in superficial emotion' (*OED*). When Richardson later described atheists as '*sentimental* Unbelievers', and when he called his didactic manual of 1755 *A Collection of . . . Moral and Instructive Sentiments*, he gave the term a pitch that involved the mind as well as the heart. A sentiment was a mental feeling, a felt thought: sentimental writing thus brought together both intellect and emotion, a point to which Samuel Johnson referred when insisting, famously, that one must read Richardson's novels 'for the sentiment, and consider the story as only giving occasion to the sentiment'. As Johnson saw, fiction of this kind not only fostered imaginative sympathy for distressed virtue but also involved the reader in a rigorous programme of instruction. It thus enlisted both heart and mind in its project of moral reform. For Adam Smith, whose *Theory of Moral Sentiments* (1759) identified sympathy as fundamental to moral and social life, Richardson and his followers were for this reason 'much better instructors' than the most eminent Stoic philosophers.

Sentimental writing did not always have such rigour, however. The following years produced a mass of emptily lachrymose fiction, of which Henry Brooke's *Fool of Quality* (1766–70), Oliver Goldsmith's *Vicar of Wakefield* (1766) and Henry Mackenzie's *Man of Feeling* (1771) mark only the most readable tip. Looking back on the period, Sir Leslie Stephen defined sentimentalism as 'the mood in which we make a luxury of grief', and few of these texts do much to repel his allegation of self-indulgence. Celebrating a virtue that resides above all in the capacity to feel, they confront the mawkish sensibilities of their heroes with scene after scene of poignant yet decorous distress. Applauding such responses as that of a character in Thomas Bridges's *Adventures of a Bank-Note* (1770–1), whose 'tears cours'd . . . down his manly cheeks, and formed a rapid current o'er his garments', they also invite their tender readers to add to the deluge themselves. Tears became an end in themselves, occasions of casual pleasure. Ostentatious sensibility could even become a polite accomplishment. 'Sophy Streatfield is never happier than when the tears trickle from her fine eyes in company', it is reported in Frances Burney's diary for 1779. Burney herself could weep when occasion demanded, 'but I must know', she insists, 'what for'.

2

Sterne's sentimental turn came late in life and at the height of his reputation. When the earliest text included in this volume (the *Memoirs*) was begun in 1758, he was a relatively obscure Yorkshire cleric. The concluding third of the *Memoirs*, by contrast, is the work of an international celebrity, written as it was in the last year of Sterne's life. Fame had come with the first instalment of *Tristram Shandy*, published in York in December 1759 and on sale in London the following month. The novel did not come out of the blue, however, for its techniques of comedy, bawdry and satire had already been tested in two preliminary texts (one unpublished in Sterne's lifetime, the other hastily withdrawn from sale), both of which are reprinted here.

A Political Romance was first printed in January 1759. Its mischievous allegory reduces the intricate ecclesiastical politics and pamphlet skirmishes of Sterne's own diocese to the scale of a rural parish, in which the Archbishop becomes a parson, the Dean his clerk, and Dr Francis Topham (an ambitious church lawyer and controversialist) the lowly sexton Trim. The plot concerns a struggle for several preferments, represented in terms of cast-off clothes, and Sterne himself has a minor role as Lorry Slim. Though quite literally parochial, *A Political Romance* remains a brilliant burlesque, and it shows a clear link between Scriblerian satire (particularly as developed by Swift in *A Tale of a Tub*) and the witty literary excess and interpretative play that was to follow in *Tristram Shandy*. The work's history is succinctly recorded in the *St James Chronicle* of 1788, supposedly in the words of an anonymous friend of Sterne's:

> a squabble breaking out at York, about opening a patent and putting in a new life, he sided with the Dean and his friends, and tried to throw the laugh on the other party, by writing The History of an Old Watchcoat; but the affair being compromised, he was desired not to publish it. About 500 copies were printed off, and all committed to the flames but three or four, he said; one of which I read, and, having some little knowledge of his *Dramatis Personae*, was highly entertained by seeing them in the light he had put them. This was a real disappointment to him; he felt it, and it was to this disappointment that the world is indebted for Tristram Shandy. For till he had finished his Watchcoat, he says, he hardly knew that he could write at all, much less with humour, so as to make his reader laugh.

A Political Romance, however, shows only hints of the hectic bawdry that made witnesses as diverse as the English bishop William Warburton and the French *philosophe* Denis Diderot react to *Tristram Shandy* by announcing Sterne 'the English Rabelais'. For this we must turn to a document first published after Sterne's death by his daughter Lydia under the title *A*

Fragment in the Manner of Rabelais. A ribald satire on learning, sermonizing and plagiarism that looks forward to the comparable concerns of *Tristram Shandy*, it was probably written shortly after *A Political Romance*, and it seems to mark an abortive early stage in the Shandy project. Where *A Political Romance* had been suppressed, however, the *Fragment* was unprintable from the start. By the time it appeared in 1775, it had been through two stages of bowdlerization. The first was by Sterne himself, who removed an obscene pun on the name of Dr John Rogers, the divine whose sermons are plagiarized when 'HOMENAS who had to preach next Sunday . . . was all this while Rogering it as hard as He could drive in the very next Room'. By the time his daughter had finished with the manuscript, its excremental tone had been expunged: a trace survives when '*broke his Neck, and fractured his Skull and beshit himself into the Bargain, by a fall from the Pulpit*' is changed to read '*befouled*'.

Also posthumously published in 1775 was *An Impromptu*, a work that has been tentatively dated to 1761 by Sterne's modern biographer Arthur Cash. A punning excursus said to have been written by Sterne 'after he had been thoroughly *soused* . . . in a few moments without stopping his pen', it treats (like *A Political Romance*, though with different implications) the ownership of a coat. Its thread of allusions concludes with a *risqué* glance at the erotic imagery of Rochester's 'Dialogue between Strephon and Daphne' in which the writer 'never can say *sub Jove* (whatever Juno might) that "it is a pleasure to *be wet*"'.

3

The Life and Opinions of Tristram Shandy, Gentleman (1759–67) brought instant fame – fame that Sterne cultivated with whimsical relish, appearing in London society as Tristram in person and in Paris as the Chevalier de Shandy. 'At present nothing is talked of, nothing admired, but . . . *Tristram Shandy*', wrote Horace Walpole in 1760, 'the great humour of which consists in the whole narration always going backwards'. Published in five large instalments, unevenly spread over the following seven years, the novel sustains a witty fiction of frustrated autobiographical effort. Vainly attempting to subject his life and opinions to narrative order, Tristram perpetually sees his writing sprawl out of control. At first he hopes to turn his trouble to advantage, resolving 'to go on leisurely, writing and publishing two volumes of my life every year; — which, if I am suffered to go on quietly, and can make a tolerable bargain with my bookseller, I shall continue to do as long as I live'. He even proposes to keep the project going 'these forty years, if it pleases the fountain of health to bless me so long with life and good spirits'. One year and several volumes into the work, however, and no further forward than his first day of life, Tristram begins to see the hopelessness of his task, computing 'that I have three hundred and sixty-four days more life to write just now, than when I first set out; so that instead of advancing, as a common writer, in my work with what I have been doing at it – on the contrary, I am just thrown so many volumes back – '. Death, moreover, is in chase. The 1761 volumes end with a promise to resume in a year's time, 'unless this vile cough kills me in the mean time'. By 1765 there is unmistakable desperation in his resolve to defy death with 'two volumes every year, provided the vile cough which then tormented me, and which to this hour I dread worse than the devil, would but give me leave . . . for I have forty volumes to write, and forty thousand things to say and do, which no body in the world will say and do for me, except thyself; and as thou seest he has got me by the throat'. Before the abrupt close of the solitary volume that appeared in 1767, defeat is acknowledged in Tristram's lament that 'Time wastes too fast: every letter I trace tells me with what rapidity Life follows my pen'. No more was written, and it remains a matter of debate whether the nine-volume work that was then left had been completed or involuntarily curtailed. What is certain is that Laurence Sterne had a cough of his own ('this vile influenza', as he told his daughter), and he died the following year.

4

There is some evidence that Sterne, and perhaps also the reading public, had simply tired of *Tristram Shandy*. It is certain that, as the project wore on, he was looking in new directions. Volume VII (1765) is an oddly autonomous digression in which Tristram takes a continental (and incipiently sentimental) tour, pursued by his own mortality, 'that death-looking, long-striding scoundrel of a scare-sinner, who is posting after me'. Writing to his banker in Paris, Sterne called the volume 'as odd a Tour thro' france, as ever was projected or executed by traveller or travell Writer, since the world began – '.

It is not only this part of *Tristram Shandy*, however, that looks forward to *A Sentimental Journey*. As early as the first instalment, Sterne had been fashioning for himself a second *alter ego* by bringing into the novel one Parson Yorick, whose name scandalously combines (as Sterne did himself) the roles of cleric and jester. In 1760, taking advantage of the Shandean vogue, he even published his own sermons under the title *The Sermons of Mr Yorick*, a whimsical gesture that drew on his head the pious wrath of reviewers. 'But are the solemn dictates of religion fit to be conveyed from the mouths of Buffoons and ludicrous Romancers?', fulminated one. 'Would any man believe that a Preacher was in earnest, who should mount the pulpit in a *Harlequin's coat*?' Despite such attacks, Yorick steadily gained ground on Tristram as Sterne's favourite self – a pliant identity always on hand to be entered or left at will. It is in this person that he pursued in 1767 his notorious sentimental liaison with Mrs Daniel Draper, addressing to her an epistolary manuscript 'wrote under the fictitious Names of Yorick & Draper' and first published in 1904 as his *Journal to Eliza*.

Eccentric tourism and Parson Yorick, then, are elements of *A Sentimental Journey* that had already been tested by Sterne. More significant still is the growing strain of sentiment that runs through *Tristram Shandy*. As early as 1762, the *Monthly Review* had singled out the Le Fever episode of volume VI for special praise, declaring that 'Since Mr. Sterne published his Sermons, we have been of opinion, that his excellence lay not so much in the humorous as in the pathetic'. By 1765, the same journal was advising that the public had tired of *Tristram Shandy*, which should be curtailed. Sterne should 'strike out a new plan' instead:

> Paint Nature in her loveliest dress – her native simplicity. Draw
> natural scenes, and interesting situations – In fine, Mr. Shandy, do,
> for surely you can, excite our passions to *laudable* purposes – awake
> our affections, engage our hearts – arouze, transport, refine, improve
> us. Let morality, let the cultivation of virtue be your aim – let wit,

humour, elegance and pathos be the means; and the grateful applause of mankind will be your reward.

Sterne himself had a keen interest in more material kinds of reward, but he was thinking on similar lines. Writing what was to prove the final volume of *Tristram Shandy* in 1766, he told one correspondent that he would suspend (though not, at this point, decisively terminate) the project, and instead 'begin a new work of four volumes, which when finish'd, I shall continue Tristram with fresh spirit'. He even seems to have incorporated in this final volume a trailer for the new work. Interrupting the main action, chapter xxiv returns to Tristram's tour through France to recollect his meeting on the road with an abandoned beauty, Maria. Though smitten by her picturesque distress, Tristram is too much concerned with his journey and the next inn to stay long, but he tantalizingly addresses to Maria his hope that 'some time . . . I may hear thy sorrows from thy own lips'. It was a hope that Yorick would fulfil.

5

Sterne's letters of 1767 describe the growth of the new work. Not uncharacteristically, his first priority was to ensure a healthy advance subscription. In February he writes with enthusiasm that the work 'will bring me a thousand guineas (au moins) – twil be an Original – in large Quarto – the Subscription half a Guinea – '. And this before writing had started, for a few days later he tells his daughter: 'I shall not begin my Sentimental Journey till I get to Coxwould – I have laid a plan for something new, quite out of the beaten track.' Like Yorick, however, Sterne seems thereafter to harmonize the rigour of his accountancy with the softer tones of a painfully responsive heart. In September he tells one reader, with showy self-approval: 'my Sentimental Journey will, I dare say, convince you that my feelings are from the heart, and that that heart is not of the worst of molds – praised be God for my sensibility ! Though it has often made me wretched, yet I would not exchange it for all the pleasures the grossest sensualist ever felt.' In November he informs another that the new work 'suits the frame of mind I have been in for some time past – I told you my design in it was to teach

us to love the world and our fellow creatures better than we do
– so it runs most upon those gentler passions and affections,
which aid so much to it'. Later in the same month, he thanks an
unknown peer

> for your letter of enquiry about Yorick – he has worn out both his
> spirits and body with the Sentimental Journey – 'tis true that an
> author must feel himself, or his reader will not – but I have torn my
> whole frame into pieces by my feelings – . . . I have long been a
> sentimental being – whatever your Lordship may think to the
> contrary. – The world has imagined, because I wrote Tristram
> Shandy, that I was myself more Shandean than I really ever was –
> 'tis a good-natured world we live in, and we are often painted
> in divers colours according to the ideas each one frames in his
> head. –

Evidently enough, the colours Sterne now wished to show the
world, or a large part of it, were those not of Tristram but of
Yorick. Characterized by a chaste and moral sensibility, *A
Sentimental Journey* would at last negate his dubious reputation
as dealer in bawdry and farce.

6

Yet is Sterne's sentimentalism so pure and simple ? On inspection, the text itself might well be thought to collapse the
distinctions between sensibility and sensuality, between the
sentimental and the Shandean, that is emphasized in these
letters. Yorick's effusive sympathies are too often on the edge of
lust ; his words and deeds are too often complicated by clever
innuendo ; he is too connoisseurly, too self-absorbed, too much
enraptured by distress for it not to seem that his sentiment is
being mocked. Henry Mackenzie, author of the impeccably
sentimental *Man of Feeling*, objected to just this combination of
'licentiousness' and 'buffoonery' in the novel, complaining that
as Sterne writes 'the fool's coat is half upon him'. To another
early critic, Vicesimus Knox, Sterne had done no more than veil
his usual grossness : 'the poison he conveys is subtle, and the
more dangerous as it is palatable.' In an excoriating tract 'On
the Moral Tendency of the Writings of Sterne', Knox added :

> That softness, that affected and excessive sympathy at first sight, that
> sentimental affection, which is but lust in disguise, and which is so

strongly inspired by the Sentimental Journey and by Tristram Shandy, have been the ruin of thousands of our countrymen and countrywomen, who fancied that, while they were breaking the laws of God and man, they were actuated by the fine feelings of sentimental affection. How much are divorces multiplied since Sterne appeared!

What seems not to have occurred to Knox is the possibility that Sterne may well have meant to present sentimental affection in just this questionable light, poking fun at the vogue of feeling even as he participated in it, and wittily stressing the closeness of what in *Tristram Shandy* he calls 'the *extreams* of DELICACY, and the *beginnings* of CONCUPISCENCE'. Only more recently has it been suggested that Yorick is less a personal ideal than a satirical butt, a figure of fun through whom Sterne alleges the self-congratulatory feeling of the sentimental tourist to be shallow, self-indulgent, exploitative of the distress on which it dwells. One might even find in the novel some more subtle anticipation of Thomas Rowlandson's cartoon 'The Man of Feeling', in which a slavering parson takes feeling to the literal point of groping a buxom peasant: sentiment is here wittily satirized, redefined not as sympathetic altruism but as mere self-gratification of the greediest kind.

Sterne nowhere speaks directly of *A Sentimental Journey* as satire, although he does use the word to describe the French expedition of *Tristram Shandy*, 'a laughing good temperd Satyr against Traveling'. In several letters, moreover, the voice of Yorick is conspicuously dropped, and the availability of more than simply a sentimental response to the *Journey* is suggested: in one notable case, Sterne even tells an unidentified reader that 'my Journey . . . shall make you cry as much as ever it made me laugh'. It is as though the book might be consumed in different ways by different categories of reader: the naive may read it as pure feeling, productive simply of tears; the sophisticated may read it as pure irony, productive rather of laughter. And that perhaps is what Sterne means when he assures his bookseller Thomas Becket that *A Sentimental Journey* is 'an Original work, and likely to take in all Kinds of Readers – the proof of the pudding is in the eating'. It will take in all readers not in the sense of deceiving or fooling them all (though it may indeed be read as an elaborate hoax passed off on the sentimental). Rather, it will take in all by catering for all, by providing for the devotees of sentiment and for the aficionados of satire a text that might simultaneously be read in contrary ways.

7

Good examples of this ambiguous mingling of sentiment and satire come with the Maria episode in *A Sentimental Journey* and its precursor in *Tristram Shandy*. For the editor of a sentimental compilation called *The Beauties of Sterne ... Selected for the Heart of Sensibility* (1782), these were among his most exquisitely lachrymose passages – passages so painful, indeed, that they threatened to 'wound the bosom of *sensibility* too deeply'. Images of Maria disseminated from the hands of such artists as Angelica Kauffmann and Joseph Wright made her a veritable icon of sentimental distress. A sixpenny pamphlet called *Sterne's Maria; A Pathetic Story* stitched together the two episodes and added for 'the inquisitive reader' a spurious continuation of her story and 'an Account of her Death, at the Castle of Valerine'.

One need only recall the mournful fortitude of Maria's words '*God tempers the wind* ... to the shorn lamb' (a speech that hauntingly renders a French proverb first recorded in 1593) to see with what skill Sterne solicits these kinds of interest. Yet the pathos of the Maria scenes is by no means without complication. She first appears when Tristram finds 'Poor Maria ... sitting upon a bank ... with her little goat beside her'. The scene of course is one of distress; yet it is set into that part of *Tristram Shandy* that is most rich in innuendo, the final book's suggestive account of Uncle Toby's amours. Nor is it sealed off from that context; quite the reverse.

> —For my uncle Toby's amours running all the way in my head, they had the same effect upon me as if they had been my own—I was in the most perfect state of bounty and good will; and felt the kindliest harmony vibrating within me, with every oscillation of the chaise alike; so that whether the roads were rough or smooth, it made no difference; every thing I saw, or had to do with, touch'd upon some secret spring either of sentiment or rapture.

Characteristically, the vibrations, oscillations and secret springs of this passage confuse sentimental and physical pleasure; and

the vaguely carnal overtones of Tristram's rapture here herald
the warmth with which he then involves himself in Maria's
exquisite woe. When Maria looks wistfully 'at me, and then at
her goat — and then at me — and then at her goat again, and so
on, alternately', the implied comparison with a traditional
emblem of lust is not to Tristram's advantage. Shortly afterwards, he seems guilty of obvious insouciance when, having
gratified his passing taste for the melancholy, he promptly then
forgets it.

> Adieu, Maria! — adieu, poor hapless damsel! — some time, but not
> *now*, I may hear thy sorrows from thy own lips — but I was deceived;
> for that moment she took her pipe and told me such a tale of woe
> with it, that I rose up, and with broken and irregular steps walk'd
> softly to my chaise.
> — What an excellent inn at Moulins!

It has often been noted what trouble this concluding sentence
caused for sentimental readers. The *Monthly Review* thought it
'an ill-tim'd stroke of levity; like a ludicrous epilogue, or
ridiculous farce, unnaturally tagged to the end of a deep
tragedy'. *The Beauties of Sterne* tactfully cut not only these
offending words but also Tristram's vibrating harmony in the
chaise. As its editor had argued, such selection was 'highly
necessary' in order to free Sterne's beauties from the levity and
grossness around them: 'his *Sentimental Journey*, in some
degree, escaped the general censure', he notes; 'though that is
not entirely free of the fault complained of.'

Nor is it. Here too sentiment is practised and parodied,
indulged and undermined; and again Maria is the perfect
example. Retracing Tristram's steps, Yorick finds that now her
plight has worsened:

> Her goat had been as faithless as her lover; and she had got a little
> dog in lieu of him, which she had kept tied by a string to her girdle;
> as I look'd at her dog, she drew him towards her with the string. —
> 'Thou shalt not leave me, Sylvio,' said she.

Maria could hardly have been brought lower, not only by the
companions who abandon her but also by the novelist who
depicts her plight. There is an almost mocking brutality in the
way Sterne now piles on yet further grief, while making its
source so laughably trivial. There is the goat again, now as false

as the lover; there is the absurdity of the lapdog's pastoral name, and the wittily casual manner of its introduction. With such details, the sentimental tableau is delicately subverted. And the effect of bathos is compounded further by the Shandean innuendoes that follow, and by the way distress seems eventually to be no more for Yorick than a source of self-regarding pleasure.

> I sat down close by her; and Maria let me wipe [her tears] away as they fell with my handkerchief. – I then steep'd it in my own – and then in hers – and then in mine – and then I wip'd hers again – and as I did it, I felt such undescribable emotions within me, as I am sure could not be accounted for from any combinations of matter and motion.
>
> I am positive I have a soul; nor can all the books with which materialists have pester'd the world ever convince me of the contrary.

Leaving aside the double-entendres and climactic rhythms (hinting perhaps at Yorick's distracted thoughts of some less polite transaction), it is hard to miss Sterne's implication in this passage. Yorick is shopping for sentimental pleasure, for erotic titillation, and in the end for some comfortable affirmation of his own benevolence and immortality. 'I am positive I have a soul': it is this, not Maria, that interests him.

8

A Sentimental Journey thus intensifies *Tristram Shandy*'s troublesome combination of effusive sentiment and undermining ironies. There is more than this, however, to the satirical edge that Sterne gives to his second Maria scene, for as well as parodying the attitudes of leisured sensibility, he also seems to parody a specific text.

Andrew Marvell's 'Nymph Complaining for the Death of Her Faun' is no blandly sentimental effusion, of course: beneath the inarticulate and uncomprehending grief of the nymph herself, the poem is shot through with complex layers of mythical, religious and political implication. Its surface, however, is simple enough. In her complaint, the nymph's pain at the loss of her 'unconstant' lover is renewed by the 'ungentle' troopers who have now killed the faun with which she had consoled herself. The faun had been her lover's gift, and she remembers how

> Unconstant *Sylvio*, when yet
> I had not found him counterfeit,
> One morning (I remember well)
> Ty'd in this silver Chain and Bell,
> Gave it to me.

Sylvio's abandonment of her then raises in her mind a fear that even the faun might do the same :

> Had it liv'd long, I do not know
> Whether it too might have done so
> As *Sylvio* did : his Gifts might be
> Perhaps as false or more than he.

In this context, Sterne's Maria takes on new interest. Abandoned by her goat, and clinging obsessively to her lapdog Sylvio, she suffers a comic intensification of the nymph's misfortune. The nymph's fear that her lover's gift might be 'Perhaps as false or more than he' has in her own case been demeaningly fulfilled : 'Her goat had been as faithless as her lover.' Bathos is deepened by her neurotic response of tying the dog, not in the nymph's 'silver Chain and Bell', but 'by a string to her girdle' ; as it is in the first place by Sterne's replacement of the pastoral faun by a goat, banal and grotesque in connotation. It hardly raises the tone that the name Sylvio is now attached not to a swain but to a dog ; and it is with this name, so exquisitely placed, that Sterne most plainly signals his allusion. Once we see it, it becomes hard to think of Maria as simply an instance of picturesque distress, or even as the object of some mildly improper rapture. She becomes instead an instance of parody, an ironically debased version of the grieving nymph. Her predicament mocks, if not Marvell's poem directly, then certainly a particular way in which the poem may well have been read.

9

It is a favourite trick of Sterne's to embed in his writing jokes available only to his more learned readers. *Tristram Shandy*'s diatribe against plagiarism can be seen in its full irony only by the reader who recognizes that the passage is itself substantially plagiarized (from Burton's *Anatomy of Melancholy*). In the case of Maria, the chances of an eighteenth-century reader catching

the Marvell allusion were smaller still, yet measurable nonethe-
less. Although Marvell's poetry did not always enjoy its modern
reputation, it was occasionally printed: 'The Nymph Complaining' appears in the *Miscellaneous Poems* of 1681, the 1726
edition of Marvell's *Works* (reprinted in 1772), and the lavish
*Works of Andrew Marvell, Esq., Poetical, Controversial, and
Political* (1776). This marked revival of interest in the 1770s
came too late to have touched a novel of 1768, of course, but
the 1776 edition marked only the culmination of a protracted
process. Throughout the 1760s, Marvell's writing, including his
poetry, had found a formidable champion in Thomas Hollis, a
maverick philanthropist memorably described by James Boswell
as 'the strenuous Whig, who used to send over Europe presents
of democratical books, with their boards stamped with daggers
and caps of liberty'. According to Francis Blackburne's *Memoirs
of Thomas Hollis, Esq.* (1780), Hollis's passion for Marvell
went back at least to 1760, when he procured through the pages
of the *York Courant* a portrait of Marvell, distributing copies
'to his friends and fellow-patriots; and to some, perhaps, who
were neither'. In 1765 Hollis held discussions with the printer
William Bowyer 'relating to a new edition of Andrew Marvell's
works'. By 1767 he was at work on Millar and Cadell. He died
with his ambition unfulfilled, but the grand edition of 1776 was
clearly indebted to his efforts. Its editor reports that Hollis 'had
once a design of making a collection of his compositions, and
advertisements were published for that purpose by the late
Andrew Millar'. He himself had worked from the manuscripts
and scarce tracts that Hollis had gathered.

It is clear that Marvell had his admirers, then, not only in the
1770s but also in the years before *A Sentimental Journey*. It is
clear, moreover, that Sterne knew these admirers well. He
became friendly with Hollis (a subscriber to the *Sermons* of
1760) early in the decade. The two first met in 1761, according
to Hollis's manuscript diary, and a second entry proudly records
'the Rev. Mr Sterne (Tristram Shandy) with me in the morning'.
Whether their acquaintance was close or lasting is not clear, but
Sterne certainly was close to Hollis's biographer Francis Blackburne, a senior churchman in Yorkshire and himself a careful
follower of the Marvell project. An interest in Marvell, moreover, was keenly enough shared by other members of Sterne's
circle for several of his literary friends to have subscribed (to the

considerable tune of three guineas) to the 1776 edition. The subscription list includes such names as Samuel Foote, David Garrick, 'John Wilkes, Esq. M.P.', 'Rev. Mr. Mason, Prebendary of York', all close to Sterne (though Mason was no friend). Most interesting of all is the inclusion of 'John Stevenson Hall, Esq.', Sterne's most intimate friend and man immortalized as the Eugenius of the novels.

It is hard not to conclude, for all Marvell's obscurity in the eighteenth century, that Sterne knew the poem in question, and knew some of his readers would know it. His wry allusion to its words leaves a telling example of the way in which *A Sentimental Journey* does indeed 'take in all Kinds of Readers'. Clearly this key episode, like the novel as a whole, was for many a straightforward case of feeling. But for a few at least of Sterne's more learned and witty friends, it must have been something more. The proof of the pudding is in the eating, as Sterne had told his bookseller, and he could not have been more assiduous in catering for differing palates and tastes. In the very act of celebrating feeling he also mocks it, and in writing the widely acknowledged masterpiece of the sentimental vogue he also writes its subtlest and most wounding critique.

10

Boswell reports an amiably brutal exchange that passed between Samuel Johnson and Mary Monckton in 1781:

Her vivacity enchanted the Sage, and they used to talk together with all imaginable ease. A singular instance happened one evening, when she insisted that some of Sterne's writings were very pathetick. Johnson bluntly denied it. 'I am sure (said she) they have affected *me*.' — 'Why (said Johnson, smiling, and rolling himself about,) that is, because, dearest, you're a dunce.'

TOM KEYMER

NOTE ON THE TEXTS

This edition is based on the first published text of each work. *A Sentimental Journey* is transcribed from the imperial-paper copy of the first edition (published 27 February 1768) in the Oates Collection, Cambridge University Library. The copy has the bookplate of Sterne's friend George Thornhill, whose name appears in the list of subscribers. This list is omitted here, but Sterne's notice to subscribers, tipped into the Thornhill copy between pages iv and v, is reprinted. A few obvious misprints have been silently corrected with reference to the second edition of 29 March 1768 and to the manuscript sources recorded in Gardner D. Stout's fine edition of the novel (Berkeley and Los Angeles : University of California Press, 1967). Full stops within chapter-titles have been dropped, but in the text itself every effort has been made to stay true to the abrupt and idiosyncratic habits of punctuation which in Sterne's writing are so important an expressive device.

A Political Romance is reprinted from the first edition of 1759, which survives in only a handful of copies. The York Minster copy has been reproduced in facsimile with an introduction by Kenneth Monkman (Menston : Scolar Press, 1971).

The *Memoirs*, the *Impromptu* and the *Fragment* were first published after Sterne's death in *Letters of the Late Rev. Mr. Laurence Sterne, to His Most Intimate Friends. With a Fragment in the Manner of Rabelais. To Which Are Prefix'd, Memoirs of His Life and Family. Written by Himself. And Published by His Daughter, Mrs. Medalle* (1775). This text is reprinted here, subject to the correction of a few minor misprints. Its source for the *Impromptu* was an imperfect transcription of Sterne's original (which is lost). In the remaining cases, Sterne's rough drafts were freely shaped into printable form, their prose regularized and (in the case of the *Fragment*) partly bowdlerized. Sterne's working papers for the *Fragment* (now in the Pierpont Morgan Library, New York) are transcribed, with invaluable commen-

tary and notes, by Melvyn New, 'Sterne's Rabelaisian Fragment:
A Text from the Holograph Manuscript', *PMLA*, 87 (1972),
1083–92. The survivng manuscript of the *Memoirs* (an unrev-
ised draft of its opening two-thirds) is reproduced, again with
invaluable commentary and notes, by Kenneth Monkman,
*Sterne's Memoirs: A Hitherto Unrecorded Holograph Now
Brought to Light in Facsimile* (Coxwold: Laurence Sterne Trust,
1985).

A

SENTIMENTAL JOURNEY

THROUGH

FRANCE AND ITALY.

BY

Mr. YORICK.

VOL. I.

LONDON:

Printed for T. Becket and P. A. De Hondt,
in the Strand. MDCCLXVIII.

ADVERTISEMENT

The Author begs leave to acknowledge to his Subscribers, that they have a further claim upon him for Two Volumes more than these delivered to them now,* and which nothing but ill health could have prevented him, from having ready along with thesé.

The Work will be compleated and delivered to the Subscribers early the next Winter.

A
SENTIMENTAL JOURNEY,
&c. &c.

— They order, said I, this matter* better in France —

— You have been in France? said my gentleman, turning quick upon me with the most civil triumph in the world. —

Strange! quoth I, debating the matter with myself, That one and twenty miles sailing, for 'tis absolutely no further from Dover to Calais, should give a man these rights — I'll look into them: so giving up the argument — I went straight to my lodgings, put up half a dozen shirts and a black pair of silk breeches — "the coat I have on, said I, looking at the sleeve, will do" — took a place in the Dover stage; and the packet sailing at nine the next morning — by three I had got sat down to my dinner upon a fricassee'd chicken so incontestably in France, that had I died that night of an indigestion, the whole world could not have suspended the effects of the [1]*Droits d'aubaine* — my shirts, and black pair of silk breeches — portmanteau and all must have gone to the King of France — even the little picture which I have so long worn, and so often have told thee, Eliza,* I would carry with me into my grave, would have been torn from my neck. — Ungenerous! — to seize upon the wreck of an unwary passenger, whom your subjects had beckon'd to their coast — by heaven! SIRE, it is not well done; and much does it grieve me, 'tis the monarch of a people so civilized and courteous, and so renown'd for sentiment and fine feelings, that I have to reason with —

But I have scarce set foot in your dominions —

CALAIS

When I had finish'd my dinner, and drank the King of France's health, to satisfy my mind that I bore him no spleen, but, on the contrary, high honour for the humanity of his temper — I rose up an inch taller for the accommodation.

---

[1] All the effects of strangers (Swiss and Scotch excepted) dying in France, are seized by virtue of this law, tho' the heir be upon the spot — the profit of these contingencies being farm'd, there is no redress.*

– No – said I – the Bourbon is by no means a cruel race : they may be misled like other people ; but there is a mildness in their blood. As I acknowledged this, I felt a suffusion of a finer kind upon my cheek – more warm and friendly to man, than what Burgundy (at least of two livres a bottle, which was such as I had been drinking) could have produced.

– Just God ! said I, kicking my portmanteau aside, what is there in this world's goods which should sharpen our spirits, and make so many kind-hearted brethren of us, fall out so cruelly as we do by the way ?

When man is at peace with man, how much lighter than a feather is the heaviest of metals in his hand ! he pulls out his purse, and holding it airily and uncompress'd, looks round him, as if he sought for an object to share it with – In doing this, I felt every vessel in my frame dilate – the arteries beat all chearily together, and every power which sustained life, perform'd it with so little friction, that 'twould have confounded the most *physical precieuse** in France : with all her materialism, she could scarce have called me a machine –

I'm confident, said I to myself, I should have overset her creed.

The accession of that idea, carried nature, at that time, as high as she could go – I was at peace with the world before, and this finish'd the treaty with myself –

– Now, was I a King of France, cried I – what a moment for an orphan to have begg'd his father's portmanteau of me !

THE MONK
CALAIS

I had scarce utter'd the words, when a poor monk of the order of St. Francis came into the room to beg something for his convent. No man cares to have his virtues the sport of contingencies – or one man may be generous, as another man is puissant – *sed non, quo ad hanc* – or be it as it may – for there is no regular reasoning upon the ebbs and flows of our humours ; they may depend upon the same causes, for ought I know, which influence the tides themselves – 'twould oft be no discredit to us, to suppose it was so : I'm sure at least for myself, that in many a case I should be more highly satisfied, to have it said by the world, "I had had an affair with the moon, in which there was neither sin nor shame," than have it pass altogether as my own act and deed, wherein there was so much of both.

– But be this as it may. The moment I cast my eyes upon him, I was predetermined not to give him a single sous; and accordingly I put my purse into my pocket – button'd it up – set myself a little more upon my centre, and advanced up gravely to him: there was something, I fear, forbidding in my look: I have his figure this moment before my eyes, and think there was that in it which deserved better.

The monk, as I judged from the break in his tonsure, a few scatter'd white hairs upon his temples, being all that remained of it, might be about seventy – but from his eyes, and that sort of fire which was in them, which seemed more temper'd by courtesy than years, could be no more than sixty – Truth might lie between – He was certainly sixty-five; and the general air of his countenance, notwithstanding something seem'd to have been planting wrinkles in it before their time, agreed to the account.

It was one of those heads, which Guido* has often painted – mild, pale – penetrating, free from all common-place ideas of fat contented ignorance looking downwards upon the earth – it look'd forwards; but look'd, as if it look'd at something beyond this world. How one of his order came by it, heaven above, who let it fall upon a monk's shoulders, best knows: but it would have suited a Bramin,* and had I met it upon the plains of Indostan, I had reverenced it.

The rest of his outline may be given in a few strokes; one might put it into the hands of any one to design, for 'twas neither elegant or otherwise, but as character and expression made it so: it was a thin, spare form, something above the common size, if it lost not the distinction by a bend forwards in the figure – but it was the attitude of Intreaty; and as it now stands presented to my imagination, it gain'd more than it lost by it.

When he had enter'd the room three paces, he stood still; and laying his left hand upon his breast, (a slender white staff with which he journey'd being in his right) – when I had got close up to him, he introduced himself with the little story of the wants of his convent, and the poverty of his order – and did it with so simple a grace – and such an air of deprecation was there in the whole cast of his look and figure – I was bewitch'd not to have been struck with it –

– A better reason was, I had predetermined not to give him a single sous.

THE MONK
CALAIS

– 'Tis very true, said I, replying to a cast upwards with his eyes, with which he had concluded his address – 'tis very true – and heaven be their resource who have no other but the charity of the world, the stock of which, I fear, is no way sufficient for the many *great claims* which are hourly made upon it.

As I pronounced the words *great claims*, he gave a slight glance with his eye downwards upon the sleeve of his tunick – I felt the full force of the appeal – I acknowledge it, said I – a coarse habit, and that but once in three years, with meagre diet – are no great matters; and the true point of pity is, as they can be earn'd in the world with so little industry, that your order should wish to procure them by pressing upon a fund which is the property of the lame, the blind, the aged and the infirm – the captive who lies down counting over and over again the days of his afflictions, languishes also for his share of it; and had you been of the *order of mercy*, instead of the order of St. Francis,* poor as I am, continued I, pointing at my portmanteau, full chearfully should it have been open'd to you, for the ransom of the unfortunate – The monk made me a bow – but of all others, resumed I, the unfortunate of our own country, surely, have the first rights; and I have left thousands in distress upon our own shore – The monk gave a cordial wave with his head – as much as to say, No doubt, there is misery enough in every corner of the world, as well as within our convent – But we distinguish, said I, laying my hand upon the sleeve of his tunick, in return for his appeal – we distinguish, my good Father! betwixt those who wish only to eat the bread of their own labour – and those who eat the bread of other people's, and have no other plan in life, but to get through it in sloth and ignorance, *for the love of God*.

The poor Franciscan made no reply: a hectic of a moment pass'd across his cheek, but could not tarry – Nature seemed to

have had done with her resentments in him; he shewed none –
but letting his staff fall within his arm, he press'd both his hands
with resignation upon his breast, and retired.

THE MONK
CALAIS

My heart smote me the moment he shut the door – Psha! said I
with an air of carelessness, three several times – but it would
not do: every ungracious syllable I had utter'd, crouded back
into my imagination: I reflected, I had no right over the poor
Franciscan, but to deny him; and that the punishment of that
was enough to the disappointed without the addition of unkind
language – I consider'd his grey hairs – his courteous figure
seem'd to re-enter and gently ask me what injury he had done
me? – and why I could use him thus – I would have given
twenty livres for an advocate – I have behaved very ill; said I
within myself; but I have only just set out upon my travels; and
shall learn better manners as I get along.

THE DESOBLIGEANT
CALAIS

When a man is discontented with himself, it has one advantage
however, that it puts him into an excellent frame of mind for
making a bargain. Now there being no travelling through France
and Italy without a chaise – and nature generally prompting us
to the thing we are fittest for, I walk'd out into the coach yard
to buy or hire something of that kind to my purpose: an old
[1]Desobligeant in the furthest corner of the court, hit my fancy at
first sight, so I instantly got into it, and finding it in tolerable
harmony with my feelings, I ordered the waiter to call Monsieur
Dessein* the master of the hôtel – but Monsieur Dessein being
gone to vespers, and not caring to face the Franciscan whom I
saw on the opposite side of the court, in conference with a lady
just arrived, at the inn – I drew the taffeta curtain betwixt us,

---

[1] A chaise, so called in France, from its holding but one person.

and being determined to write my journey, I took out my pen and ink, and wrote the preface to it in the *Desobligeant*.

PREFACE
IN THE DESOBLIGEANT

It must have been observed by many a peripatetic philosopher,* That nature has set up by her own unquestionable authority certain boundaries and fences to circumscribe the discontent of man: she has effected her purpose in the quietest and easiest manner by laying him under almost insuperable obligations to work out his ease, and to sustain his sufferings at home. It is there only that she has provided him with the most suitable objects to partake of his happiness, and bear a part of that burden which in all countries and ages, has ever been too heavy for one pair of shoulders. 'Tis true we are endued with an imperfect power of spreading our happiness sometimes beyond *her* limits, but 'tis so ordered, that from the want of languages, connections, and dependencies, and from the difference in education, customs and habits, we lie under so many impediments in communicating our sensations out of our own sphere, as often amount to a total impossibility.

It will always follow from hence, that the balance of sentimental commerce is always against the expatriated adventurer: he must buy what he has little occasion for at their own price – his conversation will seldom be taken in exchange for theirs without a large discount – and this, by the by, eternally driving him into the hands of more equitable brokers for such conversation as he can find, it requires no great spirit of divination to guess at his party –

This brings me to my point; and naturally leads me (if the see-saw of this *Desobligeant* will but let me go on) into the efficient as well as the final causes of travelling –

Your idle people that leave their native country and go abroad for some reason or reasons which may be derived from one of these general causes –

> Infirmity of body,
> Imbecility of mind, or
> Inevitable necessity.

The first two include all those who travel by land or by water, labouring with pride, curiosity, vanity or spleen, subdivided and combined *in infinitum.*

The third class includes the whole army of peregrine martyrs ; more especially those travellers who set out upon their travels with the benefit of the clergy,* either as delinquents travelling under the direction of governors recommended by the magistrate – or young gentlemen transported by the cruelty of parents and guardians, and travelling under the direction of governors recommended by Oxford, Aberdeen and Glasgow.

There is a fourth class, but their number is so small that they would not deserve a distinction, was it not necessary in a work of this nature to observe the greatest precision and nicety, to avoid a confusion of character. And these men I speak of, are such as cross the seas and sojourn in a land of strangers with a view of saving money for various reasons and upon various pretences : but as they might also save themselves and others a great deal of unnecessary trouble by saving their money at home – and as their reasons for travelling are the least complex of any other species of emigrants, I shall distinguish these gentlemen by the name of

Simple Travellers.

Thus the whole circle of travellers may be reduced to the following *Heads.*

Idle Travellers,
Inquisitive Travellers,
Lying Travellers,
Proud Travellers,
Vain Travellers,
Splenetic Travellers.

Then follow the Travellers of Necessity.

The delinquent and felonious Traveller,
The unfortunate and innocent Traveller,
The simple Traveller,

And last of all (if you please) The

Sentimental Traveller (meaning thereby myself) who have travell'd, and of which I am now sitting down to give an account – as much out of *Necessity,* and the *besoin de* Voyager, as any one in the class.

I am well aware, at the same time, as both my travels and observations will be altogether of a different cast from any of my fore-runners; that I might have insisted upon a whole nitch entirely to myself – but I should break in upon the confines of the *Vain* Traveller, in wishing to draw attention towards me, till I have some better grounds for it, than the mere *Novelty of my Vehicle*.

It is sufficient for my reader, if he has been a traveller himself, that with study and reflection hereupon he may be able to determine his own place and rank in the catalogue – it will be one step towards knowing himself; as it is great odds, but he retains some tincture and resemblance, of what he imbibed or carried out, to the present hour.

The man who first transplanted the grape of Burgundy to the Cape of Good Hope (observe he was a Dutch man) never dreamt of drinking the same wine at the Cape, that the same grape produced upon the French mountains – he was too phlegmatic for that – but undoubtedly he expected to drink some sort of vinous liquor; but whether good, bad, or indifferent – he knew enough of this world to know, that it did not depend upon his choice, but that what is generally called *chance* was to decide his success: however, he hoped for the best; and in these hopes, by an intemperate confidence in the fortitude of his head, and the depth of his discretion, *Mynheer* might possibly overset both in his new vineyard; and by discovering his nakedness,* become a laughing-stock to his people.

Even so it fares with the poor Traveller, sailing and posting through the politer kingdoms of the globe in pursuit of knowledge and improvements.

Knowledge and improvements are to be got by sailing and posting for that purpose; but whether useful knowledge and real improvements, is all a lottery – and even where the adventurer is successful, the acquired stock must be used with caution and sobriety to turn to any profit – but as the chances run prodigiously the other way both as to the acquisition and application, I am of opinion, That a man would act as wisely, if he could prevail upon himself, to live contented without foreign knowledge or foreign improvements, especially if he lives in a country that has no absolute want of either – and indeed, much grief of heart has it oft and many a time cost me, when I have observed how many a foul step the inquisitive Traveller has measured to see sights and look into discoveries; all which, as Sancho Pança said to Don Quixote,* they might have seen dryshod at home. It is an age so full of light, that there is scarce a country or corner of Europe whose beams are not crossed and interchanged with others – Knowledge in most of its branches, and in most affairs, is like music in an Italian street, whereof those may partake, who pay nothing – But there is no nation under heaven – and God is my record, (before whose tribunal I must one day come and give an account of this work) – that I do not speak it vauntingly – But there is no nation under heaven abounding with more variety of learning – where the sciences may be more fitly woo'd, or more surely won than here – where art is encouraged, and will so soon rise high – where Nature (take her all together) has so little to answer for – and, to close all, where there is more wit and variety of character to feed the mind with – Where then, my dear countrymen, are you going – *

– We are only looking at this chaise, said they – Your most obedient servant, said I, skipping out of it, and pulling off my hat – We were wondering, said one of them, who, I found, was an *inquisitive traveller* – what could occasion its motion. –

– 'Twas the agitation, said I coolly, of writing a preface – I never heard, said the other, who was a *simple traveller*, of a preface wrote in a *Desobligeant*. – It would have been better, said I, in a *Vis a Vis*.

– *As an English man does not travel to see English men*, I retired to my room.

CALAIS

I perceived that something darken'd the passage more than myself, as I stepp'd along it to my room; it was effectually Mons. Dessein, the master of the hôtel, who had just return'd from vespers, and, with his hat under his arm, was most complaisantly following me, to put me in mind of my wants. I had wrote myself pretty well out of conceit with the *Desobligeant*; and Mons. Dessein speaking of it, with a shrug, as if it would no way suit me, it immediately struck my fancy that it belong'd to some *innocent traveller*, who, on his return home, had left it to Mons. Dessein's honour to make the most of. Four months had elapsed since it had finish'd its career of Europe in the corner of Mons. Dessein's coach-yard; and having sallied out from thence but a vampt-up business at the first, though it had been twice taken to pieces on Mount Sennis,* it had not profited much by its adventures – but by none so little as the standing so many months unpitied in the corner of Mons. Dessein's coach-yard. Much indeed was not to be said for it – but something might – and when a few words will rescue misery out of her distress, I hate the man who can be a churl of them.

– Now was I the master of this hôtel, said I, laying the point of my fore-finger on Mons. Dessein's breast, I would inevitably make a point of getting rid of this unfortunate *Desobligeant* – it stands swinging reproaches at you every time you pass by it –

Mon Dieu! said Mons. Dessein – I have no interest – Except the interest, said I, which men of a certain turn of mind take, Mons. Dessein, in their own sensations – I'm persuaded, to a man who feels for others as well as for himself, every rainy night, disguise it as you will, must cast a damp upon your spirits – You suffer, Mons. Dessein, as much as the machine –

I have always observed, when there is as much *sour* as *sweet* in a compliment, that an Englishman is eternally at a loss within himself, whether to take it, or let it alone: a Frenchman never is: Mons. Dessein made me a bow.

C'est bien vrai, said he – But in this case I should only exchange one disquietude for another, and with loss: figure to yourself, my dear Sir, that in giving you a chaise which would fall to pieces before you had got half way to Paris – figure to yourself how much I should suffer, in giving an ill impression of myself to a man of honour, and lying at the mercy, as I must do, *d'un homme d'esprit*.

The dose was made up exactly after my own prescription; so I could not help taking it – and returning Mons. Dessein his bow, without more casuistry we walk'd together towards his Remise, to take a view of his magazine of chaises.

IN THE STREET
CALAIS

It must needs be a hostile kind of a world, when the buyer (if it be but of a sorry post-chaise) cannot go forth with the seller thereof into the street to terminate the difference betwixt them, but he instantly falls into the same frame of mind and views his conventionist with the same sort of eye, as if he was going along with him to Hyde-park corner to fight a duel. For my own part, being but a poor sword's-man, and no way a match for Monsieur *Dessein*, I felt the rotation of all the movements within me, to which the situation is incident – I looked at Monsieur *Dessein* through and through – ey'd him as he walked along in profile – then, *en face* – thought he look'd like a Jew – then a Turk – disliked his wig – cursed him by my gods – wished him at the devil –

– And is all this to be lighted up in the heart for a beggarly account of three or four louisd'ors, which is the most I can be over-reach'd in ? – Base passion ! said I, turning myself about, as a man naturally does upon a sudden reverse of sentiment – base, ungentle passion ! thy hand is against every man,* and every man's hand against thee – heaven forbid ! said she, raising her hand up to her forehead, for I had turned full in front upon the lady whom I had seen in conference with the monk – she had followed us unperceived – Heaven forbid indeed ! said I, offering her my own – she had a black pair of silk gloves open only at the thumb and two fore-fingers, so accepted it without reserve – and I led her up to the door of the Remise.*

Monsieur *Dessein* had *diabled* the key above fifty times before he found out he had come with a wrong one in his hand : we were as impatient as himself to have it open'd ; and so attentive to the obstacle, that I continued holding her hand almost without knowing it ; so that Monseiur *Dessein* left us together with her hand in mine, and with our faces turned towards the door of the Remise, and said he would be back in five minutes.

Now a colloquy of five minutes, in such a situation, is worth one of as many ages, with your faces turned towards the street : in the latter case, 'tis drawn from the objects and occurrences without – when your eyes are fixed upon a dead blank – you draw purely from yourselves. A silence of a single moment upon Monsieur *Dessein*'s leaving us, had been fatal to the situation – she had infallibly turned about – so I begun the conversation instantly. –

– But what were the temptations, (as I write not to apologize for the weaknesses of my heart in this tour, – but to give an account of them) – shall be described with the same simplicity, with which I felt them.

THE REMISE DOOR
CALAIS

When I told the reader that I did not care to get out of the *Desobligeant*, because I saw the monk in close conference with a lady just arrived at the inn – I told him the truth; but I did not tell him the whole truth; for I was full as much restrained by the appearance and figure of the lady he was talking to. Suspicion crossed my brain, and said, he was telling her what had passed: something jarred upon it within me – I wished him at his convent.

When the heart flies out before the understanding, it saves the judgment a world of pains – I was certain she was of a better order of beings – however, I thought no more of her, but went on and wrote my preface.

The impression returned, upon my encounter with her in the street; a guarded frankness with which she gave me her hand, shewed, I thought, her good education and her good sense; and as I led her on, I felt a pleasurable ductility about her, which spread a calmness over all my spirits –

– Good God! how a man might lead such a creature as this round the world with him! –

I had not yet seen her face – 'twas not material; for the drawing was instantly set about, and long before we had got to the door of the Remise, *Fancy* had finished the whole head, and pleased herself as much with its fitting her goddess, as if she had dived into the TIBER for it* – but thou art a seduced, and a seducing slut; and albeit thou cheatest us seven times a day with thy pictures and images, yet with so many charms dost thou do it, and thou deckest out thy pictures in the shapes of so many angels of light, 'tis a shame to break with thee.

When we had got to the door of the Remise, she withdrew her hand from across her forehead, and let me see the original – it was a face of about six and twenty – of a clear transparent brown, simply set off without rouge or powder – it was not critically handsome, but there was that in it, which in the frame of mind I was in, which attached me much more to it – it was interesting; I fancied it wore the characters of a widow'd look, and in that state of its declension, which had passed the two first paroxysms of sorrow, and was quietly beginning to reconcile itself to its loss – but a thousand other distresses might have traced the same lines; I wish'd to know what they had been – and was ready to enquire, (had the same *bon ton* of conversation permitted, as in the days of Esdras) – '*What aileth thee? and why art thou disquieted? and why is thy understanding troubled?*'* In a word, I felt benevolence for her; and resolved some way or other to throw in my mite of courtesy – if not of service.

Such were my temptations – and in this disposition to give way to them, was I left alone with the lady with her hand in mine, and with our faces both turned closer to the door of the Remise than what was absolutely necessary.

THE REMISE DOOR
CALAIS

This certainly, fair lady! said I, raising her hand up a little lightly as I began, must be one of Fortune's whimsical doings: to take two utter strangers by their hands – of different sexes, and perhaps from different corners of the globe, and in one moment place them together in such a cordial situation, as Friendship herself could scarce have atchieved for them, had she projected it for a month –

– And your reflection upon it, shews how much, Monsieur, she has embarassed you by the adventure. –

When the situation is, what we would wish, nothing is so illtimed as to hint at the circumstances which make it so: you thank Fortune, continued she – you had reason – the heart knew it, and was satisfied; and who but an English philosopher would have sent notices of it to the brain to reverse the judgment?

In saying this, she disengaged her hand with a look which I thought a sufficient commentary upon the text.

It is a miserable picture which I am going to give of the weakness of my heart, by owning, that it suffered a pain, which worthier occasions could not have inflicted. – I was mortified with the loss of her hand, and the manner in which I had lost it carried neither oil nor wine* to the wound : I never felt the pain of a sheepish inferiority so miserably in my life.

The triumphs of a true feminine heart are short upon these discomfitures. In a very few seconds she laid her hand upon the cuff of my coat, in order to finish her reply; so some way or other, God knows how, I regained my situation.

– She had nothing to add.

I forthwith began to model a different conversation for the lady, thinking from the spirit as well as moral of this, that I had been mistaken in her character; but upon turning her face towards me, the spirit which had animated the reply was fled – the muscles relaxed, and I beheld the same unprotected look of distress which first won me to her interest – melancholy ! to see such sprightliness the prey of sorrow. – I pitied her from my soul; and though it may seem ridiculous enough to a torpid heart, – I could have taken her into my arms, and cherished her, though it was in the open street, without blushing.

The pulsations of the arteries along my fingers pressing across hers,* told her what was passing within me : she looked down – a silence of some moments followed.

I fear, in this interval, I must have made some slight efforts towards a closer compression of her hand, from a subtle sensation I felt in the palm of my own – not as if she was going to withdraw hers – but, as if she thought about it – and I had infallibly lost it a second time, had not instinct more than reason directed me to the last resource in these dangers – to hold it loosely, and in a manner as if I was every moment going to release it, of myself; so she let it continue, till Monsieur *Dessein* returned with the key; and in the mean time I set myself to consider how I should undo the ill impressions which the poor monk's story, in case he had told it her, must have planted in her breast against me.

THE SNUFF-BOX
CALAIS

The good old monk was within six paces of us, as the idea of him cross'd my mind; and was advancing towards us a little out of the line, as if uncertain whether he should break in upon us or no. – He stopp'd, however, as soon as he came up to us, with a world of frankness; and having a horn snuff-box in his hand, he presented it open to me – You shall taste mine – said I, pulling out my box (which was a small tortoise one) and putting it into his hand – 'Tis most excellent, said the monk; Then do me the favour, I replied, to accept of the box and all, and when you take a pinch out of it, sometimes recollect it was the peace-offering of a man who once used you unkindly, but not from his heart.

The poor monk blush'd as red as scarlet. *Mon Dieu!* said he, pressing his hands together – you never used me unkindly. – I should think, said the lady, he is not likely. I blush'd in my turn; but from what movements, I leave to the few who feel to analyse – Excuse me, Madame, replied I – I treated him most unkindly; and from no provocations – 'Tis impossible, said the lady. – My God! cried the monk, with a warmth of asseveration which seemed not to belong to him – the fault was in me, and in the indiscretion of my zeal – the lady opposed it, and I joined with her in maintaining it was impossible, that a spirit so regulated as his, could give offence to any.

I knew not that contention could be rendered so sweet and pleasurable a thing to the nerves as I then felt it. – We remained silent, without any sensation of that foolish pain which takes place, when in such a circle you look for ten minutes in one another's faces without saying a word. Whilst this lasted, the monk rubb'd his horn box upon the sleeve of his tunick; and as soon as it had acquired a little air of brightness by the friction – he made a low bow, and said, 'twas too late to say whether it was the weakness or goodness of our tempers which had involved us in this contest – but be it as it would – he begg'd we might exchange boxes – In saying this, he presented his to me with one hand, as he took mine from me in the other; and having kiss'd it – with a stream of good nature in his eyes he put it into his bosom – and took his leave.

I guard this box, as I would the instrumental parts of my religion, to help my mind on to something better: in truth, I seldom go abroad without it; and oft and many a time have I called up by it the courteous spirit of its owner to regulate my own, in the justlings of the world; they had found full employment for his, as I learnt from his story, till about the forty-fifth year of his age, when upon some military services ill requited, and meeting at the same time with a disappointment in the tenderest of passions, he abandon'd the sword and the sex together, and took sanctuary, not so much in his convent as in himself.

I feel a damp upon my spirits, as I am going to add, that in my last return through Calais, upon inquiring after Father Lorenzo, I heard he had been dead near three months, and was buried, not in his convent, but, according to his desire, in a little cimetiery belonging to it, about two leagues off: I had a strong desire to see where they had laid him — when, upon pulling out his little horn box, as I sat by his grave, and plucking up a nettle or two at the head of it, which had no business to grow there, they all struck together so forcibly upon my affections, that I burst into a flood of tears — but I am as weak as a woman; and I beg the world not to smile, but pity me.

THE REMISE DOOR
CALAIS

I had never quitted the lady's hand all this time; and had held it so long, that it would have been indecent to have let it go, without first pressing it to my lips: the blood and spirits, which had suffer'd a revulsion from her, crouded back to her, as I did it.

Now the two travellers who had spoke to me in the coach-yard, happening at that crisis to be passing by, and observing our communications, naturally took it into their heads that we must be *man and wife* at least; so stopping as soon as they came up to the door of the Remise, the one of them, who was the inquisitive traveller, ask'd us, if we set out for Paris the next morning? — I could only answer for myself, I said; and the lady added, she was for Amiens. — We dined there yesterday, said the simple traveller — You go directly through the town, added the other, in your road to Paris. I was going to return a thousand thanks for the intelligence, *that Amiens was in the road to Paris*; but, upon pulling out my poor monk's little horn box to take a pinch of snuff — I made them a quiet bow, and wishing them a good passage to Dover — they left us alone —

— Now where would be the harm, said I to myself, if I was to beg of this distressed lady to accept of half of my chaise? — and what mighty mischief could ensue?

Every dirty passion, and bad propensity in my nature, took the alarm, as I stated the proposition – It will oblige you to have a third horse, said AVARICE, which will put twenty livres out of your pocket. – You know not who she is, said CAUTION – or what scrapes the affair may draw you into, whisper'd COWARD-ICE –

Depend upon it, Yorick! said DISCRETION, 'twill be said you went off with a mistress, and came by assignation to Calais for that purpose –

– You can never after, cried HYPOCRISY aloud, shew your face in the world – or rise, quoth MEANNESS, in the church – or be any thing in it, said PRIDE, but a lousy prebendary.

– But 'tis a civil thing, said I – and as I generally act from the first impulse, and therefore seldom listen to these cabals, which serve no purpose, that I know of, but to encompass the heart with adamant – I turn'd instantly about to the lady –

– But she had glided off unperceived, as the cause was pleading, and had made ten or a dozen paces down the street, by the time I had made the determination; so I set off after her with a long stride, to make her the proposal with the best address I was master of; but observing she walk'd with her cheek half resting upon the palm of her hand – with the slow, short-measur'd step of thoughtfulness, and with her eyes, as she went step by step, fix'd upon the ground, it struck me, she was trying the same cause herself. – God help her! said I, she has some mother-in-law, or tartufish* aunt, or nonsensical old woman, to consult upon the occasion, as well as myself: so not caring to interrupt the processe, and deeming it more gallant to take her at discretion than by surprize, I faced about, and took a short turn or two before the door of the Remise, whilst she walk'd musing on one side.

IN THE STREET
CALAIS

Having, on first sight of the lady, settled the affair in my fancy, "that she was of the better order of beings" – and then laid it down as a second axiom, as indisputable as the first, That she was a widow, and wore a character of distress – I went no further; I got ground enough for the situation which pleased me

– and had she remained close beside my elbow till midnight, I should have held true to my system, and considered her only under that general idea.

She had scarce got twenty paces distant from me, ere something within me called out for a more particular inquiry – it brought on the idea of a further separation – I might possibly never see her more – the heart is for saving what it can; and I wanted the traces thro' which my wishes might find their way to her, in case I should never rejoin her myself: in a word, I wish'd to know her name – her family's – her condition; and as I knew the place to which she was going, I wanted to know from whence she came: but there was no coming at all this intelligence: a hundred little delicacies stood in the way. I form'd a score different plans – There was no such thing as a man's asking her directly – the thing was impossible.

A little French *debonaire* captain, who came dancing down the street, shewed me, it was the easiest thing in the world; for popping in betwixt us, just as the lady was returning back to the door of the Remise, he introduced himself to my acquaintance, and before he had well got announced, begg'd I would do him the honour to present him to the lady – I had not been presented myself – so turning about to her, he did it just as well by asking her, if she had come from Paris? – No: she was going that rout, she said. – *Vous n'etez pas de Londre?* – She was not, she replied. – Then Madame must have come thro' Flanders. – *Apparamment vous etez Flammande?* said the French captain. – The lady answered, she was. – *Peutetre, de Lisle?* added he – She said, she was not of Lisle. – Nor Arras? – nor Cambray? – nor Ghent? – nor Brussels? She answered, she was of Brussels.

He had had the honour, he said, to be at the bombardment* of it last war – that it was finely situated, *pour cela* – and full of noblesse when the Imperialists were driven out by the French (the lady made a slight curtsy) – so giving her an account of the affair, and of the share he had had in it – he begg'd the honour to know her name – so made his bow.

– *Et Madame a son Mari?* – said he, looking back when he had made two steps – and without staying for an answer – danced down the street.

Had I served seven years apprenticeship to good breeding, I could not have done as much.

THE REMISE
CALAIS

As the little French captain left us, Mons. Dessein came up with
the key of the Remise in his hand, and forthwith let us into his
magazine of chaises.

The first object which caught my eye, as Mons. Dessein open'd
the door of the Remise, was another old tatter'd *Desobligeant*:
and notwithstanding it was the exact picture of that which had
hit my fancy so much in the coach-yard but an hour before –
the very sight of it stirr'd up a disagreeable sensation within me
now; and I thought 'twas a churlish beast into whose heart the
idea could first enter, to construct such a machine; nor had I
much more charity for the man who could think of using it.

I observed the lady was as little taken with it as myself: so
Mons. Dessein led us on to a couple of chaises which stood
abreast, telling us as he recommended them, that they had been
purchased by my Lord A. and B. to go the *grand tour*, but had
gone no further than Paris, so were in all respects as good as
new – They were too good – so I pass'd on to a third, which
stood behind, and forthwith began to chaffer for the price – But
'twill scarce hold two, said I, opening the door and getting in –
Have the goodness, Madam, said Mons. Dessein, offering his
arm, to step in – The lady hesitated half a second, and stepp'd
in; and the waiter that moment beckoning to speak to Mons.
Dessein, he shut the door of the chaise upon us, and left us.

THE REMISE
CALAIS

C'est bien comique, 'tis very droll, said the lady smiling, from
the reflection that this was the second time we had been left
together by a parcel of nonsensical contingencies – *c'est bien
comique*, said she –

– There wants nothing, said I, to make it so, but the comick
use which the gallantry of a Frenchman would put it to – to
make love the first moment, and an offer of his person the
second.

'Tis their *fort*: replied the lady.

It is supposed so at least – and how it has come to pass,

continued I, I know not; but they have certainly got the credit of understanding more of love, and making it better than any other nation upon earth: but for my own part I think them errant bunglers, and in truth the worst set of marksmen that ever tried Cupid's patience.

– To think of making love by *sentiments*!

I should as soon think of making a genteel suit of cloaths out of remnants: – and to do it – pop – at first sight by declaration – is submitting the offer and themselves with it, to be sifted, with all their *pours* and *contres*, by an unheated mind.

The lady attended as if she expected I should go on.

Consider then, madam, continued I, laying my hand upon hers –

That grave people hate Love for the name's sake –

That selfish people hate it for their own –

Hypocrites for heaven's –

And that all of us both old and young, being ten times worse frighten'd than hurt by the very *report* – What a want of knowledge in this branch of commerce a man betrays, whoever lets the word come out of his lips, till an hour or two at least after the time, that his silence upon it becomes tormenting. A course of small, quiet attentions, not so pointed as to alarm – nor so vague as to be misunderstood, – with now and then a look of kindness, and little or nothing said upon it – leaves Nature for your mistress, and she fashions it to her mind. –

Then I solemnly declare, said the lady, blushing – you have been making love to me all this while.

THE REMISE
CALAIS

Monsieur *Dessein* came back to let us out of the chaise, and acquaint the lady, the Count de L—— her brother was just arrived at the hotel. Though I had infinite good will for the lady, I cannot say, that I rejoiced in my heart at the event – and could not help telling her so – for it is fatal to a proposal, Madam, said I, that I was going to make you –

– You need not tell me what the proposal was, said she, laying her hand upon both mine, as she interrupted me. – A man, my good Sir, has seldom an offer of kindness to make to a woman, but she has a presentiment of it some moments before –

Nature arms her with it, said I, for immediate preservation – But I think, said she, looking in my face, I had no evil to apprehend – and to deal frankly with you, had determined to accept it. – If I had – (she stopped a moment) – I believe your good will would have drawn a story from me, which would have made pity the only dangerous thing in the journey.

I saying this, she suffered me to kiss her hand twice, and with a look of sensibility mixed with a concern she got out of the chaise – and bid adieu.

IN THE STREET
CALAIS

I never finished a twelve-guinea bargain so expeditiously in my life: my time seemed heavy upon the loss of the lady, and knowing every moment of it would be as two, till I put myself into motion – I ordered post horses directly, and walked towards the hotel.

Lord! said I, hearing the town clock strike four, and recollecting that I had been little more than a single hour in Calais –

– What a large volume of adventures may be grasped within this little span of life by him who interests his heart in every thing, and who, having eyes to see, what time and chance are perpetually holding out to him as he journeyeth on his way, misses nothing he can *fairly* lay his hands on. –

– If this won't turn out something – another will – no matter – 'tis an assay upon human nature – I get my labour for my pains – 'tis enough – the pleasure of the experiment has kept my senses, and the best part of my blood awake, and laid the gross to sleep.

I pity the man who can travel from *Dan* to *Beersheba*,* and cry, 'Tis all barren – and so it is; and so is all the world to him who will not cultivate the fruits it offers. I declare, said I, clapping my hands chearily together, that was I in a desart, I would find out wherewith in it to call forth my affections – If I could not do better, I would fasten them upon some sweet myrtle, or seek some melancholy cypress to connect myself to – I would court their shade, and greet them kindly for their protection – I would cut my name upon them, and swear they were the loveliest trees throughout the desert: if their leaves wither'd, I would teach myself to mourn, and when they rejoiced, I would rejoice along with them.

The learned SMELFUNGUS* travelled from Boulogne to Paris – from Paris to Rome – and so on – but he set out with the spleen and jaundice, and every object he pass'd by was discoloured or distorted – He wrote an account of them, but 'twas nothing but the account of his miserable feelings.

I met Smelfungus in the grand portico of the Pantheon – he was just coming out of it – *'Tis nothing but a huge cock-pit*[1], said he – I wish you had said nothing worse of the Venus of Medicis, replied I – for in passing through Florence, I had heard he had fallen foul upon the goddess, and used her worse than a common strumpet, without the least provocation in nature.*

I popp'd upon Smelfungus again at Turin, in his return home; and a sad tale of sorrowful adventures had he to tell, "wherein he spoke of moving accidents by flood and field, and of the cannibals which each other eat: the Anthropophagi"* – he had been flea'd alive,* and bedevil'd, and used worse than St. Bartholomew, at every stage he had come at –

– I'll tell it, cried Smelfungus, to the world. You had better tell it, said I, to your physician.

Mundungus,* with an immense fortune, made the whole tour; going on from Rome to Naples – from Naples to Venice – from Venice to Vienna – to Dresden, to Berlin, without one generous connection or pleasurable anecdote to tell of; but he had travell'd straight on looking neither to his right hand or his left, lest Love or Pity should seduce him out of his road.

Peace be to them! if it is to be found; but heaven itself, was it possible to get there with such tempers, would want objects to give it – every gentle spirit would come flying upon the wings of Love to hail their arrival – Nothing would the souls of Smelfungus and Mundungus hear of, but fresh anthems of joy, fresh raptures of love, and fresh congratulations of their common felicity – I heartily pity them: they have brought up no faculties for this work; and was the happiest mansion in heaven to be allotted to Smelfungus and Mundungus, they would be so

[1] Vide S——'s Travels.

far from being happy, that the souls of Smelfungus and Mundungus would do penance there to all eternity.

MONTRIUL

I had once lost my portmanteau from behind my chaise, and twice got out in the rain, and one of the times up to the knees in dirt, to help the postilion to tie it on, without being able to find out what was wanting – Nor was it till I got to Montriul, upon the landlord's asking me if I wanted not a servant, that it occurred to me, that that was the very thing.

A servant! That I do most sadly, quoth I – Because, Monsieur, said the landlord, there is a clever young fellow, who would be very proud of the honour to serve an Englishman – But why an English one, more than any other? – They are so generous, said the landlord – I'll be shot if this is not a livre out of my pocket, quoth I to myself, this very night – But they have wherewithal to be so, Monsieur, added he – Set down one livre more for that, quoth I – It was but last night, said the landlord, *qu'un my Lord Anglois presentoit un ecu a la fille de chambre – Tant pis, pour Mad*^{lle} *Janatone*, said I.*

Now Janatone being the landlord's daughter, and the landlord supposing I was young in French, took the liberty to inform me, I should not have said *tant pis* – but, *tant mieux. Tant mieux, toujours, Monsieur*, said he, when there is any thing to be got – *tant pis*, when there is nothing. It comes to the same thing, said I. *Pardonnez moi*, said the landlord.

I cannot take a fitter opportunity to observe once for all, that *tant pis* and *tant mieux* being two of the great hinges in French conversation, a stranger would do well to set himself right in the use of them, before he gets to Paris.

A prompt French Marquis at our ambassador's table demanded of Mr. H——,* if he was H—— the poet? No, said H—— mildly – *Tant pis*, replied the Marquis.

It is H—— the historian, said another – *Tant mieux*, said the Marquis. And Mr. H——, who is a man of an excellent heart, return'd thanks for both.

When the landlord had set me right in this matter, he called in La Fleur, which was the name of the young man he had spoke of – saying only first, That as for his talents, he would presume to say nothing – Monsieur was the best judge what would suit him; but for the fidelity of La Fleur, he would stand responsible in all he was worth.

The landlord deliver'd this in a manner which instantly set my mind to the business I was upon – and La Fleur, who stood waiting without, in that breathless expectation which every son of nature of us have felt in our turns, came in.

MONTRIUL

I am apt to be taken with all kinds of people at first sight; but never more so, than when a poor devil comes to offer his service to so poor a devil as myself; and as I know this weakness, I always suffer my judgment to draw back something on that very account – and this more or less, according to the mood I am in, and the case – and I may add the gender too, of the person I am to govern.

When La Fleur enter'd the room, after every discount I could make for my soul, the genuine look and air of the fellow determined the matter at once in his favour; so I hired him first – and then began to inquire what he could do: But I shall find out his talents, quoth I, as I want them – besides, a Frenchman can do every thing.

Now poor La Fleur could do nothing in the world but beat a drum, and play a march or two upon the fife. I was determined to make his talents do; and can't say my weakness was ever so insulted by my wisdom, as in the attempt.

La Fleur had set out early in life, as gallantly as most Frenchmen do, with *serving* for a few years; at the end of which, having satisfied the sentiment, and found moreover, That the honour of beating a drum was likely to be its own reward, as it open'd no further track of glory to him – he retired *a ses terres*, and lived *comme il plaisoit a Dieu* – that is to say, upon nothing.

– And so, quoth *Wisdome*, you have hired a drummer to attend you in this tour of your's thro' France and Italy! Psha! said I, and do not one half of our gentry go with a hum-drum *compagnon du voiage* the same round, and have the piper and the devil and all to pay besides? When man can extricate himself with an *equivoque* in such an unequal match – he is not ill off –

But you can do something else, La Fleur? said I – *O qu' oui!* – he could make spatterdashes, and play a little upon the fiddle – Bravo! said Wisdome – Why, I play a bass myself, said I – we shall do very well. – You can shave, and dress a wig a little, La Fleur? – He had all the dispositions in the world – It is enough for heaven! said I, interrupting him – and ought to be enough for me – So supper coming in, and having a frisky English spaniel on one side of my chair, and a French valet, with as much hilarity in his countenance as ever nature painted in one, on the other – I was satisfied to my heart's content with my empire; and if monarchs knew what they would be at, they might be as satisfied as I was.

MONTRIUL

As La Fleur went the whole tour of France and Italy with me, and will be often upon the stage, I must interest the reader a little further in his behalf, by saying, that I had never less reason to repent of the impulses which generally do determine me, than in regard to this fellow – he was a faithful, affectionate, simple soul as ever trudged after the heels of a philosopher; and notwithstanding his talents of drum-beating and spatterdash-making, which, tho' very good in themselves, happen'd to be of no great service to me, yet was I hourly recompenced by the festivity of his temper – it supplied all defects – I had a constant resource in his looks in all difficulties and distresses of my own – I was going to have added, of his too; but La Fleur was out of the reach of every thing; for whether 'twas hunger or thirst, or cold or nakedness, or watchings, or whatever stripes of ill luck La Fleur met with in our journeyings,* there was no index in his physiognomy to point them out by – he was eternally the same; so that if I am a piece of a philosopher, which Satan now and then puts it into my head I am – it always mortifies the pride of the conceit, by reflecting how much I owe to the complexional philosophy of this poor fellow, for shaming me into one of a better kind. With all this, La Fleur had a small cast of the coxcomb – but he seemed at first sight to be more a coxcomb of nature than of art; and before I had been three days in Paris with him – he seemed to be no coxcomb at all.

MONTRIUL

The next morning La Fleur entering upon his employment, I delivered to him the key of my portmanteau with an inventory of my half a dozen shirts and silk pair of breeches; and bid him fasten all upon the chaise – get the horses put to – and desire the landlord to come in with his bill.

C'est un garçon de bonne fortune, said the landlord, pointing through the window to half a dozen wenches who had got round about La Fleur, and were most kindly taking their leave of him, as the postilion was leading out the horses. La Fleur kissed all their hands round and round again, and thrice he wiped his eyes, and thrice he promised he would bring them all pardons from Rome.

The young fellow, said the landlord, is beloved by all the town, and there is scarce a corner in Montriul where the want of him will not be felt: he has but one misfortune in the world, continued he, "He is always in love." – I am heartily glad of it, said I, – 'twill save me the trouble every night of putting my breeches under my head. In saying this, I was making not so much La Fleur's eloge, as my own, having been in love with one princess or another almost all my life, and I hope I shall go on so, till I die, being firmly persuaded, that if ever I do a mean action, it must be in some interval betwixt one passion and another: whilst this interregnum lasts, I always perceive my heart locked up – I can scarce find in it, to give Misery a sixpence; and therefore I always get out of it as fast as I can, and the moment I am rekindled, I am all generosity and good will again; and would do any thing in the world either for, or with any one, if they will but satisfy me there is no sin in it.

– But in saying this – surely I am commending the passion – not myself.

A FRAGMENT*

— the town of Abdera, notwithstanding Democritus lived there trying all the powers of irony and laughter to reclaim it, was the vilest and most profligate town in all Thrace. What for poisons, conspiracies and assassinations – libels, pasquinades and tumults, there was no going there by day – 'twas worse by night.

Now, when things were at the worst, it came to pass, that the Andromeda of Euripides being represented at Abdera, the whole orchestra was delighted with it: but of all the passages which delighted them, nothing operated more upon their imaginations, than the tender strokes of nature which the poet had wrought up in that pathetic speech of Perseus,

O Cupid, prince of God and men, &c.

Every man almost spoke pure iambics the next day, and talk'd of nothing but Perseus his pathetic address – "O Cupid! prince of God and men" – in every street of Abdera, in every house – "O Cupid! Cupid!" – in every mouth, like the natural notes of some sweet melody which drops from it whether it will or no – nothing but "Cupid! Cupid! prince of God and men" – The fire caught – and the whole city, like the heart of one man, open'd itself to Love.

No pharmacopolist could sell one grain of helebore – not a single armourer had a heart to forge one instrument of death – Friendship and Virtue met together, and kiss'd each other in the street – the golden age return'd, and hung o'er the town of Abdera – every Abderite took his oaten pipe, and every Abderitish woman left her purple web, and chastly sat her down and listen'd to the song –

'Twas only in the power, says the Fragment, of the God whose empire extendeth from heaven to earth, and even to the depths of the sea, to have done this.

MONTRIUL

When all is ready, and every article is disputed and paid for in the inn, unless you are a little sour'd by the adventure, there is always a matter to compound at the door, before you can get into your chaise; and that is with the sons and daughters of poverty, who surround you. Let no man say, "let them go to the devil" – 'tis a cruel journey to send a few miserables, and they have had sufferings enow without it: I always think it better to take a few sous out in my hand; and I would counsel every gentle traveller to do so likewise: he need not be so exact in setting down his motives for giving them – they will be register'd elsewhere.

For my own part, there is no man gives so little as I do; for few that I know have so little to give: but as this was the first publick act of my charity in France, I took the more notice of it.

A well-a-way! said I. I have but eight sous in the world, shewing them in my hand, and there are eight poor men and eight poor women for 'em.

A poor tatter'd soul without a shirt on instantly withdrew his claim, by retiring two steps out of the circle, and making a disqualifying bow on his part. Had the whole parterre cried out, *Place aux dames*, with one voice, it would not have conveyed the sentiment of a deference for the sex with half the effect.

Just heaven! for what wise reasons hast thou order'd it, that beggary and urbanity, which are at such variance in other countries, should find a way to be at unity in this?

— I insisted upon presenting him with a single sous, merely for his *politesse*.

A poor little dwarfish brisk fellow, who stood over-against me in the circle, putting something first under his arm, which had once been a hat, took his snuff-box out of his pocket, and generously offer'd a pinch on both sides of him: it was a gift of consequence, and modestly declined — The poor little fellow press'd it upon them with a nod of welcomeness — *Prenez en — prenez*, said he, looking another way; so they each took a pinch — Pity thy box should ever want one! said I to myself; so I put a couple of sous into it — taking a small pinch out of his box, to enhance their value, as I did it — He felt the weight of the second obligation more than that of the first — 'twas doing him an honour — the other was only doing him a charity — and he made me a bow down to the ground for it.

— Here! said I to an old soldier with one hand, who had been campaign'd and worn out to death in the service — here's a couple of sous for thee — *Vive le Roi!* said the old soldier.

I had then but three sous left: so I gave one, simply *pour l'amour de Dieu*, which was the footing on which it was begg'd — The poor woman had a dislocated hip; so it could not be well, upon any other motive.

Mon cher et tres charitable Monsieur — There's no opposing this, said I.

My Lord Anglois — the very sound was worth the money — so I gave *my last sous for it*. But in the eagerness of giving, I had overlook'd a *pauvre honteux*, who had no one to ask a sous for him, and who, I believed, would have perish'd, ere he could have ask'd one for himself: he stood by the chaise a little without the circle, and wiped a tear from a face which I thought had seen better days – Good God! said I – and I have not one single sous left to give him – But you have a thousand! cried all the powers of nature, stirring within me – so I gave him – no matter what – I am ashamed to say *how much*, now – and was ashamed to think, how little, then: so if the reader can form any conjecture of my disposition, as these two fixed points are given him, he may judge within a livre or two what was the precise sum.

I could afford nothing for the rest, but, *Dieu vous benisse – Et le bon Dieu vous benisse encore* – said the old soldier, the dwarf, &c. The *pauvre honteux* could say nothing – he pull'd out a little handkerchief, and wiped his face as he turned away – and I thought he thank'd me more than them all.

THE BIDET

Having settled all these little matters, I got into my post-chaise with more ease than ever I got into a post-chaise in my life; and La Fleur having got one large jack-boot on the far side of a little *bidet*[1], and another on this (for I count nothing of his legs) – he canter'd away before me as happy and as perpendicular as a prince. –

– But what is happiness! what is grandeur in this painted scene of life! A dead ass, before we had got a league, put a sudden stop to La Fleur's career – his bidet would not pass by it – a contention arose betwixt them, and the poor fellow was kick'd out of his jack-boots the very first kick.

La Fleur bore his fall like a French christian, saying neither more or less upon it, than, Diable! so presently got up and came to the charge again astride his bidet, beating him up to it as he would have beat his drum.

The bidet flew from one side of the road to the other, then back again – then this way – then that way, and in short every way but by the dead ass. – La Fleur insisted upon the thing – and the bidet threw him.

[1] Post horse.

What's the matter, La Fleur, said I, with this bidet of thine? –
Monsieur, said he, *c'est un cheval le plus opiniatré du monde* –
Nay, if he is a conceited beast, he must go his own way, replied
I – so La Fleur got off him, and giving him a good sound lash,
the bidet took me at my word, and away he scamper'd back to
Montriul. – *Peste!* said La Fleur.

It is not *mal a propos* to take notice here, that tho' La Fleur
availed himself but of two different terms of exclamation in this
encounter – namely, *Diable!* and *Peste!* that there are nevertheless three, in the French language; like the positive, comparative,
and superlative, one or the other of which serve for every
unexpected throw of the dice in life.

Le Diable! which is the first, and positive degree, is generally
used upon ordinary emotions of the mind, where small things
only fall out contrary to your expectations – such as – the
throwing once doublets* – La Fleur's being kick'd off his horse,
and so forth – cuckoldom, for the same reason, is always – *Le
Diable!*

But in cases where the cast has something provoking in it, as
in that of the bidet's running away after, and leaving La Fleur
aground in jack-boots – 'tis the second degree.

'Tis then *Peste!*

And for the third – *

– But here my heart is wrung with pity and fellow-feeling,
when I reflect what miseries must have been their lot, and how
bitterly so refined a people must have smarted, to have forced
them upon the use of it. –

Grant me, O ye powers which touch the tongue with eloquence in distress! – whatever is my *cast*, Grant me but decent
words to exclaim in, and I will give my nature way.

– But as these were not to be had in France, I resolved to take
every evil just as it befell me without any exclamation at all.

La Fleur, who had made no such convenant with himself,
followed the bidet with his eyes till it was got out of sight – and
then, you may imagine, if you please, with what word he closed
the whole affair.

As there was no hunting down a frighten'd horse in jack-
boots, there remained no alternative but taking La Fleur either
behind the chaise, or into it. –

I preferred the latter, and in half an hour we got to the post-
house at Nampont.

NAMPONT
THE DEAD ASS

– And this, said he, putting the remains of a crust into his wallet – and this, should have been thy portion, said he, hadst thou been alive to have shared it with me. I thought by the accent, it had been an apostrophe to his child; but 'twas to his ass, and to the very ass we had seen dead in the road, which had occasioned La Fleur's misadventure. The man seemed to lament it much; and it instantly brought into my mind Sancho's lamentation* for his; but he did it with more true touches of nature.

The mourner was sitting upon a stone bench at the door, with the ass's pannel and its bridle on one side, which he took up from time to time – then laid them down – look'd at them and shook his head. He then took his crust of bread out of his wallet again, as if to eat it; held it some time in his hand – then laid it upon the bit of his ass's bridle – looked wistfully at the little arrangement he had made – and then gave a sigh.

The simplicity of his grief drew numbers about him, and La Fleur amongst the rest, whilst the horses were getting ready; as I continued sitting in the post-chaise, I could see and hear over their heads.

– He said he had come last from Spain, where he had been from the furthest borders of Franconia; and had got so far on his return home, when his ass died. Every one seem'd desirous to know what business could have taken so old and poor a man so far a journey from his own home.

It had pleased heaven, he said, to bless him with three sons, the finest lads in all Germany; but having in one week lost two of the eldest of them by the small-pox, and the youngest falling ill of the same distemper, he was afraid of being bereft of them all; and made a vow, if Heaven would not take him from him also, he would go in gratitude to St. Iago in Spain.*

When the mourner got thus far on his story, he stopp'd to pay nature her tribute – and wept bitterly.

He said, Heaven had accepted the conditions; and that he had set out from his cottage with this poor creature, who had been a patient partner of his journey – that it had eat the same bread with him all the way, and was unto him as a friend.*

Every body who stood about, heard the poor fellow with concern – La Fleur offered him money. – The mourner said, he did not want it – it was not the value of the ass – but the loss of him. – The ass, he said, he was assured loved him – and upon this told them a long story of a mischance upon their passage over the Pyrenean mountains which had separated them from each other three days; during which time the ass had sought him as much as he had sought the ass, and that they had neither scarce eat or drank till they met.

Thou hast one comfort, friend, said I, at least in the loss of thy poor beast; I'm sure thou hast been a merciful master to him. – Alas! said the mourner, I thought so, when he was alive – but now that he is dead I think otherwise. – I fear the weight of myself and my afflictions together have been too much for him – they have shortened the poor creature's days, and I fear I have them to answer for. – Shame on the world! said I to myself – Did we love each other, as this poor soul but loved his ass – 'twould be something. –

NAMPONT
THE POSTILLION

The concern which the poor fellow's story threw me into, required some attention: the postillion paid not the least to it, but set off upon the *pavè* in a full gallop.

The thirstiest soul in the most sandy desert of Arabia could not have wished more for a cup of cold water,* than mine did for grave and quiet movements; and I should have had an high opinion of the postillion had he but stolen off with me in something like a pensive pace. – On the contrary, as the mourner finished his lamentation, the fellow gave an unfeeling lash to each of his beasts, and set off clattering like a thousand devils.

I called to him as loud as I could, for heaven's sake to go slower – and the louder I called the more unmercifully he galloped. – The deuce take him and his galloping too – said I – he'll go on tearing my nerves to pieces till he has worked me into a foolish passion, and then he'll go slow, that I may enjoy the sweets of it.

The postillion managed the point to a miracle: by the time he had got to the foot of a steep hill about half a league from Nampont, – he had put me out of temper with him – and then with myself, for being so.

My case then required a different treatment; and a good rattling gallop would have been of real service to me. –

– Then, prithee get on – get on, my good lad, said I.

The postillion pointed to the hill – I then tried to return back to the story of the poor German and his ass – but I had broke the clue – and could no more get into it again, than the postillion could into a trot. –

– The deuce go, said I, with it all! Here am I sitting as candidly disposed to make the best of the worst, as ever wight was, and all runs counter.

There is one sweet lenitive at least for evils, which nature holds out to us; so I took it kindly at her hands, and fell asleep; and the first word which roused me was *Amiens*.

– Bless me! said I, rubbing my eyes – this is the very town where my poor lady is to come.

AMIENS

The words were scarce out of my mouth, when the Count de L***'s post-chaise, with his sister in it, drove hastily by: she had just time to make me a bow of recognition – and of that particular kind of it, which told me she had not yet done with me. She was as good as her look; for, before I had quite finished my supper, her brother's servant came into the room with a billet, in which she said, she had taken the liberty to charge me with a letter, which I was to present myself to Madame R*** the first morning I had nothing to do at Paris. There was only added, she was sorry, but from what *penchant* she had not considered, that she had been prevented telling me her story – that she still owed it me; and if my rout should ever lay through Brussels, and I had not by then forgot the name of Madame de L*** – that Madame de L*** would be glad to discharge her obligation.

Then I will meet thee, said I, fair spirit! at Brussels – 'tis only returning from Italy through Germany to Holland, by the rout of Flanders, home – 'twill scarce be ten posts out of my way; but were it ten thousand! with what a moral delight will it crown my journey, in sharing in the sickening incidents of a tale of misery told to me by such a sufferer? to see her weep! and though I cannot dry up the fountain of her tears, what an exquisite sensation is there still left, in wiping them away from off the cheeks* of the first and fairest of women, as I'm sitting with my handkerchief in my hand in silence the whole night besides her.

There was nothing wrong in the sentiment; and yet I instantly reproached my heart with it in the bitterest and most reprobate of expressions.

It had ever, as I told the reader, been one of the singular blessings of my life, to be almost every hour of it miserably in love with some one; and my last flame happening to be blown out by a whiff of jealousy on the sudden turn of a corner, I had lighted it up afresh at the pure taper of Eliza but about three months before — swearing as I did it, that it should last me through the whole journey — Why should I dissemble the matter? I had sworn to her eternal fidelity — she had a right to my whole heart — to divide my affections was to lessen them — to expose them, was to risk them: where there is risk, there may be loss — and what wilt thou have, Yorick! to answer to a heart so full of trust and confidence — so good, so gentle and unreproaching?

— I will not go to Brussels, replied I, interrupting myself — but my imagination went on — I recall'd her looks at that crisis of our separation when neither of us had power to say Adieu! I look'd at the picture she had tied in a black ribband about my neck — and blush'd as I look'd at it — I would have given the world to have kiss'd it, — but was ashamed — And shall this tender flower, said I, pressing it between my hands — shall it be smitten to its very root — and smitten, Yorick! by thee, who hast promised to shelter it in thy breast?

Eternal fountain of happiness! said I, kneeling down upon the ground — be thou my witness — and every pure spirit which tastes it, be my witness also, That I would not travel to Brussels, unless Eliza went along with me, did the road lead me towards heaven.

In transports of this kind, the heart, in spite of the understanding, will always say too much.

THE LETTER
AMIENS

Fortune had not smiled upon La Fleur; for he had been unsuccessful in his feats of chivalry – and not one thing had offer'd to signalize his zeal for my service from the time he had enter'd into it, which was almost four and twenty hours. The poor soul burn'd with impatience; and the Count de L***'s servant's coming with the letter, being the first practicable occasion which offered, La Fleur had laid hold of it; and in order to do honour to his master, had taken him into a back parlour in the Auberge, and treated him with a cup or two of the best wine in Picardy; and the Count de L***'s servant in return, and not to be behind hand in politeness with La Fleur, had taken him back with him to the Count's hôtel. La Fleur's *prevenancy* (for there was a passport in his very looks) soon set every servant in the kitchen at ease with him; and as a Frenchman, whatever be his talents, has no sort of prudery in shewing them, La Fleur, in less than five minutes, had pull'd out his fife, and leading off the dance himself with the first note, set the *fille de chambre*, the *maitre d'hotel*, the cook, the scullion, and all the household, dogs and cats, besides an old monkey, a-dancing: I suppose there never was a merrier kitchen since the flood.

Madame de L***, in passing from her brother's apartments to her own, hearing so much jollity below stairs, rung up her *fille de chambre* to ask about it; and hearing it was the English gentleman's servant who had set the whole house merry with his pipe, she order'd him up.

As the poor fellow could not present himself empty, he had loaden'd himself in going up stairs with a thousand compliments to Madame de L***, on the part of his master – added a long apocrypha of inquiries after Madame de L***'s health – told her, that Monsieur his master was *au desespoire* for her re-establishment from the fatigues of her journey – and, to close all, that Monsieur had received the letter which Madame had done him the honour – And he has done me the honour, said Madame de L***, interrupting La Fleur, to send a billet in return.

Madame de L*** had said this with such a tone of reliance upon the fact, that La Fleur had not power to disappoint her expectations – he trembled for my honour – and possibly might not altogether be unconcerned for his own, as a man capable of being attach'd to a master who could be a wanting *en egards vis a vis d'une femme*; so that when Madame de L✳✳✳ asked La Fleur if he had brought a letter – O *qu'oui,* said La Fleur : so laying down his hat upon the ground, and taking hold of the flap of his right side pocket with his left hand, he began to search for the letter with his right – then contrary-wise – *Diable!* – then sought every pocket – pocket by pocket, round, not forgetting his fob – *Peste!* – then La Fleur emptied them upon the floor – pulled out a dirty cravat – a handkerchief – a comb – a whip lash – a night-cap – then gave a peep into his hat – *Quelle etourderie!* He had left the letter upon the table in the Auberge – he would run for it, and be back with it in three minutes.

I had just finished my supper when La Fleur came in to give me an account of his adventure : he told the whole story simply as it was ; and only added, that if Monsieur had forgot (*par hazard*) to answer Madame's letter, the arrangement gave him an opportunity to recover the *faux pas* – and if not, that things were only as they were.

Now I was not altogether sure of my *etiquette,* whether I ought to have wrote or no ; but if I had – a devil himself could not have been angry : 'twas but the officious zeal of a well-meaning creature for my honour ; and however he might have mistook the road – or embarrassed me in so doing – his heart was in no fault – I was under no necessity to write – and what weighed more than all – he did not look as if he had done amiss.

– 'Tis all very well, La Fleur, said I. – 'Twas sufficient. La Fleur flew out of the room like lightening, and return'd with pen, ink, and paper, in his hand ; and coming up to the table, laid them close before me, with such a delight in his countenance, that I could not help taking up the pen.

I begun and begun again ; and though I had nothing to say, and that nothing might have been express'd in half a dozen lines, I made half a dozen different beginnings, and could no way please myself.✳

In short, I was in no mood to write.

La Fleur stepp'd out and brought a little water in a glass to dilute my ink – then fetch'd sand and seal-wax – It was all one : I wrote, and blotted, and tore off, and burnt, and wrote again –

Le Diable l'emporte! said I half to myself – I cannot write this self-same letter; throwing the pen down despairingly as I said it.

As soon as I had cast down the pen, La Fleur advanced with the most respectful carriage up to the table, and making a thousand apologies for the liberty he was going to take, told me he had a letter in his pocket wrote by a drummer in his regiment to a corporal's wife, which, he durst say, would suit the occasion.

I had a mind to let the poor fellow have his humour – Then prithee, said I, let me see it.

La Fleur instantly pull'd out a little dirty pocket-book cramm'd full of small letters and billet-doux in a sad condition, and laying it upon the table, and then untying the string which held them all together, run them over one by one, till he came to the letter in question – *La voila!* said he, clapping his hands : so unfolding it first, he laid it before me, and retired three steps from the table whilst I read it.

THE LETTER

MADAME,
Je suis penetré de la douleur la plus vive, et reduit en même temps au desespoir par ce retour imprevû du Corporal qui rend notre entrevue de ce soir la chose du monde la plus impossible.

Mais vive la joie! et toute la mienne sera de penser a vous.
L'amour n'est *rien* sans sentiment.*
Et le sentiment est encore *moins* sans amour.
On dit qu'on ne doit jamais se desesperer.
On dit aussi que Monsieur le Corporal monte la garde Mecredi : alors ce sera mon tour.

Chacun a son tour.

En attendant – Vive l'amour! et vive la bagatelle!

Je suis, MADAME,
Avec toutes les sentiments les plus respecteux
et les plus tendres tout a vous,

JACQUES ROQUE.

It was but changing the Corporal into the Count – and saying nothing about mounting guard on Wednesday – and the letter was neither right or wrong – so to gratify the poor fellow, who stood trembling for my honour, his own, and the honour of his letter, – I took the cream gently off it, and whipping it up in my own way – I seal'd it up and sent him with it to Madame de L∗∗∗ – and the next morning we pursued our journey to Paris.

PARIS

When a man can contest the point by dint of equipage, and carry all on floundering before him with half a dozen lackies and a couple of cooks – 'tis very well in such a place as Paris – he may drive in at which end of a street he will.

A poor prince who is weak in cavalry, and whose whole infantry does not exceed a single man, had best quit the field; and signalize himself in the cabinet, if he can get up into it – I say *up into it* – for there is no descending perpendicular amongst 'em with a *"Me voici! mes enfans"* – here I am – whatever many may think.

I own my first sensations, as soon as I was left solitary and alone in my own chamber in the hotel, were far from being so flattering as I had prefigured them. I walked up gravely to the window in my dusty black coat, and looking through the glass saw all the world in yellow, blue, and green, running at the ring of pleasure.∗ – The old with broken lances, and in helmets which had lost their vizards – the young in armour bright which shone like gold, beplumed with each gay feather of the east – all – all tilting at it like fascinated knights in tournaments of yore for fame and love. –

Alas, poor Yorick!∗ cried I, what art thou doing here? On the very first onset of all this glittering clatter, thou art reduced to an atom – seek – seek some winding alley, with a tourniquet at the end of it, where chariot never rolled or flambeau shot its rays – there thou mayest solace thy soul in converse sweet with some kind *grisset* of a barber's wife, and get into such coteries! –

– May I perish! if I do, said I, pulling out the letter which I had to present to Madame de R∗∗∗. – I'll wait upon this lady, the very first thing I do. So I called La Fleur to go seek me a barber directly – and come back and brush my coat.

THE WIG
PARIS

When the barber came, he absolutely refused to have any thing to do with my wig: 'twas either above or below his art: I had nothing to do, but to take one ready made of his own recommendation.

– But I fear, friend! said I, this buckle won't stand. – You may immerge it, replied he, into the ocean, and it will stand –

What a great scale is every thing upon in this city! thought I – The utmost stretch of an English periwig-maker's ideas could have gone no further than to have "dipped it into a pail of water" – What difference! 'tis like time to eternity.

I confess I do hate all cold conceptions, as I do the puny ideas which engender them; and am generally so struck with the great works of nature, that for my own part, if I could help it, I never would make a comparison less than a mountain at least. All that can be said against the French sublime in this instance of it, is this – that the grandeur is *more* in the *word*; and *less* in the *thing*. No doubt the ocean fills the mind with vast ideas; but Paris being so far inland, it was not likely I should run post a hundred miles out of it, to try the experiment – the Parisian barber meant nothing. –

The pail of water standing besides the great deep, makes certainly but a sorry figure in speech – but 'twill be said – it has one advantage – 'tis in the next room, and the truth of the buckle may be tried in it without more ado, in a single moment.

In honest truth, and upon a more candid revision of the matter, *The French expression professes more than it performs*.

I think I can see the precise and distinguishing marks of national characters more in these nonsensical *minutiæ*, than in the most important matters of state; where great men of all nations talk and stalk so much alike, that I would not give ninepence to chuse amongst them.

I was so long in getting from under my barber's hands, that it was too late to think of going with my letter to Madame R✳✳✳ that night: but when a man is once dressed at all points for going out, his reflections turn to little account, so taking down the name of the Hotel de Modene where I lodged, I walked forth without any determination where to go – I shall consider of that, said I, as I walk along.

THE PULSE
PARIS

Hail ye small sweet courtesies of life, for smooth do ye make the road of it! like grace and beauty which beget inclinations to love at first sight; 'tis ye who open this door and let the stranger in.

– Pray, Madame, said I, have the goodness to tell me which way I must turn to go to the Opera comique: – Most willingly, Monsieur, said she, laying aside her work –

I had given a cast with my eye into half a dozen shops as I came along in search of a face not likely to be disordered by such an interruption; till at last, this hitting my fancy, I had walked in.

She was working a pair of ruffles as she sat in a low chair on the far side of the shop facing the door –

– *Tres volentieres*; most willingly, said she, laying her work down upon a chair next her, and rising up from the low chair she was sitting in, with so chearful a movement and so chearful a look, that had I been laying out fifty louis d'ors with her, I should have said – "This woman is grateful."

You must turn, Monsieur, said she, going with me to the door of the shop, and pointing the way down the street I was to take – you must turn first to your left hand – *mais prenez guarde* – there are two turns; and be so good as to take the second – then go down a little way and you'll see a church, and when you are past it, give yourself the trouble to turn directly to the right, and that will lead you to the foot of the *pont neuf*, which you must cross – and there, any one will do himself the pleasure to shew you –

She repeated her instructions three times over to me with the same good natur'd patience the third time as the first; – and if *tones and manners* have a meaning, which certainly they have, unless to hearts which shut them out – she seem'd really interested, that I should not lose myself.

I will not suppose it was the woman's beauty, notwithstanding she was the handsomest grisset, I think, I ever saw, which had much to do with the sense I had of her courtesy; only I remember, when I told her how much I was obliged to her, that I looked very full in her eyes, – and that I repeated my thanks as often as she had done her instructions.

I had not got ten paces from the door, before I found I had forgot every tittle of what she had said – so looking back, and seeing her still standing in the door of the shop as if to look whether I went right or not – I returned back, to ask her whether the first turn was to my right or left – for that I had absolutely forgot. – Is is possible! said she, half laughing. – 'Tis very possible, replied I, when a man is thinking more of a woman, than of her good advice.

As this was the real truth – she took it, as every woman takes a matter of right, with a slight courtesy.

– *Attendez!* said she, laying her hand upon my arm to detain me, whilst she called a lad out of the back-shop to get ready a parcel of gloves. I am just going to send him, said she, with a packet into that quarter, and if you will have the complaisance to step in, it will be ready in a moment, and he shall attend you to the place. – So I walk'd in with her to the far side of the shop, and taking up the ruffle in my hand which she laid upon the chair, as if I had a mind to sit, she sat down herself in her low chair, and I instantly sat myself down besides her.

– He will be ready, Monsieur, said she, in a moment – And in that moment, replied I, most willingly would I say something very civil to you for all these courtesies. Any one may do a casual act of good nature, but a continuation of them shews it is a part of the temperature; and certainly, added I, if it is the same blood which comes from the heart, which descends to the extremes (touching her wrist) I am sure you must have one of the best pulses of any woman in the world – Feel it, said she, holding out her arm. So laying down my hat, I took hold of her fingers in one hand, and applied the two fore-fingers of my other to the artery –

– Would to heaven! my dear Eugenius,* thou hadst passed by, and beheld me sitting in my black coat, and in my lack-a-day-sical manner, counting the throbs of it, one by one, with as much true devotion as if I had been watching the critical ebb or flow of her fever – How wouldst thou have laugh'd and moralized upon my new profession? – and thou shouldst have laugh'd and moralized on – Trust me, my dear Eugenius, I should have said, "there are worse occupations in this world *than feeling a woman's pulse.*" – But a Grisset's! thou wouldst have said – and in an open shop! Yorick –

– So much the better : for when my views are direct, Eugenius, I care not if all the world saw me feel it.

THE HUSBAND
PARIS

I had counted twenty pulsations, and was going on fast towards the fortieth, when her husband coming unexpected from a back parlour into the shop, put me a little out in my reckoning – 'Twas no body but her husband, she said – so I began a fresh score – Monsieur is so good, quoth she, as he pass'd by us, as to give himself the trouble of feeling my pulse – The husband took off his hat, and making me a bow, said, I did him too much honour – and having said that, he put on his hat and walk'd out.

Good God! said I to myself, as he went out – and can this man be the husband of this woman ?

Let it not torment the few who know what must have been the grounds of this exclamation, if I explain it to those who do not.

In London a shopkeeper and a shopkeeper's wife seem to be one bone and one flesh : in the several endowments of mind and body, sometimes the one, sometimes the other has it, so as in general to be upon a par, and to tally with each other as nearly as man and wife need to do.

In Paris, there are scarce two orders of beings more different : for the legislative and executive powers of the shop not resting in the husband, he seldom comes there – in some dark and dismal room behind, he sits commerceless in his thrum nightcap, the same rough son of Nature that Nature left him.

The genius of a people where nothing but the monarchy is *salique*,* having ceded this department, with sundry others, totally to the women – by a continual higgling with customers of all ranks and sizes from morning to night, like so many rough pebbles shook long together in a bag, by amicable collisions, they have worn down their asperities and sharp angles, and not only become round and smooth, but will receive, some of them, a polish like a brilliant – Monsieur *le Mari* is little better than the stone under your foot –

– Surely – surely man ! it is not good for thee to sit alone* –

thou wast made for social intercourse and gentle greetings, and this improvement of our natures from it, I appeal to, as my evidence.

– And how does it beat, Monsieur? said she. – With all the benignity, said I, looking quietly in her eyes, that I expected – She was going to say something civil in return – but the lad came into the shop with the gloves – *A propos*, said I; I want a couple of pair myself.

THE GLOVES
PARIS

The beautiful Grisset rose up when I said this, and going behind the counter, reach'd down a parcel and untied it: I advanced to the side over-against her: they were all too large. The beautiful Grisset measured them one by one across my hand – It would not alter the dimensions – She begg'd I would try a single pair, which seemed to be the least – She held it open – my hand slipp'd into it at once – It will not do, said I, shaking my head a little – No, said she, doing the same thing.

There are certain combined looks of simple subtlety – where whim, and sense, and seriousness, and nonsense, are so blended, that all the languages of Babel set loose together could not express them – they are communicated and caught so instantaneously, that you can scarce say which party is the infecter. I leave it to your men of words to swell pages about it – it is enough in the present to say again, the gloves would not do; so folding our hands within our arms, we both loll'd upon the counter – it was narrow, and there was just room for the parcel to lay between us.

The beautiful Grisset look'd sometimes at the gloves, then side-ways to the window, then at the gloves – and then at me. I was not disposed to break silence – I follow'd her example: so I look'd at the gloves, then to the window, then at the gloves, and then at her – and so on alternately.

I found I lost considerably in every attack – she had a quick black eye, and shot through two such long and silken eye-lashes with such penetration, that she look'd into my very heart and reins – It may seem strange, but I could actually feel she did –

– It is no matter, said I, taking up a couple of the pairs next me, and putting them into my pocket.

I was sensible the beautiful Grisset had not ask'd above a single livre above the price – I wish'd she had ask'd a livre more, and was puzzling my brains how to bring the matter about – Do you think, my dear Sir, said she, mistaking my embarrassment, that I could ask a *sous* too much of a stranger – and of a stranger whose politeness, more than his want of gloves, has done me the honour to lay himself at my mercy ? – *M'en croyez capable?* – Faith! not I, said I; and if you were, you are welcome – So counting the money into her hand, and with a lower bow than one generally makes to a shopkeeper's wife, I went out, and her lad with his parcel followed me.

THE TRANSLATION
PARIS

There was no body in the box I was let into but a kindly old French officer. I love the character, not only because I honour the man whose manners are softened by a profession which makes bad men worse; but that I once knew one – for he is no more – and why should I not rescue one page from violation by writing his name in it, and telling the world it was Captain Tobias Shandy,* the dearest of my flock and friends, whose philanthropy I never think of at this long distance from his death – but my eyes gush out with tears. For his sake, I have a predilection for the whole corps of veterans; and so I strode over the two back rows of benches, and placed myself beside him.

The old officer was reading attentively a small pamphlet, it might be the book of the opera, with a large pair of spectacles. As soon as I sat down, he took his spectacles off, and putting them into a shagreen case, return'd them and the book into his pocket together. I half rose up, and made him a bow.

Translate this into any civilized language in the world – the sense is this:

"Here's a poor stranger come in to the box – he seems as if he knew no body; and is never likely, was he to be seven years in Paris, if every man he comes near keeps his spectacles upon his nose – 'tis shutting the door of conversation absolutely in his face – and using him worse than a German."

The French officer might as well have said it all aloud; and if he had, I should in course have put the bow I made him into French too, and told him, "I was sensible of his attention, and return'd him a thousand thanks for it."

There is not a secret so aiding to the progress of sociality, as to get master of this *short hand*, and be quick in rendering the several turns of looks and limbs, with all their inflections and delineations, into plain words. For my own part, by long habitude, I do it so mechanically, that when I walk the streets of London, I go translating all the way; and have more than once stood behind in the circle, where not three words have been said, and have brought off twenty different dialogues with me, which I could have fairly wrote down and sworn to.

I was going one evening to Martini's concert* at Milan, and was just entering the door of the hall, when the Marquesina di F*** was coming out in a sort of hurry – she was almost upon me before I saw her; so I gave a spring to one side to let her pass – She had done the same, and on the same side too; so we ran our heads together: she instantly got to the other side to get out: I was just as unfortunate as she had been; for I had sprung to that side, and opposed her passage again – We both flew together to the other side, and then back – and so on – it was ridiculous; we both blush'd intolerably; so I did at last the thing I should have done at first – I stood stock still, and the Marquesina had no more difficulty. I had no power to go into the room, till I had made her so much reparation as to wait and follow her with my eye to the end of the passage – She look'd back twice, and walk'd along it rather side-ways, as if she would make room for any one coming up stairs to pass her – No, said I – that's a vile translation: the Marquesina has a right to the best apology I can make her; and that opening is left for me to do it in – so I ran and begg'd pardon for the embarrassment I had given her, saying it was my intention to have made her way. She answered, she was guided by the same intention towards me – so we reciprocally thank'd each other. She was at the top of the stairs; and seeing no *chichesbee** near her, I begg'd to hand her to her coach – so we went down the stairs, stopping at every third step to talk of the concert and the adventure – Upon my word, Madame, said I when I had handed her in, I made six different efforts to let you go out – And I made six efforts, replied she, to let you enter – I wish to heaven you would make a seventh, said I – With all my heart, said she, making room – Life is too short to be long about the forms of it – so I instantly stepp'd in, and she carried me home with her – And what became of the concert, St. Cecilia,* who, I suppose, was at it, knows more than I.

I will only add, that the connection which arose out of that translation, gave me more pleasure than any one I had the honour to make in Italy.

THE DWARF
PARIS

I had never heard the remark made by any one in my life, except by one; and who that was,* will probably come out in this chapter; so that being pretty much unprepossessed, there must have been grounds for what struck me the moment I cast my eyes over the *parterre* – and that was, the unaccountable sport of nature in forming such numbers of dwarfs – No doubt, she sports at certain times in almost every corner of the world; but in Paris, there is no end to her amusements – The goddess seems almost as merry as she is wise.

As I carried my idea out of the *opera comique* with me, I measured every body I saw walking in the streets by it – Melancholy application! especially where the size was extremely little – the face extremely dark – the eyes quick – the nose long – the teeth white – the jaw prominent – to see so many miserables, by force of accidents driven out of their own proper class into the very verge of another, which it gives me pain to write down – every third man a pigmy! – some by ricketty heads and hump backs – others by bandy legs – a third set arrested by the hand of Nature in the sixth and seventh years of their growth – a fourth, in their perfect and natural state, like dwarf apple-trees; from the first rudiments and stamina of their existence, never meant to grow higher.

A medical traveller might say, 'tis owing to undue bandages – a splenetic one, to want of air – and an inquisitive traveller, to fortify the system, may measure the height of their houses – the narrowness of their streets, and in how few feet square in the sixth and seventh stories such numbers of the *Bourgoisie* eat and sleep together; but I remember, Mr. Shandy the elder,* who accounted for nothing like any body else, in speaking one evening of these matters, averred, that children, like other animals, might be increased almost to any size, provided they came right into the world; but the misery was, the citizens of Paris were so coop'd up, that they had not actually room enough to get them – I do not call it getting any thing, said he – 'tis getting nothing – Nay, continued he, rising in his argument, 'tis getting worse than nothing, when all you have got, after twenty or five and twenty years of the tenderest care and most nutritious aliment bestowed upon it, shall not at last be as high as my leg. Now, Mr. Shandy being very short, there could be nothing more said upon it.

As this is not a work of reasoning, I leave the solution as I found it, and content myself with the truth only of the remark, which is verified in every lane and by-lane of Paris. I was walking down that which leads from the Carousal to the Palais Royal, and observing a little boy in some distress at the side of the gutter, which ran down the middle of it, I took hold of his hand, and help'd him over. Upon turning up his face to look at him after, I perceived he was about forty – Never mind, said I; some good body will do as much for me when I am ninety.

I feel some little principles within me, which incline me to be merciful towards this poor blighted part of my species, who have neither size or strength to get on in the world – I cannot bear to see one of them trod upon; and had scarce got seated beside my old French officer, ere the disgust was exercised, by seeing the very thing happen under the box we sat in.

At the end of the orchestra, and betwixt that and the first side-box, there is a small esplanade left, where, when the house is full, numbers of all ranks take sanctuary. Though you stand, as in the parterre, you pay the same price as in the orchestra. A poor defenceless being of this order had got thrust some how or other into this luckless place – the night was hot, and he was surrounded by beings two feet and a half higher than himself.* The dwarf suffered inexpressibly on all sides; but the thing which incommoded him most, was a tall corpulent German, near seven feet high, who stood directly betwixt him and all possibility of his seeing either the stage or the actors. The poor dwarf did all he could to get a peep at what was going forwards, by seeking for some little opening betwixt the German's arm and his body, trying first one side, then the other; but the German stood square in the most unaccommodating posture that can be imagined – the dwarf might as well have been placed at the bottom of the deepest draw-well in Paris; so he civilly reach'd up his hand to the German's sleeve, and told him his distress – The German turn'd his head back, look'd down upon him as Goliah did upon David – and unfeelingly resumed his posture.

I was just then taking a pinch of snuff out of my monk's little horn box – And how would thy meek and courteous spirit, my dear monk! so temper'd to *bear and forbear!* – how sweetly would it have lent an ear to this poor soul's complaint!

The old French officer seeing me lift up my eyes with an emotion, as I made the apostrophe, took the liberty to ask me what was the matter – I told him the story in three words; and added, how inhuman it was.

By this time the dwarf was driven to extremes, and in his first transports, which are generally unreasonable, had told the German he would cut off his long queue with his knife – The German look'd back coolly, and told him he was welcome if he could reach it.

An injury sharpened by an insult, be it to who it will, makes every man of sentiment a party: I could have leaped out of the box to have redressed it. – The old French officer did it with much less confusion; for leaning a little over, and nodding to a centinel, and pointing at the same time with his finger to the distress – the centinel made his way up to it. – There was no occasion to tell the grievance – the thing told itself; so thrusting back the German instantly with his musket – he took the poor dwarf by the hand, and placed him before him. – This is noble! said I, clapping my hands together – And yet you would not permit this, said the old officer, in England.

– In England, dear Sir, said I, *we sit all at our ease.*

The old French officer would have set me at unity with myself, in case I had been at variance, – by saying it was a *bon mot* – and as a *bon mot* is always worth something at Paris, he offered me a pinch of snuff.

THE ROSE
PARIS

It was now my turn to ask the old French officer "What was the matter?" for a cry of *"Haussez les mains, Monsieur l'Abbe,"* re-echoed from a dozen different parts of the parterre, was as unintelligible to me, as my apostrophe to the monk had been to him.

He told me, it was some poor Abbe in one of the upper loges, who he supposed had got planted perdu behind a couple of grissets in order to see the opera, and that the parterre espying him, were insisting upon his holding up both his hands during the representation. – And can it be supposed, said I, that an ecclesiastick would pick the Grisset's pockets? The old French officer smiled, and whispering in my ear, open'd a door of knowledge which I had no idea of –

Good God! said I, turning pale with astonishment – is it possible, that a people so smit with sentiment should at the same time be so unclean, and so unlike themselves – *Quelle grossierte!* added I.

The French officer told me, it was an illiberal sarcasm at the church, which had begun in the theatre about the time the Tartuffe was given in it, by Moliere – but, like other remains of Gothic manners, was declining – Every nation, continued he, have their refinements and *grossiertes*, in which they take the lead, and lose it of one another by turns – that he had been in most countries, but never in one where he found not some delicacies, which other seemed to want. *Le* POUR, *et le* CONTRE *se trouvent en chaque nation*; there is a balance, said he, of good and bad every where; and nothing but the knowing it is so can emancipate one half of the world from the prepossessions which it holds against the other – that the advantage of travel, as it regarded the *sçavoir vivre*, was by seeing a great deal both of men and manners; it taught us mutual toleration; and mutual toleration, concluded he, making me a bow, taught us mutual love.

The old French officer delivered this with an air of such candour and good sense, as coincided with my first favourable impressions of his character – I thought I loved the man; but I fear I mistook the object – 'twas my own way of thinking – the difference was, I could not have expressed it half so well.

It is alike troublesome to both the rider and his beast – if the latter goes pricking up his ears, and starting all the way at every object which he never saw before – I have as little torment of this kind as any creature alive; and yet I honestly confess, that many a thing gave me pain, and that I blush'd at many a word the first month – which I found inconsequent and perfectly innocent the second.

Madame de Rambouliet,* after an acquaintance of about six weeks with her, had done me the honour to take me in her coach about two leagues out of town – Of all women, Madame de Rambouliet is the most correct; and I never wish to see one of more virtues and purity of heart – In our return back, Madame de Rambouliet desired me to pull the cord – I ask'd her if she wanted any thing – *Rien que pisser*, said Madame de Rambouliet –

Grieve not, gentle traveller, to let Madame de Rambouliet p-ss on – And, ye fair mystic nymphs! go each one *pluck your rose*,* and scatter them in your path – for Madame de Rambouliet did no more – I handed Madame de Rambouliet out of the coach; and had I been the priest of the chaste CASTALIA,* I could not have served at her fountain with a more respectful decorum.

END OF VOL. I.

A

SENTIMENTAL JOURNEY

THROUGH

FRANCE AND ITALY.

BY

Mr. YORICK.

VOL. II.

LONDON:

Printed for T. BECKET and P. A. DE HONDT,
in the Strand.   MDCCLXVIII.

THE
FILLE DE CHAMBRE
PARIS

What the old French officer had deliver'd upon travelling, bringing Polonius's advice to his son* upon the same subject into my head – and that bringing in Hamlet; and Hamlet, the rest of Shakespear's works, I stopp'd at the Quai de Conti in my return home, to purchase the whole set.

The bookseller said he had not a set in the world – *Comment!* said I; taking one up out of a set which lay upon the counter betwixt us. – He said, they were sent him only to be got bound, and were to be sent back to Versailles in the morning to the Count de B****.*

– And does the Count de B**** said I, read Shakespear? *C'est un Esprit fort*; replied the bookseller. – He loves English books; and what is more to his honour, Monsieur, he loves the English too. You speak this so civilly, said I, that 'tis enough to oblige an Englishman to lay out a Louis d'or or two at your shop – the bookseller made a bow, and was going to say something, when a young decent girl of about twenty, who by her air and dress, seemed to be *fille de chambre* to some devout woman of fashion, came into the shop and asked for *Les Egarments du Cœur & de l'Esprit*:* the bookseller gave her the book directly; she pulled out a little green sattin purse run round with a ribband of the same colour, and putting her finger and thumb into it, she took out the money, and paid for it. As I had nothing more to stay me in the shop, we both walked out at the door together.

– And what have you to do, my dear, said I, with *The Wanderings of the Heart*, who scarce know yet you have one? nor till love has first told you it, or some faithless shepherd has made it ache, can'st thou ever be sure it is so. – *Le Dieu m'en guard!* said the girl. – With reason, said I – for if it is a good one, 'tis pity it should be stolen: 'tis a little treasure to thee, and gives a better air to your face, than if it was dress'd out with pearls.

The young girl listened with a submissive attention, holding her sattin purse by its ribband in her hand all the time – 'Tis a very small one, said I, taking hold of the bottom of it – she held it towards me – and there is very little in it, my dear, said I; but be but as good as thou art handsome, and heaven will fill it: I had a parcel of crowns in my hand to pay for Shakespear; and as she had let go the purse intirely, I put a single one in; and tying up the ribband in a bow-knot, returned it to her.

The young girl made me more a humble courtesy than a low one – 'twas one of those quiet, thankful sinkings where the spirit bows itself down – the body does no more than tell it. I never gave a girl a crown in my life which gave me half the pleasure.

My advice, my dear, would not have been worth a pin to you, said I, if I had not given this along with it: but now, when you see the crown, you'll remember it – so don't, my dear, lay it out in ribbands.

Upon my word, Sir, said the girl, earnestly, I am incapable – in saying which, as is usual in little bargains of honour, she gave me her hand – *En verite, Monsieur, je mettrai cet argent apart*, said she.

When a virtuous convention is made betwixt man and woman, it sanctifies their most private walks: so notwithstanding it was dusky, yet as both our roads lay the same way, we made no scruple of walking along the Quai de Conti together.

She made me a second courtesy in setting off, and before we got twenty yards from the door, as if she had not done enough before, she made a sort of a little stop to tell me again, – she thank'd me.

It was a small tribute, I told her, which I could not avoid paying to virtue, and would not be mistaken in the person I had been rendering it to for the world – but I see innocence, my dear, in your face – and foul befal the man who ever lays a snare in its way!

The girl seem'd affected some way or other with what I said – she gave a low sigh – I found I was not impowered to enquire at all after it – so said nothing more till I got to the corner of the Rue de Nevers, where we were to part.

– But is this the way, my dear, said I, to the hotel de Modene? she told me it was – or, that I might go by the Rue de Guineygaude, which was the next turn. – Then I'll go, my dear, by the Rue de Guineygaude, said I, for two reasons; first I shall please myself, and next I shall give you the protection of my company as far on your way as I can. The girl was sensible I was civil – and said, she wish'd the hotel de Modene was in the Rue de St. Pierre – You live there? said I. – She told me she was *fille de chambre* to Madame R※※※ – Good God! said I, 'tis the very lady for whom I have brought a letter from Amiens – The girl told me that Madame R※※※, she believed expected a stranger with a letter, and was impatient to see him – so I desired the girl to present my compliments to Madame R※※※, and say I would certainly wait upon her in the morning.

We stood still at the corner of the Rue de Nevers whilst this pass'd – We then stopp'd a moment whilst she disposed of her *Egarments de Cœur,* &c. more commodiously than carrying them in her hand – they were two volumes; so I held the second for her whilst she put the first into her pocket; and then she held her pocket, and I put in the other after it.

'Tis sweet to feel by what fine-spun threads our affections are drawn together.

We set off a-fresh, and as she took her third step, the girl put her hand within my arm – I was just bidding her – but she did it of herself with that undeliberating simplicity, which shew'd it was out of her head that she had never seen me before. For my own part, I felt the conviction of consanguinity so strongly, that I could not help turning half round to look in her face, and see if I could trace out any thing in it of a family likeness – Tut! said I, are we not all relations?

When we arrived at the turning up of the Rue de Guiney-gaude, I stopp'd to bid her adieu for good an all: the girl would thank me again for my company and kindness – She bid me adieu twice – I repeated it as often; and so cordial was the parting between us, that had it happen'd any where else, I'm not sure but I should have signed it with a kiss of charity, as warm and holy as an apostle.

But in Paris, as none kiss each other but the men – I did, what amounted to the same thing –

– I bid God bless her.

THE PASSPORT
PARIS

When I got home to my hotel, La Fleur told me I had been enquired after by the Lieutenant de Police – The duce take it!

said I—I know the reason. It is time the reader should know it, for in the order of things in which it happened, it was omitted; not that it was out of my head; but that had I told it then, it might have been forgot now – and now is the time I want it.

I had left London with so much precipitation, that it never enter'd my mind that we were at war with France;* and had reach'd Dover, and look'd through my glass at the hills beyond Boulogne, before the idea presented itself; and with this in its train, that there was no getting there without a passport. Go but to the end of a street, I have a mortal aversion for returning back no wiser than I sat* out; and as this was one of the greatest efforts I had ever made for knowledge, I could less bear the thoughts of it: so hearing the Count de **** had hired the packet, I begg'd he would take me in his *suite*. The Count had some little knowledge of me, so made little or no difficulty – only said, his inclination to serve me could reach no further than Calais; as he was to return by way of Brussels to Paris: however, when I had once pass'd there, I might get to Paris without interruption; but that in Paris I must make friends and shift for myself. – Let me get to Paris, Monsieur le Count, said I – and I shall do very well. So I embark'd, and never thought more of the matter.

When La Fleur told me the Lieutenant de Police had been enquiring after me – the thing instantly recurred – and by the time La Fleur had well told me, the master of the hotel came into my room to tell me the same thing, with this addition to it, that my passport had been particularly ask'd after: the master of the hotel concluded with saying, He hoped I had one. – Not I, faith! said I.

The master of the hotel retired three steps from me, as from an infected person, as I declared this – and poor La Fleur advanced three steps towards me, and with that sort of movement which a good soul makes to succour a distress'd one – the fellow won my heart by it; and from that single *trait*, I knew his character as perfectly, and could rely upon it as firmly, as if he had served me with fidelity for seven years.

Mon seignior! cried the master of the hotel – but recollecting himself as he made the exclamation, he instantly changed the tone of it – If Monsieur, said he, has not a passport (*apparament*) in all likelihood he has friends in Paris who can procure him one. – Not that I know of, quoth I, with an air of indifference. – Then *certes*, replied he, you'll be sent to the Bastile or the Chatelet, *au moins*. Poo! said I, the king of France is a good natured soul – he'll hurt no body. – *Cela n'empeche pas*, said he – you will certainly be sent to the Bastile to-morrow morning. – But I've taken your lodgings for a month, answer'd I, and I'll not quit them a day before the time for all the kings of France in the world. La Fleur whisper'd in my ear, That no body could oppose the king of France.

Pardi! said my host, *ces Messieurs Anglois sont des gens tres extraordinaires* – and having both said and sworn it – he went out.

THE PASSPORT
THE HOTEL AT PARIS

I could not find in my heart to torture La Fleur's with a serious look upon the subject of my embarrassment, which was the reason I had treated it so cavalierly : and to shew him how light it lay upon my mind, I dropt the subject entirely ; and whilst he waited upon me at supper, talk'd to him with more than usual gaiety about Paris, and of the opera comique. – La Fleur had been there himself, and had followed me through the streets as far as the bookseller's shop ; but seeing me come out with the young *fille de chambre*, and that we walk'd down the Quai de Conti together, La Fleur deem'd it unnecessary to follow me a step further – so making his own reflections upon it, he took a shorter cut — and got to the hotel in time to be inform'd of the affair of the Police against my arrival.

As soon as the honest creature had taken away, and gone down to sup himself, I then began to think a little seriously about my situation. –

– And here, I know, Eugenius, thou wilt smile at the remembrance of a short dialogue which pass'd betwixt us the moment I was going to set out — I must tell it here.

Eugenius, knowing that I was as little subject to be overburthen'd with money as thought, had drawn me aside to interrogate me how much I had taken care for; upon telling him the exact sum, Eugenius shook his head, and said it would not do; so pull'd out his purse in order to empty it into mine. – I've enough in conscience, Eugenius, said I. — Indeed, Yorick, you have not, replied Eugenius – I know France and Italy better than you. – But you don't consider, Eugenius, said I, refusing his offer, that before I have been three days in Paris, I shall take care to say or do something or other for which I shall get clapp'd up into the Bastile, and that I shall live there a couple of months entirely at the king of France's expence. – I beg pardon, said Eugenius, drily : really, I had forgot that resource.

Now the event I treated gaily came seriously to my door.

Is it folly, or nonchalance, or philosophy, or pertinacity – or what is it in me, that, after all, when La Fleur had gone down stairs, and I was quite alone, I could not bring down my mind to think of it otherwise than I had then spoken of it to Eugenius ?

– And as for the Bastile ! the terror is in the word – Make the most of it you can, said I to myself, the Bastile is but another word for a tower – and a tower is but another word for a house you can't get out of – Mercy on the gouty ! for they are in it twice a year – but with nine livres a day, and pen and ink and paper and patience, albeit a man can't get out, he may do very well within – at least for a month or six weeks ; at the end of which, if he is a harmless fellow his innocence appears, and he comes out a better and wiser man than he went in.

I had some occasion (I forget what) to step into the court-yard, as I settled this account ; and remember I walk'd down stairs in no small triumph with the conceit of my reasoning – Beshrew the *sombre* pencil ! said I vauntingly – for I envy not its powers, which paints the evils of life with so hard and deadly a colouring. The mind sits terrified at the objects she has magnified herself, and blackened : reduce them to their proper size and hue she overlooks them – 'Tis true, said I, correcting the proposition – the Bastile is not an evil to be despised – but strip it of its towers – fill up the fossè – unbarricade the doors – call it simply a confinement, and suppose 'tis some tyrant of a distemper – and not of a man which holds you in it – the evil half vanishes, and you bear the other half without complaint.

I was interrupted in the hey-day of this soliloquy, with a voice which I took to be of a child, which complained "it could not get out." – I look'd up and down the passage, and seeing neither man, woman, or child, I went out without further attention.

In my return back through the passage, I heard the same words repeated twice over ; and looking up, I saw it was a starling hung in a little cage. – "I can't get out – I can't get out," said the starling.

I stood looking at the bird : and to every person who came through the passage it ran fluttering to the side towards which they approach'd it, with the same lamentation of its captivity – "I can't get out", said the starling – God help thee ! said I, but I'll let thee out, cost what it will ; so I turn'd about the cage to get to the door ; it was twisted and double twisted so fast with wire, there was no getting it open without pulling the cage to pieces – I took both hands to it.

The bird flew to the place where I was attempting his deliverance, and thrusting his head through the trellis, press'd his breast against it, as if impatient – I fear, poor creature ! said I, I cannot set thee at liberty – "No," said the starling – "I can't get out – I can't get out," said the starling.

I vow, I never had my affections more tenderly awakened ; nor do I remember an incident in my life, where the dissipated spirits, to which my reason had been a bubble, were so suddenly call'd home. Mechanical as the notes were, yet so true in tune to nature were they chanted, that in one moment they overthrew all my systematic reasonings upon the Bastile ; and I heavily walk'd up stairs, unsaying every word I had said in going down them.

Disguise thyself as thou wilt, still slavery ! said I – still thou art a bitter draught ; and though thousands in all ages have been made to drink of thee, thou art no less bitter on that account.*
– 'tis thou, thrice sweet and gracious goddess, addressing myself to LIBERTY, whom all in public or in private worship, whose taste is grateful, and ever wilt be so, till NATURE herself shall change – no *tint* of words can spot thy snowy mantle, or chymic power turn thy sceptre into iron – with thee to smile upon him as he eats his crust, the swain is happier than his monarch, from whose court thou art exiled – Gracious heaven ! cried I, kneeling down upon the last step but one in my ascent – grant me but health, thou great Bestower of it, and give me but this fair goddess as my companion – and shower down thy mitres, if it seems good unto thy divine providence, upon those heads which are aching for them.

THE CAPTIVE
PARIS

The bird in his cage pursued me into my room ; I sat down close to my table, and leaning my head upon my hand, I begun to figure to myself* the miseries of confinement. I was in a right frame for it, and so I gave full scope to my imagination.

I was going to begin with the millions of my fellow creatures born to no inheritance but slavery ; but finding, however affecting the picture was, that I could not bring it near me, and that the multitude of sad groups in it did but distract me. –

– I took a single captive, and having first shut him up in his dungeon, I then look'd through the twilight of his grated door to take his picture.

I beheld his body half wasted away with long expectation and confinement, and felt what kind of sickness of the heart it was which arises from hope deferr'd.* Upon looking nearer I saw him pale and feverish : in thirty years the western breeze had not once fann'd his blood – he had seen no sun, no moon in all that time – nor had the voice of friend or kinsman breathed through his lattice – his children –

– But here my heart began to bleed – and I was forced to go on with another part of the portrait.

He was sitting upon the ground upon a little straw, in the furthest corner of his dungeon, which was alternately his chair and bed : a little calender of small sticks were laid at the head notch'd all over with the dismal days and nights he had pass'd there – he had one of these little sticks in his hand, and with a rusty nail he was etching another day of misery to add to the heap. As I darkened the little light he had, he lifted up a hopeless eye towards the door, then cast it down – shook his head, and went on with his work of affliction. I heard his chains upon his legs, as he turn'd his body to lay his little stick upon the bundle – He gave a deep sigh – I saw the iron enter into his soul* – I burst into tears – I could not sustain the picture of confinement* which my fancy had drawn – I startled up from my chair, and calling La Fleur, I bid him bespeak me a *remise*, and have it ready at the door of the hotel by nine in the morning.

– I'll go directly, said I, myself to Monsieur Le Duke de Choiseul.*

La Fleur would have put me to bed ; but not willing he should see any thing upon my cheek, which would cost the honest fellow a heart ache — I told him I would go to bed by myself — and bid him go do the same.

THE STARLING
ROAD TO VERSAILLES

I got into my *remise* the hour I proposed: La Fleur got up behind, and I bid the coachman make the best of his way to Versailles.

As there was nothing in this road, or rather nothing which I look for in travelling, I cannot fill up the blank better than with a short history of this self-same bird, which became the subject of the last chapter.

Whilst the Honourable Mr. **** was waiting for a wind at Dover it had been caught upon the cliffs before it could well fly, by an English lad who was his groom; who not caring to destroy it, had taken it in his breast into the packet — and by course of feeding it, and taking it once under his protection, in a day or two grew fond of it, and got it safe along with him to Paris.

At Paris the lad had laid out a livre in a little cage for the starling, and as he had little to do better the five months his master stay'd there, he taught it in his mother's tongue the four simple words — (and no more) — to which I own'd myself so much its debtor.

Upon his master's going on for Italy — the lad had given it to the master of the hotel — But his little song for liberty, being in an *unknown* language at Paris — the bird had little or no store set by him — so La Fleur bought both him and his cage for me for a bottle of Burgundy.

In my return from Italy I brought him with me to the country in whose language he had learn'd his notes — and telling the story of him to Lord A — Lord A begg'd the bird of me — in a week Lord A gave him to Lord B — Lord B made a present of him to Lord C — and Lord C's gentleman sold him to Lord D's for a shilling — Lord D gave him to Lord E — and so on — half round the alphabet — From that rank he pass'd into the lower house, and pass'd the hands of as many commoners — But as all these wanted to *get in* — and my bird wanted to get out — he had almost as little store set by him in London as in Paris.

It is impossible but many of my readers must have heard of
him; and if any by mere chance have ever seen him – I beg leave
to inform them, that that bird was my bird – or some vile copy
set up to represent him.

I have nothing further to add upon him, but that from that
time to this, I have borne this poor starling as the crest to my
arms. – Thus :*

—And let the heralds officers twist his neck about if they
dare.

THE ADDRESS
VERSAILLES

I should not like to have my enemy take a view of my mind,
when I am going to ask protection of any man: for which
reason I generally endeavour to protect myself; but this going
to Monsieur Le Duc de C***** was an act of compulsion – had
it been an act of choice, I should have done it, I suppose, like
other people.

How many mean plans of dirty address, as I went along, did
my servile heart form! I deserved the Bastile for every one of
them.

Then nothing would serve me, when I got within sight of Versailles, but putting words and sentences together, and conceiving attitudes and tones to wreath myself into Monsieur Le Duc de C*****'s good graces – This will do – said I – Just as well, retorted I again, as a coat carried up to him by an adventurous taylor, without taking his measure – Fool! continued I – see Monsieur Le Duc's face first – observe what character is written in it; take notice in what posture he stands to hear you – mark the turns and expressions of his body and limbs – And for the tone – the first sound which comes from his lips will give it you; and from all these together you'll compound an address at once upon the spot, which cannot disgust the Duke – the ingredients are his own, and most likely to go down.

Well! said I, I wish it well over – Coward again! as if man to man was not equal, throughout the whole surface of the globe; and if in the field – why not face to face in the cabinet too? And trust me, Yorick, whenever it is not so, man is false to himself; and betrays his own succours ten times, where nature does it once. Go to the Duc de C**** with the Bastile in thy looks – My life for it, thou wilt be sent back to Paris in half an hour, with an escort.

I believe so, said I – Then I'll go to the Duke, by heaven! with all the gaity and debonairness in the world. –

– And there you are wrong again, replied I – A heart at ease, Yorick, flies into no extremes – 'tis ever on its center. – Well! well! cried I, as the coachman turn'd in at the gates – I find I shall do very well: and by the time he had wheel'd round the court, and brought me up to the door, I found myself so much the better for my own lecture, that I neither ascended the steps like a victim to justice, who was to part with life upon the topmost, – nor did I mount them with a skip and a couple of strides, as I do when I fly up, Eliza! to thee, to meet it.

As I enter'd the door of the saloon, I was met by a person who possibly might be the maitre d'hotel, but had more the air of one of the under secretaries, who told me the Duc de C**** was busy – I am utterly ignorant, said I, of the forms of obtaining an audience, being an absolute stranger, and what is worse in the present conjuncture of affairs, being an Englishman too. – He replied, that did not increase the difficulty. – I made him a slight bow, and told him, I had something of importance to say to Monsieur Le Duc. The secretary look'd towards the stairs, as if he was about to leave me to carry up this account to some one – But I must not mislead you, said I – for what I have to say is of no manner of importance to Monsieur Le Duc de C✱✱✱✱ – but of great importance to myself. – *C'est une autre affaire*, replied he – Not at all, said I, to a man of gallantry. – But pray, good sir, continued I, when can a stranger hope to have *accesse*? In not less than two hours, said he, looking at his watch. The number of equipages in the court-yard seem'd to justify the calculation, that I could have no nearer a prospect – and as walking backwards and forwards in the saloon, without a soul to commune with, was for the time as bad as being in the Bastile itself, I instantly went back to my *remise*, and bid the coachman drive me to the *cordon bleu*, which was the nearest hotel.

I think there is a fatality in it – I seldom go to the place I set out for.

LE PATISSER
VERSAILLES

Before I had got half-way down the street, I changed my mind: as I am at Versailles, thought I, I might as well take a view of the town; so I pull'd the cord, and ordered the coachman to drive round some of the principal streets – I suppose the town is not very large, said I. – The coachman begg'd pardon for setting me right, and told me it was very superb, and that numbers of the first dukes and marquises and counts had hotels – The Count de B✱✱✱✱, of whom the bookseller at the Quai de Conti had spoke so handsomely the night before, came instantly into my mind. – And why should I not go, thought I, to the Count de B✱✱✱✱, who has so high an idea of English books, and Englishmen – and tell him my story? so I changed my mind a second time – In truth it was the third; for I had intended that day for Madame de R✱✱✱✱ in the Rue St. Pierre, and had devoutly sent her word by her *fille de chambre* that I would assuredly wait upon her – but I am govern'd by circumstances – I cannot govern them: so seeing a man standing with a basket on the other side of the street, as if he had something to sell, I bid La Fleur go up to him and enquire for the Count's hotel.

La Fleur return'd a little pale; and told me it was a Chevalier de St. Louis* selling *patès* – It is impossible, La Fleur! said I. – La Fleur could no more account for the phenomenon than myself; but persisted in his story: he had seen the croix set in gold, with its red ribband, he said, tied to his button-hole – and had look'd into the basket and seen the *patès* which the Chevalier was selling; so could not be mistaken in that.

Such a reverse in man's life awakens a better principle than curiosity: I could not help looking for some time at him as I sat in the *remise* – the more I look'd at him – his croix and his basket, the stronger they wove themselves into my brain – I got out of the *remise* and went towards him.

He was begirt with a clean linen apron which fell below his knees, and with a sort of a bib went half way up his breast; upon the top of this, but a little below the hem, hung his croix. His basket of little *patès* was cover'd over with a white damask napkin; another of the same kind was spread at the bottom; and there was a look of *propreté* and neatness throughout; that one might have bought his *patès* of him, as much from appetite as sentiment.

He made an offer of them to neither; but stood still with them at the corner of a hotel, for those to buy who chose it, without solicitation.

He was about forty-eight – of a sedate look, something approaching to gravity. I did not wonder. – I went up rather to the basket than him, and having lifted up the napkin and taken one of his *patès* into my hand – I begg'd he would explain the appearance which affected me.

He told me in a few words, that the best part of his life had pass'd in the service, in which, after spending a small patrimony, he had obtain'd a company and the croix with it; but that at the conclusion of the last peace,* his regiment being reformed, and the whole corps, with those of some other regiments, left without any provision – he found himself in a wide world without friends, without a livre – and indeed, said he, without any thing but this – (pointing, as he said it, to his croix) – The poor chevalier won my pity, and he finish'd the scene, with winning my esteem too.

The king, he said, was the most generous of princes, but his generosity could neither relieve or reward every one, and it was only his misfortune to be amongst the number. He had a little wife, he said, whom he loved, who did the *patisserie*; and added, he felt no dishonour in defending her and himself from want in this way – unless Providence had offer'd him a better.

It would be wicked to with-hold a pleasure from the good, in passing over what happen'd to this poor Chevalier of St. Louis about nine months after.

It seems he usually took his stand near the iron gates which lead up to the palace, and as his croix had caught the eye of numbers, numbers had made the same enquiry which I had done – He had told them the same story, and always with so much modesty and good sense, that it had reach'd at last the king's ears – who hearing the Chevalier had been a gallant officer, and respected by the whole regiment as a man of honour and integrity – he broke up his little trade by a pension of fifteen hundred livres a year.

As I have told this to please the reader, I beg he will allow me to relate another out of its order, to please myself – the two stories reflect light upon each other, – and 'tis a pity they should be parted.

THE SWORD
RENNES

When states and empires have their periods of declension, and feel in their turns what distress and poverty is – I stop not to tell the causes which gradually brought the house d'E✳✳✳✳ in Britany into decay. The Marquis d'E✳✳✳✳ had fought up against his condition with great firmness; wishing to preserve, and still shew to the world some little fragments of what his ancestors had been – their indiscretions had put it out of his power. There was enough left for the little exigencies of *obscurity* – But he had two boys who look'd up to him for *light* – he thought they deserved it. He had tried his sword – it could not open the way – the *mounting* was too expensive – and simple œconomy was not a match for it – there was no resource but commerce.

In any other province in France, save Britany, this was smiting the root for ever of the little tree his pride and affection wish'd to see reblossom – But in Britany, there being a provision for this, he avail'd himself of it; and taking an occasion when the states were assembled at Rennes, the Marquis, attended with his two boys, enter'd the court; and having pleaded the right of an ancient law of the duchy, which, though seldom claim'd, he said, was no less in force; he took his sword from his side – Here – said he – take it; and be trusty guardians of it, till better times put me in condition to reclaim it.

The president accepted the Marquis's sword – he stay'd a few minutes to see it deposited in the archives of his house – and departed.

The Marquis and his whole family embarked the next day for Martinico, and in about nineteen or twenty years of successful application to business, with some unlook'd-for bequests from distant branches of his house – return'd home to reclaim his nobility and to support it.

It was an incident of good fortune which will never happen to any traveller, but a sentimental one, that I should be at Rennes at the very time of this solemn requisition: I call it solemn – it was so to me.

The Marquis enter'd the court with his whole family: he supported his lady – his eldest son supported his sister, and his youngest was at the other extreme of the line next his mother. – he put his handkerchief to his face twice –

– There was a dead silence. When the Marquis had approach'd within six paces of the tribunal, he gave the Marchioness to his youngest son, and advancing three steps before his family – he reclaim'd his sword. His sword was given him, and the moment he got it into his hand he drew it almost out of the scabbard – 'twas the shining face of a friend he had once given up – he look'd attentively along it, beginning at the hilt, as if to see whether it was the same – when observing a little rust which it had contracted near the point, he brought it near his eye, and bending his head down over it – I think I saw a tear fall upon the place: I could not be deceived by what followed.

"I shall find, said he, some *other way*, to get it off."

When the Marquis had said this, he return'd his sword into its scabbard, made a bow to the guardians of it – and, with his wife and daughter and his two sons following him, walk'd out.

O how I envied him his feelings!

THE PASSPORT
VERSAILLES

I found no difficulty in getting admittance to Monsieur Le Count de B****. The set of Shakespears was laid upon the table, and he was tumbling them over.* I walk'd up close to the table, and giving first such a look at the books as to make him conceive I knew what they were – I told him I had come without any one to present me, knowing I should meet with a friend in his apartment who, I trusted, would do it for me – it is my countryman the great Shakespear, said I, pointing to his works – *et ayez la bontè, mon cher ami,* apostrophizing his spirit, added I, *de me faire cet honneur la.* –

The Count smil'd at the singularity of the introduction ; and seeing I look'd a little pale and sickly, insisted upon my taking an arm-chair : so I sat down ; and to save him conjectures upon a visit so out of all rule, I told him simply of the incident in the bookseller's shop, and how that had impell'd me rather to go to him with the story of a little embarrassment I was under, than to any other man in France – And what is your embarrassment ? let me hear it, said the Count. So I told him the story just as I have told it the reader –

– And the master of my hotel, said I, as I concluded it, will needs have it, Monsieur le Count, that I shall be sent to the Bastile – but I have no apprehensions, continued I – for in falling into the hands of the most polish'd people in the world, and being conscious I was a true man, and not come to spy the nakedness of the land,* I scarce thought I laid at their mercy. – It does not suit the gallantry of the French, Monsieur le Count, said I, to shew it against invalids.

An animated blush came into the Count de B****'s cheeks, as I spoke this – *Ne craignez rien* – Don't fear, said he – Indeed I don't, replied I again – besides, continued I a little sportingly – I have come laughing all the way from London to Paris, and I do not think Monsieur le Duc de Choiseul is such an enemy to mirth, as to send me back crying for my pains.

– My application to you, Monsieur le Compte de B**** (making him a low bow) is to desire he will not.

The Count heard me with a great good nature, or I had not said half as much – and once or twice said – *C'est bien dit.* So I rested my cause there – and determined to say no more about it.

The Count led the discourse: we talk'd of indifferent things;
– of books and politicks, and men – and then of women – God
bless them all! said I, after much discourse about them – there
is not a man upon earth who loves them so much as I do: after
all the foibles I have seen, and all the satires I have read against
them, still I love them; being firmly persuaded that a man who
has not a sort of an affection for the whole sex, is incapable of
ever loving a single one as he ought.

Hèh bien! Monsieur l'Anglois, said the Count, gaily – You
are not come to spy the nakedness of the land – I believe you –
ni encore, I dare say, *that* of our women – But permit me to
conjecture – if, *par hazard*, they fell in your way – that the
prospect would not affect you.

I have something within me which cannot bear the shock of
the least indecent insinuation: in the sportability of chit-chat I
have often endeavoured to conquer it, and with infinite pain
have hazarded a thousand things to a dozen of the sex together
– the least of which I could not venture to a single one, to gain
heaven.

Excuse me, Monsieur Le Count, said I – as for the nakedness
of your land, if I saw it, I should cast my eyes over it with tears
in them – and for that of your women (blushing at the idea he
had excited in me) I am so evangelical in this, and have such a
fellow-feeling for what ever is *weak* about them, that I would
cover it with a garment, if I knew how to throw it on – But I
could wish, continued I, to spy the *nakedness* of their hearts,*
and through the different disguises of customs, climates, and
religion, find out what is good in them, to fashion my own by –
and therefore am I come.*

It is for this reason, Monsieur le Compte, continued I, that I
have not seen the Palais royal – nor the Luxembourg – nor the
Façade of the Louvre – nor have attempted to swell the
catalogues we have of pictures, statues, and churches – I
conceive every fair being as a temple, and would rather enter
in,* and see the original drawings and loose sketches hung up in
it, than the transfiguration of Raphael itself.

The thirst of this, continued I, as impatient as that which
inflames the breast of the connoisseur, has led me from my own
home into France – and from France will lead me through Italy
– 'tis a quiet journey of the heart in pursuit of NATURE, and

those affections which rise out of her, which make us love each other – and the world, better than we do.*

The Count said a great many civil things to me upon the occasion ; and added very politely how much he stood obliged to Shakespear for making me known to him – but, *a-propos*, said he – Shakespear is full of great things – He forgot a small punctillio of announcing your name – it puts you under a necessity of doing it yourself.

THE PASSPORT
VERSAILLES

There is not a more perplexing affair in life to me, than to set about telling any one who I am* – for there is scarce any body I cannot give a better account of than of myself; and I have often wish'd I could do it in a single word – and have an end of it. It was the only time and occasion in my life, I could accomplish this to any purpose – for Shakespear lying upon the table, and recollecting I was in his books, I took up Hamlet, and turning immediately to the grave-diggers scene in the fifth act, I lay'd my finger upon YORICK, and advancing the book to the Count, with my finger all the way over the name – *Me Voici!* said I.

Now whether the idea of poor Yorick's skull was put out of the Count's mind, by the reality of my own, or by what magic he could drop a period of seven or eight hundred years, makes nothing in this account – 'tis certain the French conceive better than they combine – I wonder at nothing in this world, and the less at this; inasmuch as one of the first of our own church, for whose candour and paternal sentiments I have the highest veneration, fell into the same mistake in the very same case. – "He could not bear, he said, to look into sermons wrote by the king of Denmark's jester."* – Good, my lord! said I – but there are two Yorick's. The Yorick your lordship thinks of, has been dead and buried eight hundred years ago; he flourish'd in Horwendillus's* court – the other Yorick is myself, who have flourish'd my lord in no court – He shook his head – Good God! said I, you might as well confound Alexander the Great, with Alexander the Copper-smith,* my lord – 'Twas all one, he replied –

– If Alexander king of Macedon could have translated your

lordship, said I – I'm sure your Lordship would not have said so.

The poor Count de B✻✻✻✻ fell but into the same *error* –

– *Et, Monsieur, est il Yorick?* cried the Count. – *Je le suis*, said I. – *Vous? – Moi – moi qui ai l'honneur de vous parler, Monsieur le Compte – Mon Dieu!* said he, embracing me – *Vous etes Yorick.*

The Count instantly put the Shakespear into his pocket – and left me alone in his room.

THE PASSPORT
VERSAILLES

I could not conceive why the Count de B✻✻✻✻ had gone so abruptly out of the room, any more than I could conceive why he had put the Shakespear into his pocket – *Mysteries which must explain themselves, are not worth the loss of time, which a conjecture about them takes up:* 'twas better to read Shakespear; so taking up, *"Much Ado about Nothing,"* I transported myself instantly from the chair I sat in to Messina in Sicily, and got so busy with Don Pedro and Benedick and Beatrice, that I thought not of Versailles, the Count, or the Passport.

Sweet pliability of man's spirit, that can at once surrender itself to illusions, which cheat expectation and sorrow of their weary moments! – long – long since had ye number'd out my days, had I not trod so great a part of them upon this enchanted ground: when my way is too rough for my feet, or too steep for my strength, I get off it, to some smooth velvet path which fancy has scattered over with rose-buds of delights; and having taken a few turns in it, come back strengthen'd and refresh'd – When evils press sore upon me, and there is no retreat from them in this world, then I take a new course – I leave it – and as I have a clearer idea of the elysian fields than I have of heaven, I force myself, like Eneas,* into them – I see him meet the pensive shade of his forsaken Dido – and wish to recognize it – I see the injured spirit wave her head, and turn off silent from the author of her miseries and dishonours – I lose the feelings for myself in hers – and in those affections which were wont to make me mourn for her when I was at school.

Surely this is not walking in a vain shadow * – *nor does man* *disquiet himself* in vain, *by it* – he oftener does so in trusting the issue of his commotions to reason only. – I can safely say for myself, I was never able to conquer any one single bad sensation in my heart so decisively, as by beating up as fast as I could for some kindly and gentle sensation, to fight it upon its own ground.

When I had got to the end of the third act, the Count de B**** entered with my Passport in his hand. Mons. le Duc de C****, said the Count, is as good a prophet, I dare say, as he is a statesman – *Un homme qui rit*, said the duke, *ne sera jamais dangereuz*. – Had it been for any one but the king's jester, added the Count, I could not have got it these two hours. – *Pardonnez moi*, Mons. Le Compte, said I – I am not the king's jester. – But you are Yorick ? – Yes. – *Et vous plaisantez ?* – I answered, . Indeed I did jest – but was not paid for it – 'twas entirely at my own expence.

We have no jester at court, Mons. Le Compte, said I, the last we had* was in the licentious reign of Charles the IId – since which time our manners have been so gradually refining, that our court at present is so full of patriots,* who wish for *nothing* but the honours and wealth of their country – and our ladies are all so chaste, so spotless, so good, so devout – there is nothing for a jester to make a jest of –

Voila un persiflage ! cried the Count.

THE PASSPORT
VERSAILLES

As the Passport was directed to all lieutenant governors, governors, and commandants of cities, generals of armies, justiciaries, and all officers of justice, to let Mr. Yorick, the king's jester, and his baggage, travel quietly along – I own the triumph of obtaining the Passport was not a little tarnish'd by the figure I cut in it – But there is nothing unmixt in this world ; and some of the gravest of our divines have carried it so far as to affirm, that enjoyment itself was attended even with a sigh – and that the greatest *they knew of*, terminated *in a general way*, in little better than a convulsion.

I remember the grave and learned Bevoriskius,* in his commentary upon the generations from Adam, very naturally breaks off in the middle of a note to give an account to the world of a couple of sparrows upon the out-edge of his window, which had incommoded him all the time he wrote, and at last had entirely taken him off from his genealogy.

– 'Tis strange! writes Bevoriskius; but the facts are certain, for I have had the curiosity to mark them down one by one with my pen – but the cock-sparrow during the little time that I could have finished the other half this note, has actually interrupted me with the reiteration of his caresses three and twenty times and a half.

How merciful, adds Bevoriskius, is heaven to his creatures!

Ill fated Yorick! that the gravest of thy brethren should be able to write that to the world, which stains thy face with crimson, to copy in even thy study.

But this is nothing to my travels – So I twice – twice beg pardon for it.

CHARACTER
VERSAILLES

And how do you find the French? said the Count de B****, after he had given me the Passport.

The reader may suppose that after so obliging a proof of courtesy, I could not be at a loss to say something handsome to the enquiry.

– *Mais passe, pour cela* – Speak frankly, said he; do you find all the urbanity in the French which the world give us the honour of? – I had found every thing, I said, which confirmed it – *Vraiment*, said the count. – *Les François sont polis.* – To an excess, replied I.

The count took notice of the word *excesse*; and would have it I meant more than I said. I defended myself a long time as well as I could against it – he insisted I had a reserve, and that I would speak my opinion frankly.

I believe, Mons. Le Compte, said I, that man has a certain compass, as well as an instrument; and that the social and other calls have occasion by turns for every key in him; so that if you begin a note too high or too low, there must be a want either in the upper or under part, to fill up the system of harmony. – The Count de B**** did not understand music, so desired me to explain it some other way. A polish'd nation, my dear Count, said I, makes every one its debtor; and besides urbanity itself, like the fair sex, has so many charms; it goes against the heart to say it can do ill; and yet, I believe, there is but a certain line of perfection, that man, take him altogether, is empower'd to arrive at – if he gets beyond, he rather exchanges qualities, than gets them. I must not presume to say, how far this has affected the French in the subject we are speaking of – but should it ever be the case of the English, in the progress of their refinements, to arrive at the same polish which distinguishes the French, if we did not lose the *politesse de cœur*, which inclines men more to human actions, than courteous ones – we should at least lose that distinct variety and originality of character, which distinguishes them, not only from each other, but from all the world besides.

I had a few king William's shillings as smooth as glass in my pocket; and foreseeing they would be of use in the illustration of my hypothesis, I had got them into my hand, when I had proceeded so far –

See, Mons. Le Compte, said I, rising up, and laying them before him upon the table – by jingling and rubbing one against another for seventy years together in one body's pocket or another's, they are become so much alike, you can scarce distinguish one shilling from another.

The English, like antient medals, kept more apart, and passing but few peoples hands, preserve the first sharpnesses which the fine hand of nature has given them – they are not so pleasant to feel – but in return, the legend is so visible, that at the first look you see whose image and superscription they bear. – But the French, Mons. Le Compte, added I, wishing to soften what I had said, have so many excellencies, they can the better spare this – they are a loyal, a gallant, a generous, an ingenious, and good temper'd people as is under heaven – if they have a fault – they are too *serious*.*

Mon Dieu! cried the Count, rising out of his chair.

Mais vous plaisantez, said he, correcting his exclamation. – I laid my hand upon my breast, and with earnest gravity assured him, it was my most settled opinion.

The Count said he was mortified, he could not stay to hear my reasons, being engaged to go that moment to dine with the Duc de C****.

But if it is not too far to come to Versailles to eat your soup with me, I beg, before you leave France, I may have the pleasure of knowing you retract your opinion – or, in what manner you support it. – But if you do support it, Mons. Anglois, said he, you must do it with all your powers, because you have the whole world against you. – I promised the Count I would do myself the honour of dining with him before I set out for Italy – so took my leave.

THE TEMPTATION
PARIS

When I alighted at the hotel, the porter told me a young woman with a band-box had been that moment enquiring for me. – I do not know, said the porter, whether she is gone away or no. I took the key of my chamber of him, and went up stairs; and when I had got within ten steps of the top of the landing before my door, I met her coming easily down.

It was the fair *fille de chambre* I had walked along the Quai de Conti with: Madame de R✳✳✳✳ had sent her upon some commissions to a *merchande de modes* within a step or two of the hotel de Modene; and as I had fail'd in waiting upon her, had bid her enquire if I had left Paris; and if so, whether I had not left a letter address'd to her.

As the fair *fille de chambre* was so near my door she turned back, and went into the room with me for a moment or two whilst I wrote a card.

It was a fine still evening in the latter end of the month of May – the crimson window curtains (which were of the same colour of those of the bed) were drawn close – the sun was setting and reflected through them so warm a tint into the fair *fille de chambre*'s face – I thought she blush'd – the idea of it made me blush myself – we were quite alone; and that super-induced a second blush before the first could get off.

There is a sort of a pleasing half guilty blush, where the blood is more in fault than the man – 'tis sent impetuous from the heart, and virtue flies after it – not to call it back, but to make the sensation of it more delicious to the nerves – 'tis associated. –

But I'll not describe it. – I felt something at first within me which was not in strict unison with the lesson of virtue I had given her the night before – I sought five minutes for a card – I knew I had not one. – I took up a pen – I laid it down again – my hand trembled – the devil was in me.

I know as well as any one, he is an adversary, whom if we resist, he will fly from us – but I seldom resist him at all; from a terror, that though I may conquer, I may still get a hurt in the combat – so I give up the triumph, for security; and instead of thinking to make him fly, I generally fly myself.

The fair *fille de chambre* came close up to the bureau where I was looking for a card – took up first the pen I cast down, then offered to hold me the ink: she offer'd it so sweetly, I was going to accept it – but I durst not – I have nothing, my dear, said I, to write upon. – Write it, said she, simply, upon any thing. –

I was just going to cry out, Then I will write it, fair girl! upon thy lips. –

If I do, said I, I shall perish – so I took her by the hand, and led her to the door, and begg'd she would not forget the lesson I had given her – She said, Indeed she would not – and as she utter'd it with some earnestness, she turned about, and gave me both her hands, closed together, into mine – it was impossible not to compress them in that situation – I wish'd to let them go; and all the time I held them, I kept arguing within myself against it – and still I held them on. – In two minutes I found I had all the battle to fight over again – and I felt my legs and every limb about me tremble at the idea.

The foot of the bed was within a yard and a half of the place where we were standing – I had still hold of her hands – and how it happened I can give no account, but I neither ask'd her – nor drew her – nor did I think of the bed – but so it did happen, we both sat down.

I'll just shew you, said the fair *fille de chambre*, the little purse I have been making to-day to hold your crown. So she put her hand into her right pocket, which was next me, and felt for it for some time – then into the left – "She had lost it." – I never bore expectation more quietly – it was in her right pocket at last – she pulled it out; it was of green taffeta, lined with a little bit of white quilted sattin, and just big enough to hold the crown – she put it into my hand – it was pretty; and I held it ten minutes with the back of my hand resting upon her lap – looking sometimes at the purse, sometimes on one side of it.

A stitch or two had broke out in the gathers of my stock – the fair *fille de chambre*, without saying a word, took out her little hussive, threaded a small needle, and sew'd it up – I foresaw it would hazard the glory of the day ; and as she passed her hand in silence across and across my neck in the manœuvre, I felt the laurels shake which fancy had wreath'd about my head.

A strap had given way in her walk, and the buckle of her shoe was just falling off – See, said the *fille de chambre*, holding up her foot – I could not for my soul but fasten the buckle in return, and putting in the strap – and lifting up the other foot with it, when I had done, to see both were right – in doing it too suddenly – it unavoidably threw the fair *fille de chambre* off her center – and then –

THE CONQUEST

Yes – and then – Ye whose clay-cold heads and luke-warm hearts can argue down or mask your passions – tell me, what trespass is it that man should have them? or how his spirit stands answerable, to the father of spirits, but for his conduct under them?

If nature has so wove her web of kindness, that some threads of love and desire are entangled with the piece – must the whole web be rent in drawing them out? – Whip me such stoics, great governor of nature! said I to myself – Wherever thy providence shall place me for the trials of my virtue – whatever is my danger – whatever is my situation – let me feel the movements which rise out of it, and which belong to me as a man – and if I govern them as a good one – I will trust the issues to thy justice, for thou hast made us – and not we ourselves.*

As I finish'd my address, I raised the fair *fille de chambre* up by the hand, and led her out of the room – she stood by me till I lock'd the door and put the key in my pocket – *and then* – the victory being quite decisive – and not till then, I press'd my lips to her cheek, and, taking her by the hand again, led her safe to the gate of the hotel.

THE MYSTERY
PARIS

If a man knows the heart, he will know it was impossible to go back instantly to my chamber – it was touching a cold key with a flat third to it, upon the close of a piece of musick, which had call'd forth my affections – therefore, when I let go the hand of the *fille de chambre*, I remain'd at the gate of the hotel for some time, looking at every one who pass'd by, and forming conjectures upon them, till my attention got fix'd upon a single object which confounded all kind of reasoning upon him.

It was a tall figure of a philosophic serious, adust look, which pass'd and repass'd sedately along the street, making a turn of about sixty paces on each side of the gate of the hotel – the man was about fifty-two – had a small cane under his arm – was dress'd in a dark drab-colour'd coat, waistcoat, and breeches, which seem'd to have seen some years service – they were still clean, and there was a little air of frugal *propretè* throughout him. By his pulling off his hat, and his attitude of accosting a good many in his way, I saw he was asking charity; so I got a sous or two out of my pocket ready to give him, as he took me in his turn – he pass'd by me without asking any thing – and yet did not go five steps further before he ask'd charity of a little woman – I was much more likely to have given of the two – He had scarce done with the woman, when he pull'd off his hat to another who was coming the same way. – An ancient gentleman came slowly – and, after him, a young smart one – He let them both pass, and ask'd nothing: I stood observing him half an hour, in which time he had made a dozen turns backwards and forwards, and found that he invariably pursued the same plan.

There were two things very singular in this, which set my brain to work, and to no purpose – the first was, why the man should *only* tell his story to the sex – and secondly – what kind of story it was, and what species of eloquence it could be, which soften'd the hearts of the women, which he knew 'twas to no purpose to practise upon the men.

There were two other circumstances which entangled this mystery – the one was, he told every woman what he had to say in her ear, and in a way which had much more the air of a secret than a petition – the other was, it was always successful – he never stopp'd a woman, but she pull'd out her purse, and immediately gave him something.

I could form no system to explain the phenomenon.

I had got a riddle to amuse me for the rest of the evening, so I walk'd up stairs to my chamber.

THE CASE OF CONSCIENCE
PARIS

I was immediately followed up by the master of the hotel, who came into my room to tell me I must provide lodgings else where. – How so, friend? said I. – He answer'd, I had had a young woman lock'd up with me two hours that evening in my bed-chamber, and 'twas against the rules of his house. – Very well, said I, we'll all part friends then – for the girl is no worse – and I am no worse – and you will be just as I found you. – It was enough, he said, to overthrow the credit of his hotel. – *Voyez vous, Monsieur*, said he, pointing to the foot of the bed we had been sitting upon. – I own it had something of the appearance of an evidence; but my pride not suffering me to enter into any detail of the case, I exhorted him to let his soul sleep in peace, as I resolved to let mine do that night, and that I would discharge what I owed him at breakfast.

I should not have minded, *Monsieur*, said he, if you had had twenty girls – 'Tis a score more, replied I, interrupting him, than I ever reckon'd upon – Provided, added he, it had been but in a morning. – And does the difference of the time of the day at Paris make a difference in the sin? – It made a difference, he said, in the scandal. – I like a good distinction in my heart; and cannot say I was intolerably out of temper with the man. – I own it is necessary, re-assumed the master of the hotel, that a stranger at Paris should have the opportunities presented to him of buying lace and silk stockings and ruffles, *et tout cela* – and 'tis nothing if a woman comes with a band box. – O' my conscience, said I, she had one; but I never look'd into it. – Then, *Monsieur*, said he, has bought nothing. – Not one earthly thing, replied I. – Because, said he, I could recommend one to you who would use you *en conscience*. – But I must see her this night, said I. – He made a low bow and walk'd down.

Now shall I triumph over this *maitre d'hotel*, cried I – and what then ? – Then I shall let him see I know he is a dirty fellow. – And what then ? – What then ! – I was too near myself to say it was for the sake of others. – I had no good answer left – there was more of spleen than principle in my project, and I was sick of it before the execution.

In a few minutes the Grisset came in with her box of lace – I'll buy nothing however, said I, within myself.

The Grisset would shew me every thing – I was hard to please : she would not seem to see it ; she open'd her little magazine, laid all her laces one after another before me – unfolded and folded them up again one by one with the most patient sweetness – I might buy – or not – she would let me have every thing at my own price – the poor creature seem'd anxious to get a penny ; and laid herself out to win me, and not so much in a manner which seem'd artful, as in one I felt simple and caressing.

If there is not a fund of honest cullibility in man, so much the worse – my heart relented, and I gave up my second resolution as quietly as the first – Why should I chastise one for the trespass of another ? if thou art tributary to this tyrant of an host, thought I, looking up in her face, so much harder is thy bread.

If I had not had more than four *Louis d'ors* in my purse, there was no such thing as rising up and shewing her the door, till I had first laid three of them out in a pair of ruffles.

– The master of the hotel will share the profit with her – no matter – then I have only paid as many a poor soul has *paid* before me for an act he *could* not do, or think of.

THE RIDDLE
PARIS

When La Fleur came up to wait upon me at supper, he told me how sorry the master of the hotel was for his affront to me in bidding me change my lodgings.

A man who values a good night's rest will not lay down with enmity in his heart if he can help it – So I bid La Fleur tell the master of the hotel, that I was sorry on my side for the occasion I had given him – and you may tell him, if you will, La Fleur, added I, that if the young woman should call again, I shall not see her.

This was a sacrifice not to him, but myself, having resolved,

after so narrow an escape, to run no more risks, but to leave
Paris, if it was possible, with all the virtue I enter'd in.

*C'est deroger à noblesse,** Monsieur*, said La Fleur, making
me a bow down to the ground as he said it – *Et encore
Monsieur*, said he, may change his sentiments – and if (*par
hazard*) he should like to amuse himself – I find no amusement
in it, said I, interrupting him –

Mon Dieu! said La Fleur – and took away.

In an hour's time he came to put me to bed, and was more
than commonly officious – something hung upon his lips to say
to me, or ask me, which he could not get off: I could not
conceive what it was; and indeed gave myself little trouble to
find it out, as I had another riddle so much more interesting
upon my mind, which was that of the man's asking charity
before the door of the hotel – I would have given any thing to
have got to the bottom of it; and that, not out of curiosity – 'tis
so low a principle of enquiry, in general, I would not purchase
the gratification of it with a two-sous piece – but a secret, I
thought, which so soon and so certainly soften'd the heart of
every woman you came near, was a secret at least equal to the
philosopher's stone: had I had both the Indies,* I would have
given up one to have been master of it.

I toss'd and turn'd it almost all night long in my brains to no
manner of purpose; and when I awoke in the morning, I found
my spirit as much troubled with my *dreams*, as ever the king of
Babylon* had been with his; and I will not hesitate to affirm, it
would have puzzled all the wise men of Paris, as much as those
of Chaldea, to have given its interpretation.

LE DIMANCHE
PARIS

It was Sunday; and when La Fleur came in, in the morning,
with my coffee and role and butter, he had got himself so
gallantly array'd, I scarce knew him.

I had covenanted at Montriul to give him a new hat with a
silver button and loop, and four Louis d'ors *pour s'adoniser,**
when we got to Paris; and the poor fellow, to do him justice,
had done wonders with it.

He had bought a bright, clean, good scarlet coat and a pair of breeches of the same – They were not a crown worse, he said, for the wearing – I wish'd him hang'd for telling me – they look'd so fresh, that tho' I knew the thing could not be done, yet I would rather have imposed upon my fancy with thinking I had bought them new for the fellow, than that they had come out of the *Rue de friperie*.

This is a nicety which makes not the heart sore at Paris.

He had purchased moreover a handsome blue sattin waistcoat, fancifully enough embroidered – this was indeed something the worse for the services it had done, but 'twas clean scour'd – the gold had been touch'd up, and upon the whole was rather showy than otherwise – and as the blue was not violent, it suited with the coat and breeches very well: he had squeez'd out of the money, moreover, a new bag and a solitaire; and had insisted with the *fripier*, upon a gold pair of garters to his breeches knees – He had purchased muslin ruffles, *bien brodées*, with four livres of his own money – and a pair of white silk stockings for five more – and, to top all, nature had given him a handsome figure, without costing him a sous.

He enter'd the room thus set off, with his hair dress'd in the first stile, and with a handsome *bouquet* in his breast – in a word, there was that look of festivity in every thing about him, which at once put me in mind it was Sunday – and by combining both together, it instantly struck me, that the favour he wish'd to ask of me the night before, was to spend the day, as every body in Paris spent it, besides. I had scarce made the conjecture, when La Fleur, with infinite humility, but with a look of trust, as if I should not refuse him, begg'd I would grant him the day, *pour faire le galant vis à vis de sa maitresse*.

Now it was the very thing I intended to do myself *vis à vis* Madame de R**** – I had retain'd the *remise* on purpose for it, and it would not have mortified my vanity to have had a servant so well dress'd as La Fleur was to have got up behind it: I never could have worse spared him.

But we must *feel*, not argue in these embarrassments – the sons and daughters of service part with liberty, but not with Nature in their contracts; they are flesh and blood, and have their little vanities and wishes in the midst of the house of bondage,* as well as their task-masters – no doubt, they have set their self-denials at a price – and their expectations are so unreasonable, that I would often disappoint them, but that their condition puts it so much in my power to do it.

Behold! – Behold, I am thy servant* – disarms me at once of the powers of a master –

– Thou shalt go, La Fleur! said I.

– And what mistress, La Fleur, said I, canst thou have pick'd up in so little a time at Paris? La Fleur laid his hand upon his breast, and said 'twas a *petite demoiselle* at Monsieur Le Compte de B****'s. – La Fleur had a heart made for society; and, to speak the truth of him let as few occasions slip him as his master – so that some how or other; but how – heaven knows – he had connected himself with the *demoiselle* upon the landing of the stair-case, during the time I was taken up with my Passport; and as there was time enough for me to win the Count to my interest, La Fleur had contrived to make it do to win the maid to his – the family, it seems, was to be at Paris that day, and he had made a party with her, and two or three more of the Count's houshold, upon the *boulevards*.

Happy people! that once a week at least are sure to lay down all your cares together; and dance and sing and sport away the weights of grievance, which bow down the spirit of other nations to the earth.

THE FRAGMENT
PARIS

La Fleur had left me something to amuse myself with for the day more than I had bargain'd for, or could have enter'd either into his head or mine.

He had brought the little print of butter upon a currant leaf; and as the morning was warm, and he had a good step to bring it, he had begg'd a sheet of waste paper to put betwixt the currant leaf and his hand – As that was plate sufficient, I bad him lay it upon the table as it was, and as I resolved to stay within all day I ordered him to call upon the *traiteur* to bespeak my dinner, and leave me to breakfast by myself.

When I had finish'd the butter, I threw the currant leaf out of the window, and was going to do the same by the waste paper – but stopping to read a line first, and that drawing me on to a second and third – I thought it better worth; so I shut the window, and drawing a chair up to it, I sat down to read it.

It was in the old French of Rabelais's* time, and for ought I know might have been wrote by him – it was moreover in a Gothic letter, and that so faded and gone off by damps and length of time, it cost me infinite trouble to make any thing of it – I threw it down; and then wrote a letter to Eugenius – then I took it up again, and embroiled my patience with it afresh – and then to cure that, I wrote a letter to Eliza. – Still it kept hold of me; and the difficulty of understanding it increased but the desire.

I got my dinner; and after I had enlightened my mind with a bottle of Burgundy, I at it again – and after two or three hours poring upon it, with almost as deep attention as ever Gruter or Jacob Spon* did upon a nonsensical inscription, I thought I made sense of it; but to make sure of it, the best way, I imagined, was to turn it into English, and see how it would look then – so I went on leisurely, as a trifling man does, sometimes writing a sentence – then taking a turn or two – and then looking how the world went, out of the window; so that it was nine o'clock at night before I had done it – I then begun and read it as follows.

THE FRAGMENT
PARIS

—Now as the notary's wife disputed the point with the notary with too much heat – I wish, said the notary, throwing down the parchment, that there was another notary here only to set down and attest all this—

– And what would you do then, Monsieur? said she, rising hastily up – the notary's wife was a little fume of a woman, and the notary thought it well to avoid a hurricane by a mild reply – I would go, answer'd he, to bed. – You may go to the devil, answer'd the notary's wife.

Now there happening to be but one bed in the house, the other two rooms being unfurnish'd, as is the custom at Paris, and the notary not caring to lie in the same bed with a woman who had but that moment sent him pell-mell to the devil, went forth with his hat and cane and short cloak, the night being very windy, and walk'd out ill at ease towards the *pont neuf*.

Of all the bridges which ever were built, the whole world who have pass'd over the *pont neuf*, must own, that it is the noblest – the finest – the grandest – the lightest – the longest – the broadest that ever conjoin'd land and land together upon the face of the terraqueous globe –

By this, it seems, as if the author of the fragment had not been a Frenchman.

The worst fault which divines and the doctors of the Sorbonne can allege against it, is, that if there is but a cap-full of wind in or about Paris, 'tis more blasphemously *sacre Dieu'd* there than in any other aperture of the whole city – and with reason, good and cogent Messieurs; for it comes against you without crying *garde d'eau*,* and with such unpremeditable puffs, that of the few who cross it with their hats on, not one in fifty but hazards two livres and a half, which is its full worth.

The poor notary, just as he was passing by the sentry, instinctively clapp'd his cane to the side of it, but in raising it up the point of his cane catching hold of the loop of the sentinel's hat hoisted it over the spikes of the ballustrade clear into the Seine –

– *'Tis an ill wind*, said a boatsman, who catch'd it, *which blows no body any good.*

The sentry being a gascon incontinently twirl'd up his whiskers, and levell'd his harquebuss.

Harquebusses in those days went off with matches; and an old woman's paper lanthorn at the end of the bridge happening to be blown out, she had borrow'd the sentry's match to light it – it gave a moment's time for the gascon's blood to run cool, and turn the accident better to his advantage – *'Tis an ill wind*, said he, catching off the notary's castor, and legitimating the capture with the boatman's adage.

The poor notary cross'd the bridge, and passing along the rue de Dauphine into the fauxbourgs of St. Germain, lamented himself as he walk'd along in this manner:

Luckless man! that I am, said the notary, to be the sport of hurricanes all my days – to be born to have the storm of ill language levell'd against me and my profession wherever I go – to be forced into marriage by the thunder of the church to a tempest of a woman – to be driven forth out of my house by domestic winds, and despoil'd of my castor by pontific ones – to be here, bare-headed, in a windy night at the mercy of the ebbs and flows of accidents – where am I to lay my head ? – miserable man ! what wind in the two-and-thirty points of the whole compass can blow unto thee, as it does to the rest of thy fellow creatures, good !

As the notary was passing on by a dark passage, complaining in this sort, a voice call'd out to a girl, to bid her run for the next notary – now the notary being the next, and availing himself of his situation, walk'd up the passage to the door, and passing through an old sort of a saloon, was usher'd into a large chamber dismantled of every thing but a long military pike – a breast plate – a rusty old sword, and bandoleer, hung up equi-distant in four different places against the wall.

An old personage, who had heretofore been a gentleman, and unless decay of fortune taints the blood along with it was a gentleman at that time, lay supporting his head upon his hand in his bed ; a little table with a taper burning was set close beside it, and close by the table was placed a chair – the notary sat him down in it ; and pulling out his ink-horn and a sheet or two of paper which he had in his pocket, he placed them before him, and dipping his pen in his ink, and leaning his breast over the table, he disposed every thing to make the gentleman's last will and testament.

Alas ! Monsieur le Notaire, said the gentleman, raising himself up a little, I have nothing to bequeath which will pay the expence of bequeathing, except the history of myself, which, I could not die in peace unless I left it as a legacy to the world ; the profits arising out of it, I bequeath to you for the pains of taking it from me – it is a story so uncommon, it must be read by all mankind – it will make the fortunes of your house – the notary dipp'd his pen into his ink-horn – Almighty director of every event in my life ! said the old gentleman, looking up earnestly and raising his hands towards heaven – thou whose hand has led me on through such a labyrinth of strange passages down into this scene of desolation, assist the decaying memory of an old, infirm, and broken-hearted man – direct my tongue, by the spirit of thy eternal truth, that this stranger may set down naught but what is written in that BOOK,* from whose records, said he, clasping his hands together, I am to be condemn'd or acquitted! — the notary held up the point of his pen betwixt the taper and his eye —

— It is a story, Monsieur le Notaire, said the gentleman, which will rouse up every affection in nature — it will kill the humane, and touch the heart of cruelty herself with pity —

— The notary was inflamed with a desire to begin, and put his pen a third time into his ink-horn — and the old gentleman turning a little more towards the notary, began to dictate his story in these words —

— And where is the rest of it, La Fleur? said I, as he just then enter'd the room.

THE FRAGMENT
AND THE ¹BOUQUET
PARIS

When La Fleur came up close to the table, and was made to comprehend what I wanted, he told me there were only two other sheets of it which he had wrapt round the stalks of a *bouquet* to keep it together, which he had presented to the *demoiselle* upon the *boulevards* — Then, prithee, La Fleur, said I, step back to her to the Count de B****'s hotel, and *see if you canst get* — There is no doubt of it, said La Fleur — and away he flew.

In a very little time the poor fellow came back quite out of breath, with deeper marks of disappointment in his looks than could arise from the simple irreparability of the fragment — *Juste ciel!* in less than two minutes that the poor fellow had taken his last tender farewel of her — his faithless mistress had given his *gage d'amour* to one of the Count's footmen — the footman to a young sempstress — and the sempstress to a fiddler, with my fragment at the end of it — Our misfortunes were involved together — I gave a sigh — and La Fleur echo'd it back again to my ear —

— How perfidious! cried La Fleur — How unlucky! said I. —

— I should not have been mortified, Monsieur, quoth La Fleur, if she had lost it — Nor I, La Fleur, said I, had I found it.

Whether I did or no, will be seen hereafter.

¹ Nosegay.

THE ACT OF CHARITY
PARIS

The man who either disdains or fears to walk up a dark entry may be an excellent good man, and fit for a hundred things; but he will not do to make a good sentimental traveller. I count little of the many things I see pass at broad noon day, in large and open streets. – Nature is shy, and hates to act before spectators; but in such an unobserved corner, you sometimes see a single short scene of her's worth all the sentiments of a dozen French plays compounded together – and yet they are *absolutely* fine; – and whenever I have a more brilliant affair upon my hands than common, as they suit a preacher just as well as a hero, I generally make my sermon out of 'em – and for the text – "Capadosia, Pontus and Asia, Phrygia and Pamphilia"* – is as good as any one in the Bible.

There is a long dark passage issuing out from the opera comique into a narrow street; 'tis trod by a few who humbly wait for a *fiacre*[1], or wish to get off quietly o'foot when the opera is done. At the end of it, towards the theatre, 'tis lighted by a small candle, the light of which is almost lost before you get half-way down, but near the door – 'tis more for ornament than use: you see it as a fix'd star of the least magnitude; it burns – but does little good to the world, that we know of.

In returning along this passage, I discern'd, as I approach'd within five or six paces of the door, two ladies standing arm in arm, with their backs against the wall, waiting, as I imagined, for a *fiacre* – as they were next the door, I thought they had a prior right; so edged myself up within a yard or little more of them, and quietly took my stand – I was in black, and scarce seen.

The lady next me was a tall lean figure of a woman of about thirty-six; the other of the same size and make, of about forty; there was no mark of wife or widow in any one part of either of them – they seem'd to be two upright vestal sisters, unsapp'd by caresses, unbroke in upon by tender salutations: I could have wish'd to have made them happy – their happiness was destin'd, that night, to come from another quarter.

A low voice, with a good turn of expression, and sweet

[1] Hackney-coach.

cadence at the end of it, begg'd for a twelve-sous piece betwixt them, for the love of heaven. I thought it singular, that a beggar should fix the quota of an alms — and that the sum should be twelve times as much as what is usually given in the dark. They both seemed astonish'd at it as much as myself. — Twelve sous! said one — a twelve-sous piece! said the other — and made no reply.

The poor man said, He knew not how to ask less of ladies of their rank; and bow'd down his head to the ground.

Poo! said they — we have no money.

The beggar remained silent for a moment or two, and renew'd his supplication.

Do not, my fair young ladies, said he, stop your good ears against me — Upon my word, honest man! said the younger, we have no change — Then God bless you, said the poor man, and multiply those joys which you can give to others without change! — I observed the elder sister put her hand into her pocket — I'll see, said she, if I have a sous. — A sous! give twelve, said the supplicant; Nature has been bountiful to you, be bountiful to a poor man.

I would, friend, with all my heart, said the younger, if I had it.

My fair charitable! said he, addressing himself to the elder — What is it but your goodness and humanity which makes your bright eyes so sweet, that they outshine the morning even in this dark passage? and what was it which made the Marquis de Santerre and his brother say so much of you both as they just pass'd by?

The two ladies seemed much affected; and impulsively at the same time they both put their hands into their pocket, and each took out a twelve-sous piece.

The contest betwixt them and the poor supplicant was no more — it was continued betwixt themselves, which of the two should give the twelve-sous piece in charity — and to end the dispute, they both gave it together, and the man went away.

THE RIDDLE EXPLAINED
PARIS

I stepp'd hastily after him: it was the very man whose success in asking charity of the women before the door of the hotel had so puzzled me – and I found at once his secret, or at least the basis of it – 'twas flattery.

Delicious essence! how refreshing art thou to nature! how strongly are all its powers and all its weaknesses on thy side! how sweetly dost thou mix with the blood, and help it through the most difficult and tortuous passages to the heart!

The poor man, as he was not straighten'd for time, had given it here in a larger dose: 'tis certain he had a way of bringing it into less form, for the many sudden cases he had to do with in the streets; but how he contrived to correct, sweeten, concentre, and qualify it – I vex not my spirit with the inquiry – it is enough, the beggar gain'd two twelve-sous pieces – and they can best tell the rest, who have gain'd much greater matters by it.

PARIS

We get forwards in the world not so much by doing services, as receiving them: you take a withering twig, and put it in the ground; and then you water it, because you have planted it.

Mons. Le Compte de B****, merely because he had done me one kindness in the affair of my passport, would go on and do me another, the few days he was at Paris, in making me known to a few people of rank; and they were to present me to others, and so on.

I had got master of my *secret*, just in time to turn these honours to some little account; otherwise, as is commonly the case, I should have din'd or supp'd a single time or two round, and then by *translating* French looks and attitudes into plain English, I should presently have seen, that I had got hold of the *couvert*[1] of some more entertaining guest; and in course, should have resigned all my places one after another, merely upon the principle that I could not keep them. – As it was, things did not go much amiss.

---

[1] Plate, napkin, knife, fork, and spoon.

I had the honour of being introduced to the old Marquis de B✻✻✻ : in days of yore he had signaliz'd himself by some small feats of chivalry in the *Cour d'amour*, and had dress'd himself out to the idea of tilts and tournaments ever since – the Marquis de B✻✻✻ wish'd to have it thought the affair was somewhere else than in his brain. "He could like to take a trip to England," and ask'd much of the English ladies. Stay where you are, I beseech you, Mons. le Marquise, said I – Les Messrs. Angloise can scarce get a kind look from them as it is. – The Marquis invited me to supper.

Mons. P✻✻✻ the farmer-general* was just as inquisitive about our taxes. – They were very considerable, he heard – If we knew but how to collect them, said I, making him a low bow.

I could never have been invited to Mons. P✻✻✻'s concerts upon any other terms.

I had been misrepresented to Madame de Q✻✻✻ as an *esprit* – Madam de Q✻✻✻ was an *esprit* herself; she burnt with impatience to see me, and hear me talk. I had not taken my seat, before I saw she did not care a sous whether I had any wit or no – I was let in, to be convinced she had. – I call heaven to witness I never once open'd the door of my lips.

Madame de Q✻✻✻ vow'd to every creature she met, "She had never had a more improving conversation with a man in her life."

There are three epochas in the empire of a French-woman – She is coquette – then deist – then *devôte :* the empire during these is never lost – she only changes her subjects : when thirty-five years and more have unpeopled her dominions of the slaves of love, she re-peoples it with slaves of infidelity – and then with the slaves of the Church.

Madame de V✻✻✻ was vibrating betwixt the first of these epochas : the colour of the rose was shading fast away – she ought to have been a deist five years before the time I had the honour to pay my first visit.

She placed me upon the same sopha with her, for the sake of disputing the point of religion more closely. – In short, Madame de V✻✻✻ told me she believed nothing.

I told Madame de V✻✻✻ it might be her principle; but I was sure it could not be her interest to level the outworks, without which I could not conceive how such a citadel as hers could be defended – that there was not a more dangerous thing in the world, than for a beauty to be a deist – that it was a debt I owed my creed, not to conceal it from her – that I had not been five minutes sat upon the sopha besides her, but I had begun to form designs – and what is it, but the sentiments of religion, and the persuasion they had existed in her breast, which could have check'd them as they rose up.

We are not adamant, said I, taking hold of her hand – and there is need of all restraints, till age in her own time steals in and lays them on us – but, my dear lady, said I, kissing her hand – 'tis too – too soon –

I declare I had the credit all over Paris of unperverting Madame de V✳✳✳. – She affirmed to Mons. D✳✳✳ and the Abbe M✳✳✳, that in one half hour I had said more for revealed religion, than all their Encyclopedia* had said against it – I was listed directly into Madame de V✳✳✳'s *Coterie* – and she put off the epocha of deism for two years.

I remember it was in this *Coterie*, in the middle of a discourse, in which I was shewing the necessity of a *first cause*, that the young Count de Faineant* took me by the hand to the furthest corner of the room, to tell me my *solitaire* was pinn'd too strait about my neck – It should be *plus badinant*, said the Count, looking down upon his own – but a word, Mons. Yorick, to *the wise* –

– And from the wise, Mons. Le Compte, replied I, making him a bow – *is enough*.

The Count de Faineant embraced me with more ardour than ever I was embraced by mortal man.

For three weeks together, I was of every man's opinion I met. – *Pardi! ce Mons. Yorick a autant d'esprit que nous autres.* – *Il raisonne bien*, said another. – *C'est un bon enfant*, said a third. – And at this price I could have eaten and drank and been merry all the days of my life at Paris; but 'twas a dishonest *reckoning* – I grew ashamed of it – it was the gain of a slave – every sentiment of honour revolted against it – the higher I got, the more was I forced upon my *beggarly system* – the better the *Coterie* – the more children of Art – I languish'd for those of Nature: and one night, after a most vile prostitution of myself to half a dozen different people, I grew sick – went to bed – order'd La Fleur to get me horses in the morning to set out for Italy.

MARIA
MOULINES

I never felt what the distress of plenty was in any one shape till now – to travel it through the Bourbonnois, the sweetest part of France – in the hey-day of the vintage, when Nature is pouring her abundance into every one's lap, and every eye is lifted up – a journey through each step of which music beats time to *Labour*, and all her children are rejoicing as they carry in their clusters – to pass through this with my affections flying out, and kindling at every group before me – and every one of 'em was pregnant with adventures.

Just heaven! – it would fill up twenty volumes – and alas! I have but a few small pages left of this to croud it into – and half of these must be taken up with the poor Maria my friend, Mr. Shandy, met with near Moulines.*

The story he had told of that disorder'd maid affect'd me not a little in the reading; but when I got within the neighbourhood where she lived, it returned so strong into my mind, that I could not resist an impulse which prompted me to go half a league out of the road to the village where her parents dwelt to enquire after her.

'Tis going, I own, like the Knight of the Woeful Countenance,* in quest of melancholy adventures – but I know not how it is, but I am never so perfectly conscious of the existence of a soul within me, as when I am entangled in them.

The old mother came to the door, her looks told me the story before she open'd her mouth – She had lost her husband; he had died, she said, of anguish, for the loss of Maria's senses about a month before. – She had feared at first, she added, that it would have plunder'd her poor girl of what little understanding was left – but, on the contrary, it had brought her more to herself – still she could not rest – her poor daughter, she said, crying, was wandering somewhere about the road –

– Why does my pulse beat languid as I write this? and what made La Fleur, whose heart seem'd only to be tuned to joy, to pass the back of his hand twice across his eyes, as the woman stood and told it? I beckon'd to the postilion to turn back into the road.

When we had got within half a league of Moulines, at a little opening in the road leading to a thicket, I discovered poor Maria sitting under a poplar – she was sitting with her elbow in her lap, and her head leaning on one side within her hand – a small brook ran at the foot of the tree.

I bid the postilion go on with the chaise to Moulines – and La Fleur to bespeak my supper – and that I would walk after him.

She was dress'd in white, and much as my friend described her, except that her hair hung loose, which before was twisted within a silk net. – She had, superadded likewise to her jacket, a pale green ribband which fell across her shoulder to the waist; at the end of which hung her pipe. – Her goat had been as faithless as her lover; and she had got a little dog in lieu of him, which she had kept tied by a string to her girdle; as I look'd at her dog, she drew him towards her with the string. – "Thou shalt not leave me, Sylvio," said she.* I look'd in Maria's eyes, and saw she was thinking more of her father than of her lover or her little goat; for as she utter'd them the tears trickled down her cheeks.

I sat down close by her; and Maria let me wipe them away as they fell with my handkerchief. – I then steep'd it in my own – and then in hers – and then in mine – and then I wip'd hers again – and as I did it, I felt such undescribable emotions* within me, as I am sure could not be accounted for from any combinations of matter and motion.

I am positive I have a soul; nor can all the books with which materialists have pester'd the world ever convince me of the contrary.

MARIA

When Maria had come a little to herself, I ask'd her if she remember'd a pale thin person of a man who had sat down betwixt her and her goat about two years before? She said, she was unsettled much at that time, but remember'd it upon two accounts – that ill as she was she saw the person pitied her; and next, that her goat had stolen his handkerchief, and she had beat him for the theft – she had wash'd it, she said, in the brook, and kept it ever since in her pocket to restore it to him in case she should ever see him again, which, she added, he had half promised her. As she told me this, she took the handkerchief out of her pocket to let me see it; she had folded it up neatly in a couple of vine leaves, tied round with a tendril – on opening it, I saw an S mark'd in one of the corners.

She had since that, she told me, stray'd as far as Rome, and walk'd round St. Peter's once – and return'd back – that she found her way alone across the Apennines – had travell'd over all Lombardy without money – and through the flinty roads of Savoy without shoes – how she had borne it, and how she had got supported, she could not tell – but *God tempers the wind*, said Maria, to the shorn lamb.*

Shorn indeed! and to the quick, said I; and wast thou in my own land, where I have a cottage, I would take thee to it and shelter thee: thou shouldst eat of my own bread, and drink of my own cup* – I would be kind to thy Sylvio – in all thy weaknesses and wanderings I would seek after thee and bring thee back – when the sun went down I would say my prayers, and when I had done thou shouldst play thy evening song upon thy pipe, nor would the incense of my sacrifice be worse accepted* for entering heaven along with that of a broken heart.

Nature melted within me, as I utter'd this; and Maria observing, as I took out my handkerchief, that it was steep'd too much already to be of use, would needs go wash it in the stream. – And where will you dry it, Maria? said I – I'll dry it in my bosom, said she – 'twill do me good.

And is your heart still so warm, Maria? said I.

I touch'd upon the string on which hung all her sorrows – she look'd with wistful disorder for some time in my face; and then, without saying any thing, took her pipe, and play'd her service to the Virgin – The string I had touch'd ceased to vibrate – in a moment or two Maria returned to herself – let her pipe fall – and rose up.

And where art you going, Maria? said I. – She said to Moulines. – Let us go, said I, together. – Maria put her arm within mine, and lengthening the string, to let the dog follow – in that order we entered Moulines.

MARIA
MOULINES

Tho' I hate salutations and greetings in the market-place,* yet when we got into the middle of this, I stopp'd to take my last look and last farewel of Maria.

Maria, tho' not tall, was nevertheless of the first order of fine forms – affliction had touch'd her looks with something that was scarce earthly – still she was feminine – and so much was there about her of all that the heart wishes, or the eye looks for in woman, that could the traces be ever worn out of her brain, and those of Eliza's out of mine, she should *not only eat of my bread and drink of my own cup*, but Maria should lay in my bosom, and be unto me as a daughter.*

Adieu, poor luckless maiden! – imbibe the oil and wine* which the compassion of a stranger, as he journieth on his way, now pours into thy wounds – the being who has twice bruised thee can only bind them up for ever.

THE BOURBONNOIS

There was nothing from which I had painted out for myself so joyous a riot of the affections, as in this journey in the vintage, through this part of France; but pressing through this gate of sorrow to it, my sufferings had totally unfitted me: in every scene of festivity I saw Maria in the back-ground of the piece, sitting pensive under her poplar; and I had got almost to Lyons before I was able to cast a shade across her –

– Dear sensibility! source inexhausted of all that's precious in our joys, or costly in our sorrows! thou chainest thy martyr down upon his bed of straw – and 'tis thou who lifts him up to HEAVEN – eternal fountain of our feelings! – 'tis here I trace thee – and this is thy divinity which stirs within me – not, that in some sad and sickening moments, *"my soul shrinks back upon herself, and startles at destruction"** – mere pomp of words! – but that I feel some generous joys and generous cares beyond myself – all comes from thee, great – great SENSORIUM of the world! which vibrates, if a hair of our heads but falls upon the ground,* in the remotest desert of thy creation. – Touch'd with thee, Eugenius draws my curtain* when I languish

– hears my tale of symptoms, and blames the weather for the disorder of his nerves. Thou giv'st a portion of it sometimes to the roughest peasant who traverses the bleakest mountains – he finds the lacerated lamb of another's flock – This moment I beheld him leaning with his head against his crook, with piteous inclination looking down upon it – Oh! had I come one moment sooner! – it bleeds to death – his gentle heart bleeds with it –

Peace to thee, generous swain! – I see thou walkest off with anguish – but thy joys shall balance it – for happy is thy cottage – and happy is the sharer of it – and happy are the lambs which sport about you.

THE SUPPER

A shoe coming loose from the fore-foot of the thill-horse, at the beginning of the ascent of mount Taurira, the postilion dismounted, twisted the shoe off, and put it in his pocket; as the ascent was of five or six miles, and that horse our main dependence, I made a point of having the shoe fasten'd on again, as well as we could; but the postilion had thrown away the nails, and the hammer in the chaise-box, being of no great use without them, I submitted to go on.

He had not mounted half a mile higher, when coming to a flinty piece of road, the poor devil lost a second shoe, and from off his other fore-foot; I then got out of the chaise in good earnest; and seeing a house about a quarter of a mile to the left-hand, with a great deal to do, I prevailed upon the postilion to turn up to it. The look of the house, and of every thing about it, as we drew nearer, soon reconciled me to the disaster. – It was a little farm-house surrounded with about twenty acres of vineyard, about as much corn – and close to the house, on one side, was a *potagerie* of an acre and a half, full of every thing which could make plenty in a French peasant's house – and on the other side was a little wood which furnished wherewithal to dress it. It was about eight in the evening when I got to the house – so I left the postilion to manage his point as he could – and for mine, I walk'd directly into the house.

The family consisted of an old grey-headed man and his wife, with five or six sons and sons-in-law and their several wives, and a joyous genealogy out of 'em.

They were all sitting down together to their lentil-soup; a large wheaten loaf was in the middle of the table; and a flaggon of wine at each end of it promised joy thro' the stages of the repast — 'twas a feast of love.

The old man rose up to meet me, and with a respectful cordiality would have me sit down at the table; my heart was sat down the moment I enter'd the room; so I sat down at once like a son of the family; and to invest myself in the character as speedily as I could, I instantly borrowed the old man's knife, and taking up the loaf cut myself a hearty luncheon; and as I did it I saw a testimony in every eye, not only of an honest welcome, but of a welcome mix'd with thanks that I had not seem'd to doubt it.

Was it this; or tell me, Nature, what else it was which made this morsel so sweet — and to what magick I owe it, that the draught I took of their flaggon was so delicious with it, that they remain upon my palate to this hour?

If the supper was to my taste — the grace which follow'd it was much more so.

THE GRACE

When supper was over, the old man gave a knock upon the table with the haft of his knife — to bid them prepare for the dance: the moment the signal was given, the women and girls ran all together into a back apartment to tye up their hair — and the young men to the door to wash their faces, and change their sabots; and in three minutes every soul was ready upon a little esplanade before the house to begin — The old man and his wife came out last, and, placing me betwixt them, sat down upon a sopha of turf by the door.

The old man had some fifty years ago been no mean performer upon the vielle — and at the age he was then of, touch'd it well enough for the purpose. His wife sung now-and-then a little to the tune — then intermitted — and joined her old man again as their children and grand-children danced before them.

It was not till the middle of the second dance, when, from some pauses in the movement wherein they all seemed to look up, I fancied I could distinguish an elevation of spirit different from that which is the cause or the effect of simple jollity. — In a word, I thought I beheld *Religion* mixing in the dance – but as I had never seen her so engaged, I should have look'd upon it now, as one of the illusions of an imagination which is eternally misleading me, had not the old man, as soon as the dance ended, said, that this was their constant way; and that all his life long he had made it a rule, after supper was over, to call out his family to dance and rejoice; believing, he said, that a chearful and contented mind was the best sort of thanks to heaven that an illiterate peasant could pay – *

– Or a learned prelate either, said I.

THE CASE OF DELICACY

When you have gained the top of mount Taurira, you run presently down to Lyons – adieu then to all rapid movements! 'Tis a journey of caution; and it fares better with sentiments, not to be in a hurry with them; so I contracted with a Voiturin to take his time with a couple of mules, and convey me in my own chaise safe to Turin through Savoy.

Poor, patient, quiet, honest people! fear not; your poverty, the treasury of your simple virtues, will not be envied you by the world, nor will your vallies be invaded by it. – Nature! in the midst of thy disorders, thou art still friendly to the scantiness thou hast created – with all thy great works about thee, little hast thou left to give, either to the scithe or to the sickle – but to that little, thou grantest safety and protection; and sweet are the dwellings which stand so shelter'd.

Let the way-worn traveller vent his complaints upon the sudden turns and dangers of your roads – your rocks – your precipices – the difficulties of getting up – the horrors of getting down – mountains impracticable – and cataracts, which roll down great stones from their summits, and block up his road. – The peasants had been all day at work in removing a fragment of this kind between St. Michael and Madane; and by the time my Voiturin got to the place, it wanted full two hours of compleating before a passage could any how be gain'd: there was nothing but to wait with patience – 'twas a wet and tempestuous night; so that by the delay, and that together, the Voiturin found himself obliged to take up five miles short of his stage at a little decent kind of an inn by the road side.

I forthwith took possession of my bed-chamber – got a good fire – order'd supper; and was thanking heaven it was no worse – when a voiture arrived with a lady in it and her servant-maid.*

As there was no other bed-chamber in the house, the hostess, without much nicety, led them into mine, telling them, as she usher'd them in, that there was no body in it but an English gentleman – that there were two good beds in it, and a closet within the room which held another – the accent in which she spoke of this third bed did not say much for it – however, she said, there were three beds, and but three people – and she durst say, the gentleman would do any thing to accommodate matters. – I left not the lady a moment to make a conjecture about it – so instantly made a declaration I would do any thing in my power.

As this did not amount to an absolute surrender of my bed-chamber, I still felt myself so much the proprietor, as to have a right to do the honours of it – so I desired the lady to sit down – pressed her into the warmest seat – call'd for more wood – desired the hostess to enlarge the plan of the supper, and to favour us with the very best wine.

The lady had scarce warm'd herself five minutes at the fire, before she began to turn her head back, and give a look at the beds; and the oftener she cast her eyes that way, the more they return'd perplex'd – I felt for her – and for myself; for in a few minutes, what by her looks, and the case itself, I found myself as much embarrassed as it was possible the lady could be herself.

That the beds we were to lay in were in one and the same room, was enough simply by itself to have excited all this – but the position of them, for they stood parallel, and so very close to each other as only to allow space for a small wicker chair betwixt them, render'd the affair still more oppressive to us – they were fixed up moreover near the fire, and the projection of the chimney on one side, and a large beam which cross'd the room on the other, form'd a kind of recess for them that was no way favourable to the nicety of our sensations – if any thing could have added to it, it was, that the two beds were both of 'em so very small, as to cut us off from every idea of the lady and the maid lying together; which in either of them, could it have been feasible, my lying besides them, tho' a thing not to be wish'd, yet there was nothing in it so terrible which the imagination might not have pass'd over without torment.

As for the little room within, it offer'd little or no consolation to us; 'twas a damp cold closet, with a half dismantled window shutter, and with a window which had neither glass or oil paper in it to keep out the tempest of the night. I did not endeavour to stifle my cough when the lady gave a peep into it; so it reduced the case in course to this alternative – that the lady should sacrifice her health to her feelings, and take up with the closet herself, and abandon the bed next mine to her maid – or that the girl should take the closet, &c. &c.

The lady was a Piedmontese of about thirty, with a glow of health in her cheeks. – The maid was a Lyonoise of twenty, and as brisk and lively a French girl as ever moved. – There were difficulties every way – and the obstacle of the stone in the road, which brought us into the distress, great as it appeared whilst the peasants were removing it, was but a pebble to what lay in our ways now – I have only to add, that it did not lessen the weight which hung upon our spirits, that we were both too delicate to communicate what we felt to each other upon the occasion.

We sat down to supper; and had we not had more generous wine to it than a little inn in Savoy could have furnish'd, our tongues had been tied up, till necessity herself had set them at liberty – but the lady having a few bottles of Burgundy in her voiture sent down her Fille de Chambre for a couple of them; so that by the time supper was over, and we were left alone, we felt ourselves inspired with a strength of mind sufficient to talk, at least, without reserve upon our situation. We turn'd it every way, and debated and considered it in all kind of lights in the course of a two hours negociation; at the end of which the articles were settled finally betwixt us, and stipulated for in form and manner of a treaty of peace – and I believe with as much religion and good faith on both sides, as in any treaty which as yet had the honour of being handed down to posterity.

They were as follows:

First. As the right of the bed-chamber is in Monsieur – and he thinking the bed next to the fire to be the warmest, he insists upon the concession on the lady's side of taking up with it.

Granted, on the part of Madame; with a proviso, That as the curtains of that bed are of a flimsy transparent cotton, and appear likewise too scanty to draw close, that the Fille de Chambre, shall fasten up the opening, either by corking pins, or needle and thread, in such manner as shall be deemed a sufficient barrier on the side of Monsieur.

2dly. It is required on the part of Madame, that Monsieur shall lay the whole night through in his robe de chambre.

Rejected: inasmuch as Monsieur is not worth a robe de chambre; he having nothing in his portmanteau but six shirts and a black silk pair of breeches.

The mentioning the silk pair of breeches made an entire change of the article – for the breeches were accepted as an equivalent for the robe de chambre, and so it was stipulated and agreed upon that I should lay in my black silk breeches all night.

3dly. It was insisted upon, and stipulated for by the lady, that after Monsieur was got to bed, and the candle and fire extinguished, that Monsieur should not speak one single word the whole night.

Granted; provided Monsieur's saying his prayers might not be deem'd an infraction of the treaty.

There was but one point forgot in this treaty, and that was the manner in which the lady and myself should be obliged to undress and get to bed – there was but one way of doing it, and that I leave to the reader to devise; protesting as I do it, that if it is not the most delicate in nature, 'tis the fault of his own imagination – against which this is not my first complaint.

Now when we were got to bed, whether it was the novelty of the situation, or what it was, I know not; but so it was, I could not shut my eyes; I tried this side and that, and turn'd and turn'd again, till a full hour after midnight; when Nature and patience both wearing out – O my God! said I –

– You have broke the treaty, Monsieur, said the lady, who had no more slept than myself. – I begg'd a thousand pardons – but insisted it was no more than an ejaculation – she maintain'd 'twas an entire infraction of the treaty – I maintain'd it was provided for in the clause of the third article.

The lady would by no means give up her point, tho' she weakened her barrier by it; for in the warmth of the dispute, I could hear two or three corking pins fall out of the curtain to the ground.

Upon my word and honour, Madame, said I – stretching my arm out of bed, by way of asseveration –

– (I was going to have added, that I would not have trespass'd against the remotest idea of decorum for the world) –

– But the Fille de Chambre hearing there were words between us, and fearing that hostilities would ensue in course, had crept silently out of her closet, and it being totally dark, had stolen so close to our beds, that she had got herself into the narrow passage which separated them, and had advanc'd so far up as to be in a line betwixt her mistress and me –

So that when I stretch'd out my hand, I caught hold of the Fille de Chambre's

END* OF VOL. II.

A
Political Romance,

Addreſſed

To ——— ————, *Eſq;*

OF

Y O R K.

To which is ſubjoined a

K E Y.

Ridiculum acri
Fortius et melius magnas plerumque ſecat Res.*

Y O R K:
Printed in the Year MDCCLIX.

[Price ONE SHILLING.]

A
POLITICAL ROMANCE
&c.

In my last, for want of something better to write about, I told
you what a World of Fending and Proving we have had of late,
in this little Village of ours, about an *old-cast-Pair-of-black-
Plush-Breeches*,* which *John*, our Parish-Clerk, about ten Years
ago, it seems, had made a Promise of to one *Trim*, who is our
Sexton and Dog-Whipper. — To this you write me Word, that
you have had more than either one or two Occasions to know a
good deal of the shifty Behaviour of this said Master *Trim*, —
and that you are astonished, nor can you for your Soul conceive,
how so worthless a Fellow, and so worthless a Thing into the
Bargain, could become the Occasion of such a Racket as I have
represented.

Now, though you do not say expressly, you could wish to
hear any more about it, yet I see plain enough that I have
raised your Curiosity; and therefore, from the same Motive,
that I slightly mentioned it at all in my last Letter, I will, in this,
give you a full and very circumstantial Account of the whole
Affair.

But, before I begin, I must first set you right in one very
material Point, in which I have missled you, as to the true Cause
of all this Uproar amongst us; — which does not take its Rise, as
I then told you, from the Affair of the *Breeches*; — but, on the
contrary, the whole Affair of the *Breeches* has taken its Rise
from it: — To understand which, you must know, that the first
Beginning of the Squabble was not between *John* the Parish-
Clerk and *Trim* the Sexton, but betwixt the Parson of the Parish
and the said Master *Trim*, about an old *Watch-Coat*,* which
had many Years hung up in the Church, which *Trim* had set his
Heart upon; and nothing would serve *Trim* but he must take it
home, in order to have it converted into a *warm Under-Petticoat*
for his Wife, and a *Jerkin* for himself, against Winter; which, in
a plaintive Tone, he most humbly begg'd his Reverence would
consent to.

I need not tell you, Sir, who have so often felt it, that a

Principle of strong Compassion transports a generous Mind sometimes beyond what is strictly right, – the Parson was within an Ace of being an honourable Example of this very Crime; – for no sooner did the distinct Words – *Petticoat—poor Wife— warm— Winter* strike upon his Ear, —but his Heart warmed, – and, before *Trim* had well got to the End of his Petition, (being a Gentleman of a frank and open Temper) he told him he was welcome to it, with all his Heart and Soul. But, *Trim*, says he, as you see I am but just got down to my Living, and am an utter Stranger to all Parish-Matters, know nothing about this old Watch-Coat you beg of me, having never seen it in my Life, and therefore cannot be a Judge whether 'tis fit for such a Purpose ; or, if it is, in Truth, know not whether 'tis mine to bestow upon you or not; —you must have a Week or ten Days Patience, till I can make some Inquiries about it; – and, if I find it is in my Power, I tell you again, Man, your Wife is heartily welcome to an Under-Petticoat out of it, and you to a Jerkin, was the Thing as good again as you represent it.

It is necessary to inform you, Sir, in this Place, That the Parson was earnestly bent to serve *Trim* in this Affair, not only from the Motive of Generosity, which I have justly ascribed to him, but likewise from another Motive ; and that was by way of making some Sort of Recompence for a Multitude of small Services which *Trim* had occasionally done, and indeed was continually doing, (as he was much about the House) when his own Man was out of the Way. For all these Reasons together, I say, the Parson of the Parish intended to serve *Trim* in this Matter to the utmost of his Power: All that was wanting was previously to inquire, if any one had a *Claim* to it; – or whether, as it had, Time immemorial, hung up in the Church, the taking it down might not raise a Clamour in the Parish. These Inquiries were the very Thing that *Trim* dreaded in his Heart. – He knew very well that if the Parson should but say one Word to the Church-Wardens about it, there would be an End of the whole Affair. For this, and some other Reasons not necessary to be told you, at present, *Trim* was for allowing no Time in this Matter; – but, on the contrary, doubled his Diligence and Importunity at the Vicarage-House; – plagued the whole Family to Death; – pressed his Suit Morning, Noon, and Night; and, to shorten my Story, teazed the poor Gentleman, who was but in an ill State of Health, almost out of his Life about it.

You will not wonder, when I tell you, that all this Hurry and Precipitation, on the Side of Master *Trim*, produced its natural Effect on the Side of the Parson, and that was, a Suspicion that all was not right at the Bottom.

He was one Evening sitting alone in his Study, weighing and turning this Doubt every Way in his Mind; and, after an Hour and a half's serious Deliberation upon the Affair, and running over *Trim's* Behaviour throughout, – he was just saying to himself, *It must be so*; – when a sudden Rap at the Door put an End to his Soliloquy, – and, in a few Minutes, to his Doubts too; for a Labourer in the Town, who deem'd himself past his fifty-second Year, had been returned by the Constable in the Militia-List, – and he had come, with a Groat in his Hand, to search the Parish Register for his Age. – The Parson bid the poor Fellow put the Groat into his Pocket, and go into the Kitchen: – Then shutting the Study Door, and taking down the Parish Register, – *Who knows*, says he, *but I may find something here about this self-same Watch-Coat?* – He had scarce unclasped the Book, in saying this, when he popp'd upon the very Thing he wanted, fairly wrote on the first Page, pasted to the Inside of one of the Covers, whereon was a Memorandum about the very Thing in Question, in these express Words:

MEMORANDUM

The great Watch-Coat was purchased and given above two hundred Years ago, by the Lord of the Manor, to this Parish-Church, to the sole Use and Behoof of the poor Sextons thereof, and their Successors, for ever, to be worn by them respectively in winterly cold Nights, in ringing Complines, Passing-Bells, &c. **which the said Lord of the Manor had done, in Piety, to keep the poor Wretches warm, and for the Good of his own Soul, for which they were directed to pray,** &c. &c. &c. &c. *Just Heaven!* said the Parson to himself, looking upwards, *What an Escape have I had! Give this for an Under-Petticoat to* Trim's *Wife! I would not have consented to such a Desecration to be Primate of all* England; *nay, I would not have disturb'd a single Button of it for half my Tythes!*

Scarce were the Words out of his Mouth, when in pops *Trim* with the whole Subject of the Exclamation under both his Arms. – I say, under both his Arms; – for he had actually got it ripp'd and cut out ready, his own Jerkin under one Arm, and the Petticoat under the other, in order to be carried to the Taylor to be made up, – and had just stepp'd in, in high Spirits, to shew the Parson how cleverly it had held out.

There are many good Similies now subsisting in the World, but which I have neither Time to recollect or look for, which would give you a strong Conception of the Astonishment and honest Indignation which this unexpected Stroke of *Trim's* Impudence impress'd upon the Parson's Looks. – Let it suffice to say, That it exceeded all fair Description, – as well as all Power of proper Resentment, – except this, that *Trim* was ordered, in a stern Voice, to lay the Bundles down upon the Table, – to go about his Business, and wait upon him, at his Peril, the next Morning at Eleven precisely : – Against this Hour, like a wise Man, the Parson had sent to desire *John* the Parish-Clerk, who bore an exceeding good Character as a Man of Truth, and who having, moreover, a pretty Freehold of about eighteen Pounds a Year in the Township, was a leading Man in it ; and, upon the whole, was such a one of whom it might be said, – That he rather did Honour to his Office, – than that his Office did Honour to him. – Him he sends for, with the Church-Wardens, and one of the Sides-Men, a grave, knowing, old Man,* to be present : – For as *Trim* had with-held the whole Truth from the Parson, touching the Watch-Coat, he thought it probable he would as certainly do the same Thing to others ; though this, I said, was wise, the Trouble of the Precaution might have been spared, – because the Parson's Character was unblemish'd, – and he had ever been held by the World in the Estimation of a Man of Honour and Integrity. – *Trim's* Character, on the contrary, was as well known, if not in the World, yet, at least, in all the Parish, to be that of a little, dirty, pimping, pettifogging, ambidextrous Fellow, – who neither cared what he did or said of any, provided he could get a Penny by it. – This might, I say, have made any Precaution needless ; – but you must know, as the Parson had in a Manner but just got down to his Living,* he dreaded the Consequences of the least ill Impression on his first Entrance amongst his Parishioners, which would have disabled him from doing them the Good he wished ; – so that, out of Regard to his Flock, more than the necessary Care due to himself, – he was resolv'd not to lie at the Mercy of what Resentment might vent, or Malice lend an Ear to. – Accordingly the whole Matter was rehearsed from first to last by the Parson, in the Manner I've told you, in the Hearing of *John* the Parish-Clerk, and in the Presence of *Trim*.

Trim had little to say for himself, except "That the Parson had absolutely promised to befriend him and his Wife in the Affair, to the utmost of his Power : That the Watch-Coat was certainly in his Power, and that he might still give it him if he pleased."

To this, the Parson's Reply was short, but strong, "That nothing was in his *Power* to do, but what he could do *honestly* : – That in giving the Coat to him and his Wife, he should do a manifest Wrong to the *next* Sexton ; the great Watch-Coat being the most comfortable Part of the Place : – That he should, moreover, injure the Right of his own Successor, who would be just so much a worse Patron, as the Worth of the Coat amounted to ; – and, in a Word, he declared, that his whole Intent in promising that Coat, was Charity to *Trim* ; but *Wrong* to no Man ; that was a Reserve, he said, made in all Cases of this Kind : – and he declared solemnly, *in Verbo Sacerdotis*, That this was his Meaning, and was so understood by *Trim* himself."

With the Weight of this Truth, and the great good Sense and strong Reason which accompanied all the Parson said upon the Subject, – poor *Trim* was driven to his last Shift, – and begg'd he might be suffered to plead his Right and Title to the Watch-Coat, if not by *Promise*, at least by *Services*. – It was well known how much he was entitled to it upon these Scores : That he had black'd the Parson's Shoes without Count, and greased his Boots above fifty Times : – That he had run for Eggs into the Town upon all Occasions; – whetted the Knives at all Hours; – catched his Horse and rubbed him down : – That for his Wife she had been ready upon all Occasions to charr for them; – and neither he nor she, to the best of his Remembrance, ever took a Farthing, or any thing beyond a Mug of Ale. – To this Account of his Services he begg'd Leave to add those of his Wishes, which, he said, had been equally great. – He affirmed, and was ready, he said, to make it appear, by Numbers of Witnesses, "He had drank his Reverence's Health a thousand Times, (by the bye, he did not add out of the Parson's own Ale) : That he not only drank his Health, but wish'd it ; and never came to the House, but ask'd his Man kindly how he did ; that in particula,,about half a Year ago, when his Reverence cut his Finger in paring an Apple, he went half a Mile to ask a cunning Woman, what was good to stanch Blood, and actually returned with a Cobweb in his Breeches Pocket : — Nay, says *Trim*, it was not a Fortnight ago, when your Reverence took that violent Purge, that I went to the far End of the whole Town to borrow you a Close-stool, — and came back, as my Neighbours, who flouted me, will all bear witness, with the Pan upon my Head, and never thought it too much."

Trim concluded his pathetick Remonstrance with saying, "He hoped his Reverence's Heart would not suffer him to requite so many faithful Services by so unkind a Return : — That if it was so, as he was the first, so he hoped he should be the last, Example of a Man of his Condition so treated." — This Plan of *Trim's* Defence, which *Trim* had put himself upon, — could admit of no other Reply but a general Smile.

Upon the whole, let me inform you, That all that could be said, *pro* and *con*, on both Sides, being fairly heard, it was plain, That *Trim*, in every Part of this Affair, had behaved very ill ; — and *one* Thing, which was never expected to be known of him, happening in the Course of this Debate to come out against him ; — namely, That he had gone and told the Parson, efrre he had ever set Foot in his Parish, That *John* his Parish-Clerk, — his Church-Wardens, and some of the Heads of the Parish, were a Parcel of Scoundrels. — Upon the Upshot, *Trim* was kick'd out of Doors ; and told, at his Peril, never to come there again.

At first *Trim* huff'd and bounced most terribly; — swore he would get a Warrant; — then nothing would serve him but he would call a Bye-Law, and tell the whole Parish how the Parson had misused him; — but cooling of that, as fearing the Parson might possibly bind him over to his good Behaviour, and, for aught he knew, might send him to the House of Correction, — he let the Parson alone ; and, to revenge himself, falls foul upon his Clerk, who had no more to do in the Quarrel than you or I; — rips up the Promise of the old-cast-Pair-of-black-Plush-Breeches, and raises an Uproar in the Town about it,* notwithstanding it had slept ten Years. — But all this, you must know, is look'd upon in no other Light, but as an artful Stroke of Generalship in *Trim*, to raise a Dust, and cover himself under the disgraceful Chastisement he has undergone.

If your Curiosity is not yet satisfied, — I will now proceed to relate the *Battle* of the Breeches, in the same exact Manner I have done *that* of the Watch-Coat.

Be it known then, that, about ten Years ago, when *John* was appointed Parish-Clerk of this Church, this said Master *Trim* took no small Pains to get into *John's* good Graces; in order, as it afterwards appeared, to coax a Promise out of him of a Pair of Breeches, which *John* had then by him, of black Plush, not much the worse for wearing; – *Trim* only begging for God's Sake to have them bestowed upon him when *John* should think fit to cast them.

Trim was one of those kind of Men who loved a Bit of Finery in his Heart, and would rather have a tatter'd Rag of a Better Body's, than the best plain whole Thing his Wife could spin him.

John, who was naturally unsuspicious, made no more Difficulty of promising the Breeches, than the Parson had done in promising the Great Coat; and, indeed, with something less Reserve, – because the Breeches were *John's own*, and he could give them, without Wrong, to whom he thought fit.

It happened, I was going to say unluckily, but, I should rather say, most luckily, for *Trim*, for he was the only Gainer by it, – that a Quarrel, about some six or eight Weeks after this, broke out between *the late* Parson of the Parish* and *John* the Clerk. Somebody (and it was thought to be Nobody but *Trim*) had put it into the Parson's Head, "That *John's* Desk in the Church was, at the least, four Inches higher than it should be: – That the Thing gave Offence, and was indecorous, inasmuch as it approach'd too near upon a Level with the Parson's Desk itself. This Hardship the Parson complained of loudly, – and told *John* one Day after Prayers, – "He could bear it no longer: – And would have it alter'd and brought down as it should be." *John* made no other Reply, but, "That the Desk was not of his raising: – That 'twas not one Hair Breadth higher than he found it; – and that as he found it, so would he leave it: – In short, he would neither make an Encroachment, nor would he suffer one."

The *late* Parson might have his Virtues, but the leading Part of his Character was not *Humility*; so that *John's* Stiffness in this Point was not likely to reconcile Matters. – This was *Trim's* Harvest.

After a friendly Hint to *John* to stand his Ground, – away hies *Trim* to make his Market at the Vicarage: – What pass'd there, I will not say, intending not to be uncharitable; so shall content myself with only guessing at it, from the sudden Change that appeared in *Trim's* Dress for the better; – for he had left his old ragged Coat, Hat and Wig, in the Stable, and was come forth strutting across the Church-yard, y'clad in a good creditable cast Coat, large Hat and Wig,* which the Parson had just given him. – Ho! Ho! Hollo! *John!* cries *Trim*, in an insolent Bravo, as loud as ever he could bawl – See here, my Lad! how fine I am. – The more Shame for you, answered *John*, seriously. – Do you think, *Trim*, says he, such Finery, gain'd by such Services, becomes you, or can wear well? – Fye upon it, *Trim*; – I could not have expected this from you, considering what Friendship you pretended, and how kind I have ever been to you: – How many Shillings and Sixpences I have generously lent you in your Distresses? – Nay, it was but t'other Day that I promised you these black Plush Breeches I have on. – Rot your Breeches, quoth *Trim*; for *Trim's* Brain was half turn'd with his new Finery: – Rot your Breeches, says he, – I would not take them up, were they laid at my Door; – give 'em, and be d—d to you, to whom you like; – I would have you to know I can have a better Pair at the Parson's any Day in the Week: – *John* told him plainly, as his Word had once pass'd him, he had a Spirit above taking Advantage of his Insolence, in giving them away to another: – But, to tell him his Mind freely, he thought he had got so many Favours of that Kind, and was so likely to get many more for the same Services, of the Parson, that he had better give up the Breeches, with good Nature, to some one who would be more thankful for them.

Here *John* mentioned *Mark Slender*,* (who, it seems, the Day before, had ask'd *John* for 'em) not knowing they were under Promise to *Trim*. – "Come, *Trim*, says he, let poor *Mark* have 'em, – You know he has not a Pair to his A— : Besides, you see he is just of my Size, and they will fit him to a T; whereas, if I give 'em to you, – look ye, they are not worth much; and, besides, you could not get your Backside into them, if you had them, without tearing them all to Pieces."

Every Tittle of this was most undoubtedly true; for *Trim*, you must know, by foul Feeding, and playing the good Fellow at the Parson's, was grown somewhat gross about the lower Parts, *if not higher*: So that, as all *John* said upon the Occasion was fact, *Trim*, with much ado, and after a hundred Hum's and Hah's, at last, out of mere Compassion to *Mark, signs, seals, and delivers up* all Right, Interest, and Pretensions whatsoever, in and to the said Breeches; thereby binding his Heirs, Executors, Administrators, and Assignes, never more to call the said Claim in Question.

All this Renunciation was set forth in an ample Manner, to be in pure Pity to *Mark*'s Nakedness; – but the Secret was, *Trim* had an Eye to, and firmly expected in his own Mind, the great Green Pulpit-Cloth and old Velvet Cushion,* which were that very Year to be taken down; – which, by the Bye, could he have wheedled *John* a second Time out of 'em, as he hoped, he had made up the Loss of his Breeches Seven-fold.

Now, you must know, this Pulpit-Cloth and Cushion were not in *John*'s Gift, but in the Church-Wardens, *&c.* – However, as I said above, that *John* was a leading Man in the Parish, *Trim* knew he could help him to them if he would: – But *John* had got a Surfeit of him; – so, when the Pulpit-Cloth, *&c.* were taken down, they were immediately given (*John* having a great Say in it) to *William Doe*,* who understood very well what Use to make of them.

As for the old Breeches, poor *Mark Slender* lived to wear them but a short Time, and they got into the Possession of *Lorry Slim*,* an unlucky Wight, by whom they are still worn; – in Truth, as you will guess, they are very thin by this Time: – But *Lorry* has a light Heart; and what recommends them to him, is this, that, as thin as they are, he knows that *Trim*, let him say what he will to the contrary, still envies the *Possessor* of them, – and, with all his Pride, would be very glad to wear them after *him*.

Upon this Footing have these Affairs slept quietly for near ten Years, – and would have slept for ever, but for the unlucky Kicking-Bout; which, as I said, has ripp'd this Squabble up afresh: So that it was no longer ago than last Week, that *Trim* met and insulted *John* in the public Town-Way, before a hundred People; – tax'd him with the Promise of the old-cast-Pair-of-black-Breeches, notwithstanding *Trim's* solemn Renunciation; twitted him with the Pulpit-Cloth and Velvet Cushion, – as good as told him, he was ignorant of the common Duties of his Clerkship; adding, very insolently, That he knew not so much as to give out a common Psalm in Tune. –

John contented himself with giving a plain Answer to every Article that *Trim* had laid to his Charge, and appealed to his Neighbours who remembered the whole Affair; – and as he knew there was never any Thing to be got in wrestling with a

Chimney-Sweeper, – he was going to take Leave of *Trim* for ever. – But, hold, – the Mob by this Time had got round them, and their High Mightinesses insisted upon having *Trim* tried upon the Spot. – *Trim* was accordingly tried; and, after a full Hearing, was convicted a second Time, and handled more roughly by one or more of them, than even at the Parson's.

Trim, says one, are you not ashamed of yourself, to make all this Rout and Disturbance in the Town, and set Neighbours together by the Ears, about an old-worn-out-Pair-of-cast-Breeches, not worth Half a Crown? – Is there a cast-Coat, or a Place in the whole Town, that will bring you in a Shilling, but what you have snapp'd up, like a greedy Hound as you are?*

In the first Place, are you not Sexton and Dog-Whipper, worth Three Pounds a Year? – Then you begg'd the Church-Wardens to let your Wife have the Washing and Darning of the Surplice and Church-Linen, which brings you in Thirteen Shillings and Four Pence. – Then you have Six Shillings and Eight Pence for oiling and winding up the Clock, both paid you at *Easter*. – The Pinder's Place, which is worth Forty Shillings a Year, – you have got that too. – You are the Bailiff, which the late Parson got you, which brings you in Forty Shillings more. – Besides all this, you have Six Pounds a Year, paid you Quarterly for being Mole-Catcher to the Parish. – Aye, says the luckless Wight above-mentioned, (who was standing close to him with his Plush Breeches on) "You are not only Mole-Catcher, *Trim*, but you catch STRAY CONIES too in the *Dark*; and you pretend a *Licence* for it, which, I trow, will be look'd into at the next Quarter Sessions." I maintain it, I have a Licence, says *Trim*, blushing as red as Scarlet: – I have a Licence, – and as I farm a Warren in the next Parish, I will catch Conies every Hour of the Night. – *You catch Conies*!* cries a toothless old Woman, who was just passing by. –

This set the Mob a laughing, and sent every Man home in perfect good Humour, except *Trim*, who waddled very slowly off with that Kind of inflexible Gravity only to be equalled by one Animal in the whole Creation, – and surpassed by none. I am,

SIR,

Yours, &c. &c.

FINIS.

POSTSCRIPT

I have broke open my Letter to inform you, that I miss'd the Opportunity of sending it by the Messenger, who I expected would have called upon me in his Return through this Village to *York*, so it has laid a Week or ten Days by me.

— I am not sorry for the Disappointment, because something has since happened, in Continuation of this Affair, which I am thereby enabled to transmit to you, all under one Trouble.

When I finished the above Account, I thought (as did every Soul in the Parish) *Trim* had met with so thorough a Rebuff from *John* the Parish-Clerk and the Town's Folks, who all took against him, that *Trim* would be glad to be quiet, and let the Matter rest.

But, it seems, it is not half an Hour ago since *Trim* sallied forth again; and, having borrowed a Sow-Gelder's Horn,* with hard Blowing he got the whole Town round him, and endeavoured to raise a Disturbance, and fight the whole Battle over again: — That he had been used in the last Fray worse than a Dog; — not by *John* the Parish-Clerk, — for I shou'd not, quoth *Trim*, have valued him a Rush single Hands: — But all the Town sided with him, and twelve Men in *Buckram* set upon me all at once, and kept me in Play at Sword's Point for three Hours together. — Besides, quoth *Trim*, there were two misbegotten Knaves in *Kendal Green*,* who lay all the while in Ambush in *John's* own House, and they all *sixteen* came upon my Back, and let drive at me together. — A Plague, says *Trim*, of all Cowards! — *Trim* repeated this Story above a Dozen Times; — which made some of the Neighbours pity him, thinking the poor Fellow crack-brain'd, and that he actually believed what he said. After this *Trim* dropp'd the Affair of the *Breeches*, and begun a fresh Dispute about the *Reading-Desk*, which I told you had occasioned some small Dispute between the *late* Parson and *John*, some Years ago.

This *Reading-Desk*, as you will observe, was but an Episode wove into the main Story by the Bye; — for the main Affair was the *Battle of the Breeches* and *Great Watch-Coat*. — However, *Trim* being at last driven out of these two Citadels, — he has seized hold, in his Retreat, of this *Reading-Desk*, with a View, as it seems, to take Shelter behind it.

I cannot say but the Man has fought it out obstinately

enough; — and, had his Cause been good, I should have really pitied him. For when he was driven out of the *Great Watch-Coat*, — you see, he did not run away; — no, — he retreated behind the *Breeches*; — and, when he could make nothing of it behind the *Breeches*, — he got behind the *Reading-Desk*. — To what other Hold *Trim* will next retreat, the Politicians of this Village are not agreed. — Some think his next Move will be towards the Rear of the Parson's Boot; — but, as it is thought he cannot make a long Stand there, — others are of Opinion, That *Trim* will once more in his Life get hold of the Parson's Horse, and charge upon him, or perhaps behind him. — But as the Horse is not easy to be caught, the more general Opinion is, That, when he is driven out of the *Reading-Desk*, he will make his last Retreat in such a Manner as, if possible, to gain the *Close-Stool*, and defend himself behind it to the very last Drop. If *Trim* should make this Movement, by my Advice he should be left besides his Citadel, in full Possession of the Field of Battle; — where, 'tis certain, he will keep every Body a League off, and may pop by himself till he is weary: Besides, as *Trim* seems bent upon *purging* himself, and may have Abundance of foul Humours to work off, I think he cannot be better placed.

But this is all Matter of Speculation. — Let me carry you back to Matter of Fact, and tell you what Kind of a Stand *Trim* has actually made behind the said *Desk*.

"Neighbours and Townsmen all, I will be sworn before my Lord Mayor, That *John* and his nineteen Men in *Buckram*, have abused me worse than a Dog; for they told you that I play'd fast and go-loose with the *late* Parson and him, in that old Dispute of theirs about the *Reading-Desk*; and that I made Matters worse between them, and not better."

Of this Charge, *Trim* declared he was as innocent as the Child that was unborn: That he would be Book-sworn he had no Hand in it. He produced a strong Witness; — and, moreover, insinuated, that *John* himself, instead of being angry for what he had done in it, had actually thank'd him. Aye, *Trim*, says the Wight in the Plush Breeches, but that was, *Trim*, the Day before *John* found thee out. — Besides, *Trim*, there is nothing in that: — For, the very Year that thou wast made Town's Pinder, thou knowest well, that I both thank'd thee myself; and, moreover, gave thee a good warm Supper for turning *John Lund*'s Cows and Horses out of my Hard-Corn Close; which if thou had'st not done, (as thou told'st me) I should have lost my whole Crop: Whereas, *John Lund* and *Thomas Patt*, who are both here to testify, and will take their Oaths on't, That thou thyself wast the very Man who set the Gate open; and, after all, – it was not thee, *Trim*, – 'twas the Blacksmith's poor Lad who turn'd them out: So that a Man may be thank'd and rewarded too for a good Turn which he never did, nor ever did intend.

Trim could not sustain this unexpected Stroke; – so *Trim* march'd off the Field, without Colours flying, or his Horn sounding, or any other Ensigns of Honour whatever.

Whether after this *Trim* intends to rally a second Time, – or whether *Trim* may not take it into his Head to claim the Victory, – no one but *Trim* himself can inform you: – However, the general Opinion, upon the whole, is this, – That, in three several pitch'd Battles, *Trim* has been so *trimm'd*, as never disastrous Hero was trimm'd before him.

THE KEY

This *Romance* was, by some Mischance or other, dropp'd in the *Minster-Yard, York,* and pick'd up by a Member of a small Political Club* in that City; where it was carried, and publickly read to the Members the last Club Night.

It was instantly agreed to, by a great Majority, That it was a *Political Romance*; but concerning what State or Potentate, could not so easily be settled amongst them.

The President of the Night, who is thought to be as clear and quick-sighted as any one of the whole Club in Things of this Nature, discovered plainly, That the Disturbances therein set forth, related to those on the *Continent*: — That *Trim* could be Nobody but the King of *France*, by whose shifting and intriguing Behaviour, all *Europe* was set together by the Ears: — That *Trim*'s Wife was certainly the *Empress*, who are as kind together, says he, as any Man and Wife can be for their Lives. — The more Shame for 'em, says an Alderman, low to himself. — Agreeable to this Key, continues the President, — The *Parson*, who I think is a most excellent Character, — is His Most Excellent Majesty King *George*; — *John*, the Parish-Clerk, is the King of *Prussia*; who, by the Manner of his first entering *Saxony*, shew'd the World most evidently, — That he did know how to lead out the Psalm, and in Tune and Time too, notwithstanding *Trim*'s vile Insult upon him in that Particular. — But who do you think, says a Surgeon and Man-Midwife, who sat next him, (whose Coat-Button the President, in the Earnestness of this Explanation, had got fast hold of, and had thereby partly drawn him over to his Opinion) Who do you think, Mr. President, says he, are meant by the *Church-Wardens, Sides-Men, Mark Slender, Lorry Slim, & c.* — Who do I think? says he, Why, — Why, Sir, as I take the Thing, — the *Church-Wardens* and *Sides-Men*, are the *Electors* and the other *Princes* who form the *Germanick Body.* — And as for the other subordinate Characters of *Mark Slim*, — the *unlucky Wight* in the Plush Breeches, — the *Parson's Man* who was so often out of the Way, *&c. &c.* — these, to be sure, are the several *Marshals* and *Generals*, who fought, or should have fought, under them the last Campaign. — The Men in *Buckram*, continued the President, are the Gross of the King of *Prussia*'s Army, who are as *stiff* a Body of Men as are in the World: — And *Trim*'s saying they were twelve, and then nineteen, is a Wipe for the *Brussels Gazetteer*, who, to my Knowledge, was never two Weeks in the same Story, about that or any thing else.

As for the rest of the *Romance*, continued the President, it sufficiently explains itself, – *The Old-cast-Pair-of-Black-Plush-Breeches* must be *Saxony*, which the *Elector*, you see, *has left off wearing*: – And as for the *Great Watch-Coat*, which, you know, covers all, it signifies all *Europe*; comprehending, at least, so many of its different States and Dominions, as we have any Concern with in the present War.

I protest, says a Gentleman who sat next but one to the President, and who, it seems, was the Parson of the Parish, a Member not only of the Political, but also of a Musical Club in the next Street; – I protest, says he, if this Explanation is right, which I think it is, – That the whole makes a very fine Symbol. – You have always some Musical Instrument or other in your Head, I think, says the Alderman. – Musical Instrument! replies the Parson, in Astonishment, – Mr Alderman, I mean an Allegory; and I think the greedy Disposition of *Trim* and his Wife, in ripping the *Great Watch-Coat* to Pieces, in order to convert it into a Petticoat for the one, and a Jerkin for the other, is one of the most beautiful of the Kind I ever met with; and will shew all the World what have been the true Views and Intentions of the Houses of *Bourbon* and *Austria* in this abominable Coalition, – I might have called it Whoredom: – Nay, says the Alderman, 'tis downright Adulterydom, or nothing.

This Hypothesis of the President's explain'd every Thing in the *Romance* extreamly well; and, withall, was delivered with so much Readiness and Air of Certainty, as begot an Opinion in two Thirds of the Club, that Mr. President was actually the Author of the *Romance* himself: But a Gentleman who sat on the opposite Side of the Table, who had come piping-hot from reading the History of King *William*'s and Queen *Anne*'s Wars, and who was thought, at the Bottom, to envy the President the Honour both of the *Romance* and Explanation too, gave an entire new Turn to it all. He acquainted the Club, That Mr. President was altogether wrong in every Supposition he had made, except that one, where the *Great Watch-Coat* was said by him to represent *Europe*, or at least a great Part of it: – So far he acknowledged he was pretty right; but that he had not gone far enough backwards into our History to come at the Truth. He then acquainted them, that the dividing the *Great Watch-Coat* did, and could, allude to nothing else in the World but the *Partition-Treaty* ;* which, by the Bye, he told them, was the most unhappy and scandalous Transaction in all King *William*'s Life : It was that false Step, and that only, says he, rising from his Chair, and striking his Hand upon the Table with great Violence ; it was that false Step, says he, knitting his Brows and throwing his Pipe down upon the Ground, that has laid the Foundation of all the Disturbances and Sorrows we feel and lament at this very Hour ; and as for *Trim*'s giving up the *Breeches*, look ye, it is almost Word for Word copied from the *French* King and *Dauphin*'s Renunciation of *Spain* and the *West-Indies*, which all the World knew (as was the very Case of the *Breeches*) were renounced by them on purpose to be reclaim'd when Time should serve.

This Explanation had too much Ingenuity in it to be altogether slighted ; and, in Truth, the worst Fault it had, seem'd to be the prodigious Heat of it ; which (as an Apothecary, who sat next the Fire, observ'd, in a very low Whisper to his next Neighbour) was so much incorporated into every Particle of it, that it was impossible, under such Fermentation, it should work its desired Effect.

This, however, no way intimidated a little valiant Gentleman, though he sat the very next Man, from giving an Opinion as diametrically opposite as *East* is from *West*.

This Gentleman, who was by much the best Geographer in the whole Club, and, moreover, second Cousin to an Engineer, was positive the *Breeches* meant *Gibraltar* ; for, if you remember, Gentlemen, says he, tho' possibly you don't, the Ichnography and Plan of that Town and Fortress, it exactly resembles a Pair of Trunk-Hose, the two Promontories forming the two Slops, *&c. &c.* – Now we all know, continued he, that King *George* the First made a Promise of that important Pass to the King of *Spain* : — So that the whole Drift of the *Romance*, according to my Sense of Things, is merely to vindicate the King and the Parliament in that Transaction, which made so much Noise in the World.

A Wholesale Taylor, who from the Beginning had resolved not to speak at all in the Debate, – was at last drawn into it, by something very unexpected in the last Person's Argument.

He told the Company, frankly, he did not understand what *Ichnography* meant: — But as for the Shape of a *Pair of Breeches*, as he had had the Advantage of cutting out so many hundred Pairs in his Life-Time, he hoped he might be allowed to know as much of the Matter as another Man.

Now, to my Mind, says he, there is nothing in all the Terraqueous Globe (a Map of which, it seems, hung up in his Work-Shop) so like a *Pair of Breeches* unmade up, as the Island of *Sicily*: — Nor is there any thing, if you go to that, quoth an honest Shoe-maker, who had the Honour to be a Member of the Club, so much like a *Jack-Boot*, to my Fancy, as the Kingdom of *Italy*. — What the Duce has either *Italy* or *Sicily* to do in the Affair? cries the President, who, by this Time, began to tremble for this Hypothesis, — What have they to do? — Why, answered the *Partition-Treaty* Gentleman, with great Spirit and Joy sparkling in his Eyes, — They have just so much, Sir, to do in the Debate as to overthrow your Suppositions, and to establish the Certainty of mine beyond the Possibility of a Doubt: For, says he, (with an Air of Sovereign Triumph over the President's Politicks) — By the *Partition-Treaty*, Sir, both *Naples* and *Sicily* were the very Kingdoms made to devolve upon the *Dauphin*; — and *Trim*'s *greasing the Parson's Boots*, is a Devilish Satyrical Stroke; — for it exposes the Corruption and Bribery made Use of at that Juncture, in bringing over the several States and Princes of *Italy* to use their Interests at *Rome*, to stop the Pope from giving the Investitures of those Kingdoms to any Body else. — The Pope has not the Investiture of *Sicily*, cries another Gentleman. — I care not, says he, for that.

Almost every one apprehended the Debate to be now ended, and that no one Member would venture any new Conjecture upon the *Romance*, after so many clear and decisive Interpretations had been given. But, hold, — Close to the Fire, and opposite to where the Apothecary sat, there sat also a Gentleman of the Law, who, from the Beginning to the End of the Hearing of this Cause, seem'd no way satisfied in his Conscience with any one Proceeding in it. This Gentleman had not yet opened his Mouth, but had waited patiently till they had all gone thro' their several Evidences on the other Side; — reserving himself, like an expert Practitioner, for the last Word in the Debate. When the *Partition-Treaty*-Gentleman had finish'd what he had to say, — He got up, — and, advancing towards the Table, told them, That the

Error they had all gone upon thus far, in making out the several Facts in the *Romance*, – was in looking too high ; which, with great Candor, he said, was a very natural Candor, he said, was a very natural Thing, and very excusable withall, in such a Political Club as theirs : For Instance, continues he, you have been searching the *Registers*, and looking into the *Deeds* of *Kings* and *Emperors*, – as if Nobody had any *Deeds* to shew or compare the *Romance* to but themselves. – This, continued the Attorney, is just as much out of the Way of good Practice, as if I should carry a Thing slap-dash into the House of Lords, which was under forty Shillings, and might be decided in the next County-Court for six Shillings and Eight-pence. – He then took the *Romance* in his Left Hand, and pointing with the Fore-Finger of his Right towards the second Page, he humbly begg'd Leave to observe, (and, to do him Justice, he did it in somewhat of a *forensic Air*) That the *Parson, John*, and *Sexton*, shewed incontestably the Thing to be *Tripartite* ; now, if you will take Notice, Gentlemen, says he, these several Persons, who are Parties to this Instrument, are merely Ecclesiastical ; that the *Reading-Desk, Pulpit-Cloth*, and *Velvet Cushion*, are tripartite too ; and are, by Intendment of Law, Goods and Chattles merely of an Ecclesiastick Nature, belonging and appertaining "only unto them," *and to them only.* – So that it appears very plain to me, That the *Romance*, neither directly nor indirectly, goes upon Temporal, but altogether upon Church-Matters. – And do not you think, says he, softening his Voice a little, and addressing himself to the Parson with a forced Smile, – Do not you think Doctor, says he, That the Dispute in the *Romance*, between the *Parson* of the Parish and *John*, about the Height of *John*'s Desk, is a very fine Panegyrick upon the *Humility* of *Church-Men* ? – I think, says the Parson, it is much of the same Fineness with that which your Profession is complimented with, in the pimping, dirty, pettyfogging Character of *Trim*, – which, in my Opinion, Sir, is just such another Panegyrick upon the *Honesty* of *Attornies*.

Nothing whets the Spirits like an Insult : – Therefore the Parson went on with a visible Superiority and an uncommon Acuteness. – As you are so happy, Sir, continues he, in making Applications, – pray turn over a Page or two to the black Law-Letters in the *Romance*. – What do you think of them, Sir ? – Nay, – pray read the Grant of the *Great Watch-Coat* – and

Trim's Renunciation of the *Breeches*. – Why, there is downright
Lease and **Release** for you, – 'tis the very Thing, Man; – only with
this small Difference, – and in which consists the whole Strength
of the Panegyric, – That the Author of the *Romance* has convey'd and reconvey'd, in about ten Lines, – what you, with the
glorious Prolixity of the Law, could not have crowded into as
many Skins of Parchment.

The Apothecary, who had paid the Attorney, the same
Afternoon, a Demand of Three Pounds Six Shillings and Eight-
Pence, for much such another Jobb, – was so highly tickled with
the Parson's Repartee in that particular Point, – that he rubb'd
his Hands together most fervently, – and laugh'd most trium-
phantly thereupon.

This could not escape the Attorney's Notice, any more than
the Cause of it did escape his Penetration.

I think, Sir, says he, (dropping his Voice a Third) you might
well have spared this immoderate Mirth, since you and your
Profession have the least Reason to triumph here of any of us. –
I beg, quoth he, that you would reflect a Moment upon the
Cob-Web which *Trim* went so far for, and brought back with
an Air of so much Importance, in his Breeches Pocket, to lay
upon the Parson's cut Finger. – This said Cob-Web, Sir, is a
fine-spun Satyre, upon the flimsy Nature of one Half of the
Shop-Medicines, with which you make a Property of the Sick,
the Ignorant, and the Unsuspecting. – And as for the Moral of
the *Close-Stool-Pan*, Sir, 'tis too plain, – Does not nine Parts in
ten of the whole Practice, and of all you vend under *its Colours*,
pass into and concenter in that one nasty Utensil? – And let me
tell you, Sir, says he, raising his Voice, – had not your unseason-
able Mirth blinded you, you might have seen that *Trim*'s
carrying the Close-Stool-Pan upon his Head the whole Length
of the Town, without blushing, is a pointed Raillery, – and one
of the sharpest Sarcasms, Sir, that ever was thrown out upon
you; – for it unveils the solemn Impudence of the whole
Profession, who, I see, are ashamed of nothing which brings in
Money.

There were two Apothecaries in the Club, besides the Surgeon
mentioned before, with a Chemist and an Undertaker, who all
felt themselves equally hurt and aggrieved by this discourteous
Retort: – And they were all five rising up together from their
Chairs, with full Intent of Heart, as it was thought, to return the

Reproof Valiant* thereupon. – But the President, fearing it would end in a general Engagement, he instantly call'd out, *To Order*; – and gave Notice, That if there was any Member in the Club, who had not yet spoke, and yet did desire to speak upon the main Subject of the Debate, – that he should immediately be heard.

This was a happy Invitation for a stammering Member, who, it seems, had but a weak Voice at the best; and having often attempted to speak in the Debate, but to no Purpose, had sat down in utter Despair of an Opportunity.

This Member, you must know, had got a sad Crush upon his Hip, in the late *Election*, which gave him intolerable Anguish; – so that, in short, he could think of nothing else : – For which Cause, and others, he was strongly of Opinion, That the whole *Romance* was a just Gird at the late *York* Election ; and I think, says he, that the *Promise* of the *Breeches* broke, may well and truly signify *Somebody's else Promise*, which was broke, and occasion'd so much Disturbance amongst us.

– Thus every Man turn'd the Story to what was swimming uppermost in his own Brain; – so that, before all was over, there were full as many Satyres spun out of it, – and as great a Variety of Personages, Opinions, Transactions, and Truths, found to lay hid under the dark Veil of its Allegory, as ever were discovered in the thrice-renowned History of the Acts of *Gargantua* and *Pantagruel.**

At the Close of all, and just before the Club was going to break up, – Mr. President rose from his Chair, and begg'd Leave to make the two following Motions, which were instantly agreed to, without any Division.

First, Gentlemen, says he, as *Trim*'s Character in the *Romance*, of a shuffling intriguing Fellow, – whoever it was drawn for, is, in Truth, as like the *French King* as it can stare, – I move, That the *Romance* be forthwith *printed :* – For, continues he, if we can but once turn the Laugh against him, and make him asham'd of what he has done, it may be a great Means, with the Blessing of God upon our Fleets and Armies, to save the Liberties of *Europe*.

In the *second* Place, I move, That Mr. Attorney, our worthy Member, be desired to take Minutes, upon the Spot, of every Conjecture which has been made upon the the *Romance*, by the several Members who have spoke; which, I think, says he, will answer two good Ends:

1st, It will establish the Political Knowledge of our Club for ever, and place it in a respectable Light to all the World.

In the *next* Place, it will furnish what will be wanted; that is, a *Key* to the *Romance*. — In troth you might have said a whole Bunch of *Keys*, quoth a Whitesmith, who was the only Member in the Club who had not said something in the Debate: But let me tell you, Mr. President, says he, That the *Right Key*, if it could but be found, would be worth the whole Bunch put together.

To _____ _____, *Esq* ;*

of YORK

SIR,

You write me Word that the Letter I wrote to you, and now stiled *The Political Romance** is printing; and that, as it was drop'd by Carelessness, to make some Amends, you will over-look the Printing of it yourself, and take Care to see that it comes right into the World.

I was just going to return you Thanks, and to beg, withal, you would take Care That the Child be not laid at my Door. – But having, this Moment, perused the *Reply* to the *Dean* of *York*'s *Answer*, – it has made me alter my Mind in that respect; so that, instead of making you the Request I intended, I do here desire That the Child be filiated upon me, *Laurence Sterne*, Prebendary of *York*, &c. &c. And I do, accordingly, own it for my own true and lawful Offspring.

My Reason for this is plain; – for as, you see, the *Writer* of that *Reply*, has taken upon him to invade this *incontested Right* of another Man's in a Thing of this Kind, it is high Time for every Man to look to his own – Since, upon the *same Grounds*, and with half the Degree of Anger, that he affirms the Produc-tion of that very Reverend Gentleman's, to be the Child of many Fathers,* some one in his Spight (for I am not without my Friends of that Stamp) may run headlong into the other Extream, and swear, That mine had no Father at all : – And therefore, to make use of *Bays*'s Plea in the *Rehearsal*, for *Prince Pretty-Man*; I merely do it, as he says, "for fear it should be said to be no Body's Child at all."*

I have only to add two Things : – First, That, at your Peril, you do not presume to alter or transpose one Word, nor rectify one false Spelling, nor so much as add or diminish one Comma or Tittle, in or to my *Romance :* – For if you do, – In case any of the Descendents of *Curl** should think fit to invade my Copy-Right, and print it over again in my Teeth, I may not be able, in a Court of Justice, to swear strictly to my own Child, after you had *so large a Share* in the begetting it.

In the next Place, I do not approve of your *quaint Conceit** at the Foot of the Title Page of my *Romance*, – It would only set People on smiling a Page or two before I give them Leave; – and besides, all Attempts either at Wit or Humour, in that Place, are a Forestalling of what slender Entertainment of those Kinds are prepared within : Therefore I would have it stand thus :

Y O R K :
Printed in the Year 1759.
(Price One Shilling.)

I know you will tell me, That it is set too high ; and as a Proof, you will say, That this last *Reply* to the *Dean's Answer* does consist of near as many Pages as mine ; and yet is all sold for Six-pence. — But mine, my dear Friend, is quite a *different Story* : — It is a Web wrought out of my own Brain, of twice the Fineness of this which he has spun out of his ; and besides, I maintain it, it is of a more curious Pattern, and could not be afforded at the Price that his is sold at, by any *honest* Workman in *Great-Britain.*

   Moreover, Sir, you do not consider, That the Writer is interested in his *Story*, and that it is his Business to set it a-going at *any Price* : And indeed, from the Information of Persons conversant in Paper and Print, I have very good Reason to believe, if he should sell every Pamphlet of them, he would inevitably be a *Great Loser* by it. This I believe verily, and am,

> *Dear Sir,*
>
>   *Your obliged Friend*
>
>   *and humble Servant,*
>
>   LAURENCE STERNE

Sutton on the Forest,
Jan. 20, 1759.

To Dr. TOPHAM

SIR,

Though the *Reply* to the *Dean* of *York* is not declared, in the *Title-Page*, or elsewhere, to be wrote by you, – Yet I take that Point for granted; and therefore beg Leave, in this public Manner, to write to you in Behalf of myself; with Intent to set you right in two Points where I stand concerned in this Affair; and which I find you have misapprehended, and consequently (as I hope) misrepresented.

The *First* is, in respect of some Words, made use of in the Instrument, signed by Dr. *Herring*, Mr. *Berdmore** and myself. – Namely, *to the best of our Remembrance and Belief*, which Words you have caught hold of, as implying some Abatement of our Certainty as to the Facts therein attested. Whether it was so with the other two Gentlemen who signed that Attestation with me, it is not for me to say; they are able to answer for themselves, and I desire to do so for myself; and therefore I declare to you, and to all Mankind, "That the Words in the first Paragraph, *to the best of our Remembrance and Belief*, implied no Doubt remaining upon my Mind, nor any Distrust whatever of my Memory, from the Distance of Time; – Nor, in short, was it my Intention to attest the several Facts therein, as Matters of Belief – But as Matters of as much Certainty as a Man was capable of having, or giving Evidence to. In Consequence of this Explanation of myself, I do declare myself ready to attest the same Instrument over again, striking out the Words *to the best of our Remembrance and Belief*, which I see, have raised this Exception to it.

Whether I was mistaken or no, I leave to better Judges; but I understood those Words were a very common Preamble to Attestations of Things, to which we bore the clearest Evidence: – However, Dr. *Topham*, as you have claimed just such another Indulgence yourself, in the Case of begging the *Dean*'s Authority to say, what, as you affirm, you had sufficient Authority to say without, as a modest and Gentleman-like Way of Affirmation; – I wish you had spared either the one or the other of your Remarks upon these two Passages:

*– Veniam petimus, demusque vicissim.**

There is another Observation relating to this Instrument, which I perceive has escaped your Notice; which I take the Liberty to point out to you, namely, That the Words, *To the best of our Remembrance and Belief*, if they imply any Abatement of Certainty, seem only confined to that Paragraph, and to what is immediately attested after them in it: — For in the second Paragraph, wherein the main Points are minutely attested, and upon which the whole Dispute, and main Charge against the *Dean*, turns, it is introduced thus:

"*We do particularly remember*, That as soon as Dinner was over, *&c.*"

In the second Place you affirm, "That it is not said, That Mr. *Sterne* could affirm he had heard you charge the *Dean* with a Promise, in its own Nature so very extraordinary, as of the Commissaryship of the Dean and Chapter:" — To this I answer, That my true Intent in subscribing that very Instrument, and I suppose of others, was to attest this *very Thing*; and I have just now read that Part of the Instrument over; and cannot, for my Life, affirm it either more directly or expresly, than in the Words as they there stand; — therefore please to let me transcribe them.

— "But being press'd by Mr. *Sterne* with an undeniable Proof, That he, (Dr. *Topham*) did propagate the said Story, (viz. *of a Promise from the Dean to Dr.* Topham *of the Dean and Chapter's Commissaryship*) — Dr. *Topham* did at last acknowledge it; adding, as his Reason or Excuse for so doing, That he apprehended (or Words to that Effect) he had a *Promise* under the *Dean's own Hand*, of the *Dean and Chapter's Commissaryship*."

This I have attested, and what Weight the Sanction of an Oath will add to it, I am willing and ready to give.

As for Mr. *Ricard's** feeble Attestation, brought to shake the Credit of this firm and solemn one, I have nothing to say to it, as it is only an Attestation of Mr. *Ricard's* Conjectures upon the Subject. — But this I can say, That I had the Honour to be at the Deanery with the learned Counsel, when Mr. *Ricard* underwent that *most formidable* Examination you speak of; — and I solemnly affirm, That he then said, He knew nothing at all about the Matter, one Way or the other; and the Reasons he gave for his utter Ignorance, were, first, That he was then so full of Concern, at the Difference which arose between two Gentlemen, both his Friends, that he did not attend to the Subject Matter of it, — and of which he declared again he knew nothing at all. And secondly, If he had understood it then, the Distance would have put it out of his Head by this Time.

He has since scower'd his Memory, I ween; for now he says, That he apprehended the Dispute regarded something in the Dean's Gift, as he could not *naturally* suppose, *&c.* 'Tis certain, at the Deanery, he had *naturally* no Suppositions in his Head about this Affair; so that I wish this may not prove one of the After-Thoughts you speak of, and not so much a *natural* as an *artificial* Supposition of my good Friend's.

As for the *formidable* Enquiry you represent him as under-going, – let me intreat you to give me Credit in what I say upon it, — namely, — That it was as much the Reverse to every Idea that ever was couch'd under that Word, as Words can represent it to you. As for the learned Counsel and myself, who were in the Room all the Time, I do not remember that we, either of us, spoke ten Words. The Dean was the only one that ask'd Mr. *Ricard* what he remembered about the Affair of the Sessions Dinner; which he did in the most Gentleman-like and candid Manner, – and with an Air of as much Calmness and seeming Indifference, as if he had been questioning him about the News in the last *Brussels Gazette.*

What Mr. *Ricard* saw to terrify him so sadly, I cannot apprehend, unless the Dean's *Gothic* Book-Case, – which I own has an odd Appearance to a Stranger; so that if he came terrified in his Mind there, and with a Resolution not to *plead*, he might *naturally suppose* it to be a great Engine brought there on purpose to exercise the *Peine fort et dure** upon him. — But to be serious; if Mr. *Ricard* told you, That this Enquiry was *most formidable, He* was much to blame; – and if you have said it, without his express Information, then *You* are much to blame.

This is all, I think, in your *Reply*, which concerns me to answer: – As for the many coarse and unchristian Insinuations scatter'd throughout your *Reply*, – as it is my Duty to beg God to forgive you, so I do from my Heart: Believe me, Dr. *Topham*, they hurt yourself more than the Person they are aimed at; and when the *first Transport* of Rage is a little over, they will grieve you more too.

*—prima est hæc Ultio.**

But these I hold to be no answerable Part of a Controversy; — and for the little that remains unanswered in yours, — I believe I could, in another half Hour, set it right in the Eyes of the World: — But this is not my Business. — And if it is thought worth the while, which I hope it never will, I know no one more able to do it than the very Reverend and Worthy Gentleman whom you have so unhandsomely insulted upon that Score.

As for the *supposed Compilers*, whom you have been so wrath and so unmerciful against, I'll be answerable for it, as they are Creatures of your own Fancy, they will bear you no Malice. However, I think the more positively any Charge is made, let it be against whom it will, the better it should be supported; and therefore I should be sorry, for your own Honour, if you have not some better Grounds for all you have thrown out about them, than the mere Heat of your Imagination or Anger. To tell you truly, your Suppositions on this Head oft put me in Mind of *Trim*'s twelve Men in *Buckram*, which his disordered Fancy represented as laying in Ambush in *John* the Clerk's House, and letting drive at him all together. I am,

SIR,

Your most obedient

And most humble Servant,

LAWRENCE STERNE.

Sutton on the Forest,
Jan. 20, 1759.

P.S. I beg Pardon for *clapping* this upon the *Back* of the *Romance*, — which is done out of no Disrespect to you. — But the *Vehicle* stood ready at the Door, — and as I was to pay the whole Fare, and there was Room enough behind it, — it was the cheapest and readiest Conveyance I could think of.

FINIS.

LETTERS

OF THE LATE

Rev. Mr. LAURENCE STERNE,

To his most intimate FRIENDS.

WITH A

FRAGMENT in the Manner of *Rabelais*.

To which are prefix'd,

Memoirs of his Life and Family.

Written by HIMSELF.

And Published by his Daughter, Mrs. MEDALLE.

In THREE VOLUMES.

VOL. I.

LONDON:

Printed for T. BECKET, the Corner of the Adelphi, in the Strand, 1775.

MEMOIRS OF THE LIFE AND FAMILY
OF THE LATE
REV. MR. LAURENCE STERNE

Roger Sterne, (grandson to Archbishop Sterne) Lieutenant in Handaside's regiment,* was married to Agnes Hebert,* widow of a captain of a good family: her family name was (I believe) Nuttle – though, upon recollection, that was the name of her father-in-law, who was a noted sutler in Flanders, in Queen Ann's wars, where my father married his wife's daughter (N.B. he was in debt to him) which was in September 25, 1711, Old Stile.* – This Nuttle had a son by my grandmother – a fine person of a man but a graceless whelp – what became of him I know not. – The family (if any left), live now at Clomwel* in the south of Ireland, at which town I was born November 24th, 1713, a few days after my mother arrived from Dunkirk. – My birth-day was ominous to my poor father, who was, the day after our arrival, with many other brave officers broke, and sent adrift into the wide world with a wife and two children – the elder of which was Mary; she was born in Lisle in French Flanders, July the tenth, one thousand seven hundred and twelve, New Stile. – This child was most unfortunate – she married one Weemans in Dublin – who used her most unmercifully – spent his substance, became a bankrupt, and left my poor sister to shift for herself, – which she was able to do but for a few months, for she went to a friend's house in the country, and died of a broken heart. She was a most beautiful woman – of a fine figure, and deserved a better fate. – The regiment, in which my father served, being broke, he left Ireland as soon as I was able to be carried, with the rest of the family, and came to the family seat at Elvington, near York, where his mother lived. She was daughter to Sir Roger Jaques, and an heiress. There we sojourned for about ten months, when the regiment was established, and our household decamped with bag and baggage for Dublin – within a month of our arrival, my father left us, being ordered to Exeter, where, in a sad winter, my mother and her two children followed him, travelling from Liverpool by land to Plymouth. (Melancholy description of this journey not necessary to be transmitted here). In twelve months we were all sent back to Dublin. – My mother, with three of us, (for she laid in at Plymouth of a boy, Joram), took ship at Bristol, for Ireland, and had a narrow escape from being cast away by a leak springing up in the vessel. – At length, after many perils, and struggles, we got to Dublin. – There my father took a large house, furnished it, and in a year and a half's time spent a great deal of money. – In the year one thousand seven hundred and nineteen, all unhing'd again ; the regiment was ordered, with many others, to the Isle of Wight, in order to embark for Spain in the Vigo expedition.* We accompanied the regiment, and was driven into Milford Haven, but landed at Bristol, from thence by land to Plymouth again, and to the Isle of Wight – where I remember we stayed encamped some time before the embarkation of the troops – (in this expedition from Bristol to Hampshire we lost poor Joram – a pretty boy, four years old, of the small-pox), my mother, sister, and myself, remained at the Isle of Wight during the Vigo Expedition, and until the regiment had got back to Wicklow in Ireland, from whence my father sent for us. – We had poor Joram's loss supplied during our stay in the Isle of Wight, by the birth of a girl, Anne, born September the twenty-third, one thousand seven hundred and nineteen. – This pretty blossom fell at the age of three years, in the Barracks of Dublin – she was, as I well remember, of a fine delicate frame, not made to last long, as were most of my father's babes. – We embarked for Dublin, and had all been cast away by a most violent storm ; but through the intercessions of my mother, the captain was prevailed upon to turn back into Wales, where we stayed a month, and at length got into Dublin, and travelled by land to Wicklow, where my father had for some Weeks given us over for lost. – We lived in the barracks at Wicklow, one year, (one thousand seven hundred and twenty) when Devijeher (so called after Colonel Devijeher,) was born ; from thence we decamped to stay half a year with Mr. Fetherston, a clergyman, about seven miles from Wicklow, who being a relation of my mother's, invited us to his parsonage at Animo. – It was in this parish, during our stay, that I had that wonderful escape in falling through a mill-race whilst the mill was going, and of being taken up unhurt – the story is incredible, but known for truth in all that part of Ireland – where hundreds of the common people flocked to see me. – From hence we followed the regiment to Dublin, where we lay in the barracks a year. – In this year, one

thousand seven hundred and twenty-one, I learned to write, &c.
– The regiment, ordered in twenty-two, to Carrickfergus in the
north of Ireland; we all decamped, but got no further than
Drogheda, thence ordered to Mullengar, forty miles west, where
by Providence we stumbled upon a kind relation, a collateral
descendant from Archbishop Sterne, who took us all to his
castle and kindly entreated us for a year – and sent us to the
regiment at Carrickfergus, loaded with kindnesses, &c. – a most
rueful and tedious journey had we all, in March, to Carrickfergus, where we arrived in six or seven days – little Devijeher here
died, he was three years old – He had been left behind at nurse
at a farmhouse near Wicklow, but was fetch'd to us by my
father the summer after – another child sent to fill his place,
Susan; this babe too left us behind in this weary journey – The
autumn of that year, or the spring afterwards, (I forget which)
my father got leave of his colonel to fix me at school – which he
did near Halifax, with an able master; with whom I staid some
time, 'till by God's care of me my cousin Sterne, of Elvington,
became a father to me, and sent me to the university, &c., &c.
To pursue the thread of our story, my father's regiment was the
year after ordered to Londonderry, where another sister was
brought forth, Catherine, still living, but most unhappily
estranged from me by my uncle's wickedness, and her own folly
– from this station the regiment was sent to defend Gibraltar, at
the seige,* where my father was run through the body by
Captain Phillips, in a duel, (the quarrel begun about a goose)
with much difficulty he survived – tho' with an impaired
constitution, which was not able to withstand the hardships it
was put to – for he was sent to Jamaica, where he soon fell by
the country fever, which took away his senses first, and made a
child of him, and then, in a month or two, walking about
continually without complaining, till the moment he sat down
in an arm chair, and breathed his last – which was at Port
Antonio, on the north of the island. – My father was a little
smart man – active to the last degree, in all exercises – most
patient of fatigue and disappointments, of which it pleased God
to give him full measure – he was in his temper somewhat rapid,
and hasty – but of a kindly, sweet disposition, void of all design;
and so innocent in his own intentions, that he suspected no one;
so that you might have cheated him ten times in a day, if nine
had not been sufficient for your purpose – my poor father died

in March 1731* – I remained at Halifax 'till about the latter
end of that year, and cannot omit mentioning this anecdote of
myself, and school-master – He had had the cieling of the
school-room new white-washed – the ladder remained there – I
one unlucky day mounted it, and wrote with a brush in large
capital letters, LAU. STERNE, for which the usher severely
whipped me. My master was very much hurt at this, and said,
before me, that never should that name be effaced, for I was a
boy of genius, and he was sure I should come to preferment –
this expression made me forget the stripes I had received – In
the year thirty-two my cousin sent me to the university, where I
staid some time. 'Twas there that I commenced a friendship
with Mr H. . .,* which has been most lasting on both sides – I
then came to York, and my uncle got me the living of Sutton –
and at York I became acquainted with your mother, and courted
her for two years – she owned she liked me, but thought herself
not rich enough, or me too poor, to be joined together – she
went to her sister's in S——,* and I wrote to her often – I believe
then she was partly determined to have me, but would not say
so – at her return she fell into a consumption – and one evening
that I was sitting by her with an almost broken heart to see her
so ill, she said, "my dear Lawrey, I can never be yours, for I
verily believe I have not long to live – but I have left you every
shilling of my fortune;" – upon that she shewed me her will –
this generosity overpowered me. – It pleased God that she
recovered, and I married her in the year 1741. My uncle and
myself were then upon very good terms, for he soon got me the
Prebendary of York – but he quarrelled with me afterwards,
because I would not write paragraphs in the newspapers –
though he was a party-man, I was not, and detested such dirty
work : thinking it beneath me – from that period, he became my
bitterest enemy. – By my wife's means I got the living of
Stillington – a friend of her's in the south had promised her,
that if she married a clergyman in Yorkshire, when the living
became vacant, he would make her a compliment of it. I
remained near twenty years at Sutton, doing duty at both places
– I had then very good health. – Books, painting, fiddling, and
shooting were my amusements ; as to the 'Squire of the parish, I
cannot say we were upon a very friendly footing – but at
Stillington, the family of the C——s* shewed us every kindness
– 'twas most truly agreeable to be within a mile and a half of an

amiable family, who were ever cordial friends – In the year 1760, I took a house at York for your mother and yourself, and went up to London to publish my two first volumes of Shandy. In that year Lord F——*presented me with the curacy of Coxwold – a sweet retirement in comparison of Sutton. In sixty-two I went to France before the peace* was concluded, and you both followed me. – I left you both in France, and in two years after I went to Italy for the recovery of my health – and when I called upon you, I tried to engage your mother to return to England, with me – she and yourself are at length come – and I have had the inexpressible joy of seeing my girl every thing I wished her.

I have set down these particulars relating to my family, and self, for my Lydia, in case hereafter she might have a curiosity, or a kinder motive to know them.

TO MR. B.*

Exeter, July, 1775.

SIR,

This was quite an *Impromptu* of Yorick's after he had been thoroughly *soused*. – He drew it up in a few moments without stopping his pen. I should be glad to see it in your intended collection of Mr. Sterne's memoirs, &c. If you should have a copy of it, you will be able to rectify a misapplication of a term that Mr. Sterne could never be guilty of, as one great excellence of his writing lies in the most happy choice of metaphors and allusions – such as shewed his philosophic judgement, at the same time that they displayed his wit and genius – but it is not for me to comment on, or correct so great an original. I should have sent this fragment as soon as I saw Mrs. Medalle's advertisement,* had I not been at a distance from my papers. I expect much entertainment from this posthumous work of a man to whom no one is more indebted for amusement and instruction, than,

Sir,

Your humble servant,

S. P.

AN IMPROMPTU

No – not one farthing would I give for such a coat in wet weather, or dry – If the sun shines you are sure of being melted, because it closes so tight about one – if it rains it is no more a defence than a cobweb – a very sieve, o' my conscience! that lets through every drop, and like many other things that are put on only for a cover, mortifies you with disappointment and makes you curse the impostor, when it is too late to avail one's self of the discovery. Had I been wise I should have examined the claim the coat had to the title of "defender of the body"* – before I had trusted my body in it – I should have held it up to the light like other suspicious matters to have seen how much it was likely to admit of that which I wanted to keep out – whether it was no more than such a frail, flimsy contexture of flesh and blood, as I am fated to carry about with me through every tract of this dirty world, and could have comfortably and safely dispensed with in so short a journey – taking into my account the chance of spreading trees – thick hedges o'erhanging the road – with twenty other coverts that a man may thrust his head under – if he is not violently pushed on by that d – d stimulus – you know where – that will not let a man sit still in one place for half a minute together – but like a young nettlesome tit is eternally on the fret, and is for pushing on still farther – or if the poor scared devil is not hunted tantivy by a hue and cry with gives and a halter dangling before his eyes – now in either case he has not a minute to throw away in standing still, but like king Lear* must brave "the peltings of a pitiless storm" and give heaven leave to "rumble its belly full – spit fire – or spout rain"　as spitefully as it pleaseth, without finding the inclination or the resolution to slacken his pace lest something should be lost that might have been gained, or more gotten than he well knows how to get rid of – Now had I acted with as much prudence as some other good folks – I could name many of them who have been made b – ps within my remembrance for having been hooded and muffled up in a larger quantity of this dark drab of mental manufacture than ever fell to my share – and absolutely for nothing else – as will be seen when they are undressed another day – Had I had but as much as might have been taken out of their cloth without lessening much of the size, or injuring in the least the shape, or contracting aught of the doublings and foldings, or confining to a less circumference, the superb sweep of any one cloak that any one b – p ever wrapt himself up in – I should never have given this coat a place upon my shoulders. I should have seen by the light at one glance, how little it would keep out of rain, by how little it would keep in of darkness – This a coat for a rainy day ? do pray madam hold it up to that window – did you ever see such an *illustrious* coat since the day you could distinguish between a coat and a pair of breeches ? – My lady did not understand derivatives, and so she could not see quite through my splendid pun.* Pope Sixtus would have blinded her with the same "darkness of excessive light."* What a flood of it breaks in thro' this rent ? what an

irradiation beams through that? what twinklings – what spark-
lings as you wave it before your eyes in the broad face of the
sun? Make a fan out of it for the ladies to look at their gallants
with at church – It has not served me for one purpose – it will
serve them for two – This is coarse stuff – of worse manufacture
than the cloth – put it to its proper use, for I love when things
sort and join well – make a philtre[1] of it – while there is a drop
to be extracted – I know but one thing in the world that will
draw, drain, or suck like it – and that is – neither wool nor flax
– make – make any thing of it, but a vile, hypocritical coat for
me – for I never can say *sub Jove* (whatever Juno might) that "it
is a pleasure to *be wet*."*

L. STERNE

[1] This allusion is improper. A philtre originally signifies a love potion – and it is used
as a noun from the verb *philtrate* – it must signify a *strainer*, not a *sucker* – cloth is
sometimes used for the purpose of *draining* by means of its pores or capillary tubes, but its
action is contrary to philtration. His meaning is obvious enough; but as he drew up this
fragment without stopping his pen, as I was informed, it is no wonder he erred in the
application of some of his terms.

THE FRAGMENT
CHAP. I

Shewing two Things; first, what a Rabelaic Fellow LONGINUS
RABELAICUS *is, and secondly, how cavalierly he begins his Book.*

My dear and thrice reverend brethren, as well archbishops and
bishops, as the *rest* of the inferior clergy! would it not be a
glorious thing, if any man of genius and capacity amongst us for
such a work, was fully bent within himself, to sit down
immediately and compose a thorough-stitch'd system of the
KERUKOPAEDIA,* fairly* setting forth, to the best of his wit and
memory, and collecting for that purpose all that is needful to be
known, and understood of that art? — Of what art cried PAN-
URGE? Good God! answered LONGINUS (making an exclamation, but taking care at the same time to moderate his voice)*
why, of the art of making all kinds of your theological,
hebdodomical, rostrummical, humdrummical what d'ye call
'ems — I will be shot, quoth EPISTEMON, if all this story of thine
of a roasted horse,* is simply no more than S—— Sausages?
quoth PANURGE. Thou hast fallen twelve feet and about five
inches below the mark, answer'd EPISTEMON, for I hold them to
be *Sermons* — which said word, (as I take the matter) being but
a word of low degree, for a book of high rhetoric — LONGINUS
RABELAICUS was foreminded to usher and lead into his disser-
tation, with as much pomp and parade as he could afford; and
for my own part, either I know no more of Latin than my
horse,* or the KERUKOPAEDIA is nothing but the art of making
'em — And why not, quoth GYMNAST, of preaching them when
we have done? — Believe me, dear souls, this is half in half — and
if some skilful body would but put us in a way to do this to
some *tune* — Thou wouldst not have them *chanted* surely, quoth
TRIBOULET, laughing? — No, nor *canted* neither, quoth GYM-
NAST, crying! — but what I mean, my friends,* says LONGINUS
RABELAICUS (who is certainly one of the greatest criticks in the
western world, and as Rabelaic a fellow as ever existed)* what I
mean, says he, interrupting them both and resuming his discourse, is this, that if all the scatter'd rules of the KERUKOPAEDIA
could be but once carefully collected into one code, as thick as

PANURGE'S head, and the whole *cleanly* digested – (pooh, says PANURGE,* who felt himself aggrieved) and bound up continued LONGINUS, by way of a regular institute, and then put into the hands of every licensed preacher in Great Britain, and Ireland, just before he began to compose, I maintain it – I deny it flatly, quoth PANURGE – What? answer'd LONGINUS RABELAICUS with all the temper in the world.

CHAP. II.

In which the Reader will begin to form a Judgement, of what an Historical, Dramatical, Anecdotical, Allegorical, and Comical Kind of a Work he has got hold of.

HOMENAS who had to preach next Sunday* (before God knows whom) knowing nothing at all of the matter – was all this while at it as hard as he could drive in the very next room : – for having fouled two clean sheets of his own, and being quite stuck fast in the entrance upon his third general *division*, and finding himself unable to get either forwards or backwards with any grace – "Curse it,"* says he, (thereby excommunicating every mother's son who should think differently) "why may not a man lawfully call in for help in this, as well as any other human emergency?" – So without any more argumentation, except starting up and nimming down from the top shelf but one, the second volume of CLARK* – tho' without any felonious intention in so doing, he had begun to clap me in (making a joint first) five whole pages, nine round paragraphs, and a dozen and a half of good thoughts all of a row; and because there was a confounded high gallery – was transcribing it away like a little devil. – Now – quoth HOMENAS to himself "tho' I hold all this to be fair and square, yet, if I am found out, there will be the deuce and all to pay." – *Why are the bells ringing backwards, you lad? what is all that crowd about, honest man?* HOMENAS *was got upon Doctor* CLARK'S *back, sir – and what of that, my lad? Why an please you, he has broke his neck, and fractured his skull, and befouled* himself into the bargain, by a fall from the pulpit two stories high.* Alas! poor HOMENAS! HOMENAS has done his business! – HOMENAS will never preach more while breath is in his body. – No, faith, I shall never again be able to tickle it off as I have done. I may sit up whole winter nights baking my blood with hectic watchings, and write as solid as a FATHER of the church — or, I may sit down whole summer days evaporating my spirits into the finest thoughts, and write as florid as a MOTHER of it. — In a word, I may compose myself off my legs, and preach till I burst — and when I have done, it will be worse than if not done at all. — *Pray Mr. Such-a-one, who held forth last Sunday? Doctor* CLARK, *I trow; says one. Pray what Doctor* CLARK *says a second? Why* HOMENAS'S *Doctor* CLARK, *quoth a third.* O rare HOMENAS! cries a fourth; your *servant* Mr. HOMENAS, quoth a *fifth.* — 'Twill be all over with me, by Heav'n — I may as well put the book from whence I took it.* — Here HOMENAS burst into a flood of tears, which falling down helter skelter, ding dong without any kind of intermission for six minutes and almost twenty five seconds, had a marvellous effect upon his discourse; for the aforesaid tears, do you mind, did so temper the wind* that was rising upon the aforesaid discourse, but falling for the most part perpendicularly, and hitting the spirits at right angles, which were mounting horizontally all over the surface of his harangue, they not only play'd the devil and all with the sublimity — but moreoever the said tears, by their nitrous quality, did so refrigerate, precipitate, and hurry down to the bottom of his soul, all the unsavory particles which lay fermenting (as you saw) in the middle of his conception, that he went on in the coolest and chastest stile (for a *soliloquy* I think) that ever mortal man uttered.

"This is really and truly a very hard case, continued HOMENAS to himself" — PANURGE, by the bye, and all the company in the next room hearing all along every syllable he spoke; for you must know, that notwithstanding PANURGE had open'd his mouth as wide as he could for his blood, in order to give a round answer to LONGINUS RABELAICUS's interrogation, which concluded the last chapter — yet HOMENAS's rhetoric had pour'd in so like a torrent, slap-dash thro' the wainscot amongst them, and happening at that *uncritical* crisis, when PANURGE had just put his ugly face into the above-said posture of defence — that he stopt short — he did indeed, and tho' his head was full of matter, and he had screw'd up every nerve and muscle belonging to it, till all cryed *crack* again, in order to give a due projectile force to what he was going to let fly, full in LONGINUS RABELAICUS's teeth who sat over against him. — Yet for all that, he had the continence to contain himself, for he stopt short, I say, without uttering one word except, Z .... ds* — many reasons may be assign'd for this, but the most true, the most strong, the most hydrostatical, and the most philosophical reason, why PANURGE did not go on, was — that the fore-mention'd *torrent* did so *drown* his voice, that he had none left to go on with. — God help him, poor fellow! so he stopt short, (as I have told you before) and all the time HOMENAS was speaking he said not another word, good or bad, but stood gaping, and staring, like what you please — so that the break, mark'd thus — which HOMENAS's grief had made in the middle of his discourse, which he could no more help than he could fly — produced no other change in the room where LONGINUS RABELAICUS, EPISTEMON, GYMNAST, TRIBOULET, and nine or ten more honest blades had got Kerukopædizing together, but that it gave time to GYMNAST to give PANURGE a good squashing chuck under his double chin; which PANURGE taking in good part, and just as it was meant by GYMNAST, he forthwith shut his mouth — and gently sitting down upon a stool* though somewhat excentrically and out of neighbours row, but listening, as all the rest did, with might and main, they plainly and distinctly heard every syllable of what you will find recorded in the very next chapter.

NOTES

p. 2 The promise of further volumes was no doubt sincere, though it is appropriately Shandean that *A Sentimental Journey through France and Italy* should end with its protagonist yet to reach the second country. Sterne's death in March 1768 left no chance to complete the work.

p. 3 Ian Jack has noted that *Yorick's Sentimental Journey Continued by Eugenius* (1769), a spurious sequel, identifies 'this matter' as 'the inconvenience of drinking healths whilst at meal, and toasts afterwards' (*TLS*, 4 February 1977, 131).

p. 3 The footnote recalls Smollett's complaint: 'If a foreigner dies in France, the king seizes all his effects, even though his heir should be upon the spot; and this tyranny is called the *droit d'aubaine* (*Travels through France and Italy* (1766), letter ii). On 'farming', see below, note to p. 93.

p. 3 In reference to Mrs Elizabeth Draper (1744–78), with whom Sterne pursued a sentimental liaison in 1767. See his *Journal to Eliza*, 'wrote under the fictitious Names of Yorick & Draper – and sometimes of the Bramin & Bramine – but tis a Diary of the miserable feelings of a person separated from a Lady for whose Society he languish'd – ' (*Letters of Laurence Sterne*, ed. L. P. Curtis (Oxford, 1935), p. 322). Later in the *Journal* Sterne refers to 'a portrait, (which by the by, I have immortalized in my Sentimental Journey)', adding that 'Some Annotator . . . in this place will take occasion, to speak of the Friendship wch Subsisted so long & faithfully betwixt Yorick & the Lady he speaks of' (*Letters*, pp. 357, 358).

p. 4 Molière's *Les Précieuses ridicules* (1659), a satire on fashionable learning and affectation, had recently been translated in Samuel Foote's *Comic Theatre* (1762) as *The Conceited Ladies*. Yorick imagines a more modern *précieuse*, caught up perhaps in the materialistic philosophy of La Mettrie's *L'Homme machine* (1748).

p. 5 Guido Reni (1575–1642), Bolognese baroque painter (mentioned in *Tristram Shandy*, III, xii). Noting that Guido's St Michael had 'all the air of a French dancing-master', Smollett complained that 'his expression is often erroneous, and his attitudes are always affected and unnatural' (*Travels*, letter xxxi).

p. 5 Member of the Hindu priestly caste, proverbially wise and austere, as in Pope's *Epistle to Bathurst* (1733), lines 185–6: 'If Cotta liv'd on pulse, it was no more / Than Bramins, Saints and Sages did before.' Also a pseudonym, in the *Journal to Eliza*, for Sterne himself.

p. 6 Contrasting the mendicant Franciscans with the Order of Our Lady of Mercy, founded in 1218 to raise ransoms for Christians held by the Moors. See *Tristram Shandy*, V, i.

p. 7 The entrepreneurial Pierre Quillacq, *dit* Dessin, lessee (and, in 1764, probable arsonist) of the Lyon d'Argent in Calais. Proprietor from 1765 of the popular Hôtel d'Angleterre, where he is reported to have claimed, in 1782, that Sterne 'gain moche money by his Journey of Sentiment – mais moi – I – make more through de means of dat, than he, by all his ouvrages reunies – Ha ha!' (A. H. Cash, *Laurence Sterne: The Later Years* (1986), p. 229).

p. 8 The phrase links Yorick's rambles, jestingly, with the Aristotelian or peripatetic school, so named after its founder's practice of teaching while perambulating.

p. 9 Literally, clerical exemption from the jurisdiction of the ordinary courts of the law; Yorick turns the phrase to the practice of sending young aristocrats on the Grand Tour under clerical supervision.

p. 10 Alluding to the drunkenness of Noah, Genesis 9: 20–23.

p. 11 Cervantes, *Don Quixote* (1605–15), Part II, v, where Sancho in fact addresses his wife.

p. 11 Recalling the animadversions of Joseph Hall in *Quo Vadis? A Just Censure of Travel* (1617), on which the preceding paragraph is partly based.

p. 12 Mt Cenis, on the Franco-Italian border, to cross which coaches were sometimes dismantled and carried on mules.

p. 13 cf. Genesis 16: 12.

p. 13 'True delicate double entendre is not where yᵉ Word bears two meanings but where a modest Expression leaves incidentally a Lewd Idea upon yᵉ Mind', wrote John Scott (1739–98), Earl of Clonmell, in his copy at this point (P. Franssen, 'Great Lessons of Political Instruction', *Shandean*, 2 (1990), 166).

p. 14 Compare the workings of Fancy in *Tristram Shandy*, VI, xxxviii and VIII, v. The bed of the Tiber was a fruitful archaeological resource, having been 'considerably raised by the rubbish of old Rome' (Smollett, *Travels*, letter xxix).

p. 15 cf. 2 Esdras 10 : 31 (Apocrypha).

p. 16 Unlike the good Samaritan of Luke 10 : 34.

p. 16 Compare the sensual fingerings of *Tristram Shandy*, VIII, xvi.

p. 19 After the sanctimonious hypocrite of Molière's *Le Tartuffe, ou L'Imposteur* (1664–7). See *Tristram Shandy*, V, i and VIII, ii ; *Letters*, p. 411.

p. 20 Brussels suffered its severest bombardment by the French in 1695 ; they besieged the city again during the War of the Austrian Succession (1740–8), taking it from the Imperialist allies in February 1746.

p. 23 Distant points, as in Judges 20 : 1, in which the far-flung tribes of Israel are gathered 'from Dan even to Beersheba' ; see also *Tristram Shandy*, VIII, xvi.

p. 24 Tobias Smollett (1721–71), in whose unsentimental *Travels through France and Italy* (1766) the landscape around Rome is 'almost a desert' and 'nothing but a naked withered down' (letter xxix).

p. 24 Smollett was disappointed at the Pantheon, which 'looks like a huge cockpit, open at top' (letter xxxi). He criticizes the features and attitude of the Venus de' Medici, but quotes with unusual relish a classical encomium on the statue's 'back parts': 'Heavens! what a beautifull back! the loins, with what exuberance they fill the grasp! how finely arc the swelling buttocks rounded . . . !' (letter xxviii).

p. 24 cf. *Othello*, I.iii.134–44.

p. 24 Punning on Smollett's description of 'Bartholomew flaed alive, and a hundred other pictures equally frightful' and on his complaints at flea-ridden inns in which he 'was half devoured by vermin' (letter xxxiv). See also Slawkenbergius's tale, where 'the several sisterhoods had scratch'd and mawl'd themselves all to death – they got out of their beds almost flead alive' (*Tristram Shandy*, IV).

p. 24 Mundungus's fortune and itinerary make implausible the traditional identification with Dr Samuel Sharp, author of *Letters from Italy* (1766). Stout notes that in 1766 Sterne was invited to accompany the wealthy tourist Henry Errington from Naples to England 'by Venice, Vienna, Saxony, Berlin' (*Letters*, 269), but Mundungus may simply represent a general type of wealthy *arrivisme*. The play on 'dunghill' in his name identifies his fortune as brash new money, as when the seat of the *parvenu* Harlowes in Richardson's *Clarissa*

(1747–8) is 'sprung up from a dunghil, within every elderly person's remembrance' (3rd edn, I, letter xxxiv).

p. 25 cf. *Tristram Shandy*, VII, ix.

p. 25 John Home (1722–1808), poet and tragedian, and the historian and philosopher David Hume (1711–76), sometimes called 'the two Humes' (as in Smollett's *Humphry Clinker* (1771), letter of 8 August). Sterne saw Home's *Siege of Aquileia* performed in London in 1760; on meeting Hume in Paris in 1764, he praised 'this amiable turn of his character, that has given more consequence and force to his scepticism, than all the arguments of his sophistry' (*Letters*, p. 218).

p. 27 cf. 2 Corinthians 11 : 23–7.

p. 28 Adapted from Robert Burton, *The Anatomy of Melancholy* (1621–51), Part. 3, Sect. 2, Memb. 2, Subs. 4.

p. 32 A pair of ones, i.e. the lowest score at dice.

p. 32 A third term would be *Bougre!*, perhaps, or *Foutre!*, as in *Tristram Shandy*, VII, xxv.

p. 33 *Don Quixote*, Part I, xxiii; see also Part II, lv; also *Tristram Shandy*, VII, xxxii and VII, xxxvi.

p. 33 Santiago de Compostella, shrine of St James.

p. 33 cf. 2 Samuel 12 : 3; see also second note to p. 98 below.

p. 34 cf. Proverbs 25 : 25.

p. 36 cf. Isaiah 25 : 8; *Letters*, p. 386.

p. 38 Yorick's epistolary block recalls (perhaps in parody) the famous disintegration of the heroine's letters in Richardson's *Clarissa*. Where Yorick 'had nothing to say . . . I made half a dozen different beginnings, and could no way please myself', Clarissa 'sat down to say a great deal . . . I did not know what to say first . . . so I can write nothing at all.' And where Yorick 'wrote, and blotted, and tore off, and burnt, and wrote again', Clarissa's captor describes how 'what she writes she tears, and throws the paper in fragments under the table, either as not knowing what she does, or disliking it : Then gets up, wrings her hands, weeps . . . returns to her table, sits down, and writes again' (3rd edn, V, letter xxxvi).

p. 39 See *Letters*, p. 256.

p. 40 A chivalric exercise in which a horseman lances a suspended ring. The innuendo (reinforced here by the broken lances, lost vizards and Boswellian armour that follow) is more pointed in Rabelais, *Gargantua* and *Pantagruel* (tr. 1653–94), II, i, and also in *Tristram*

Shandy: 'They are running at the ring of pleasure, said I, giving him a prick' (VII, xliii).

p. 40 *Hamlet*, V.i.178 ; *Tristram Shandy*, I, xii.

p. 43 In reference to Sterne's libertine friend John Hall-Stevenson (1718–85). Apostrophes to Eugenius are more frequent in *Tristram Shandy*, where it is he who has inscribed on Yorick's grave the text 'Alas, poor YORICK !' (I, xii).

p. 44 Law excluding women from succession to the French throne.

p. 45 cf. *Genesis* 2 : 18.

p. 46 Uncle Toby, the amiable *mutilé de guerre* of *Tristram Shandy*.

p. 47 Giambattista Martini (1706–84), Franciscan friar and a noted composer.

p. 47 *Cicisbeo*, 'the recognised gallant or *cavalier servente* of a married woman' (*OED*) – a connection Yorick attempts with commendable persistence in the following lines.

p. 48 Patron saint of music.

p. 48 The medical, splenetic and inquisitive traveller Smollett, whose views on the causes of deformity (*Travels*, letter xxx) are satirized later in the chapter.

p. 49 Tristram's father Walter, whose frustrated perfectionism in the art of begetting is a concern of *Tristram Shandy*. A strained conversation with his wife concerns their son's inexplicable height · 'I am very short myself, – continued my father, gravely' (VI, xviii).

p. 49 An incident seemingly based on Scarron's *Roman comique* (1651), II, xvii.

p. 52 Mischievously recalling Catherine de Vivonne (1588–1665), Marquise de Rambouillet, a leading *précieuse*.

p. 52 Euphemistic, as in Swift's 'Strephon and Chloe' : 'None ever saw her pluck a Rose. / Her dearest Comrades never caught her / Squat on her Hams, to make Maid's Water' (lines 16–18).

p. 52 Nymph who escapes Apollo's addresses by plunging into a spring on Mt Parnassus. The spring was held sacred, and was entered by many pilgrims.

p. 55 *Hamlet*, I.iii.55–81.

p. 55 Claude de Thiard (1721–1810), comte de Bissy, soldier, academician and anglophile, who seems to have speeded Sterne's own application for a passport in Paris in January 1762.

p. 55 *Les Egarements du Coeur et de l'Esprit* (1736), novel by Claude-Prosper-Jolyot de Crébillon (1707–77), *dit* Crébillon *fils*. Translated as *The Wanderings of the Heart and Mind* (1751), it was widely seen as licentious. Having met Crébillon in 1762, Sterne told Garrick: 'he has agreed to write me an expostulatory letter upon the indecorums of T. Shandy – which is to be answered by recrimination upon the liberties in his own works – these are to be printed together – Crebillion against Sterne – Sterne against Crebillion – the copy to be sold, and the money equally divided' (*Letters*, p. 162).

p. 58 The Seven Years War, formally ended by the Treaty of Paris in February 1763. For Sterne's own difficulties in France in January 1762, see Cash, *Later Years*, pp. 116–23.

p. 58 Past tense of *to set*, 'frequent in inferior writers of the second half of the eighteenth century' (*OED*).

p. 61 cf. *The Sermons of Mr Yorick* (1760), II, 98–9 ('Job's Account of . . . Life, Considered'). In 1766 Sterne received a letter from Ignatius Sancho, an African freedman, who quoted with approval the sermon in question ('Consider Slavery – what it is, – how bitter a draught! and how many millions have been made to drink of it – ') and urged him to resume the subject (*Letters*, pp. 282–3). Sterne replied that he would 'not forget yr Letter' (p. 287), and he seems to remember it here.

p. 62 Compare Sancho's confidence that 'in me, you behold the uplifted hands of Millions of my moorish brethren – Grief (you pathetically observe) is eloquent – figure to yourself their attitudes – hear their supplicatory address – humanity must comply' (*Letters*, p. 283). See also *Sermons*, II, 98–9 and II, 102 ('Millions of our fellow creatures, born to no inheritance but poverty and trouble').

p. 62 cf. Proverbs 13 : 12.

p. 62 cf. Psalm 105 : 18 (Book of Common Prayer).

p. 62 See the response of Joseph Wright to Yorick's painterly terms in his 'Captive, from Sterne' (1774), reproduced in J. Egerton, *Wright of Derby* (1990), p. 108.

p. 62 César-Gabriel de Choiseul (1712–85), duc de Choiseul-Praslin, Minister for Foreign Affairs 1761–6.

p. 64 Sterne plays on his own heraldic inheritance, and on an association between *starling* (*starn* in Yorkshire dialect) and *Sterne*: see M. J. O'Shea, 'Laurence Sterne's Display of Heraldry', *Shandean*, 3 (1991), 61–9.

p. 67 The Order of St Louis, founded by Louis XIV in 1693 to reward military merit.

p. 67 The Treaty of Aix-la-Chapelle (1748), ending the War of the Austrian Succession.

p. 70 "Twas an odd incident when I was introduced to the Count de Bissie, which I was at his desire – I found him reading Tristram – ', Sterne told Garrick in 1762 (*Letters*, p. 151).

p. 70 'Ye are spies; to see the nakedness of the land ye are come' (Genesis 42 : 9).

p. 71 cf. *Tristram Shandy*, I, xxiii.

p. 71 See above, second note to p. 70.

p. 71 Yorick alludes indelicately to biblical images of the body as temple (John 2 : 21 ; 1 Corinthians 6 : 19, etc.).

p. 72 See *Letters*, p. 401.

p. 72 cf. *Tristram Shandy*, VII, xxxiii.

p. 72 Compare the *Monthly Review*'s objections to the title of *The Sermons of Mr Yorick*, by which Sterne scandalously seemed to 'mount the pulpit in a *Harlequin's coat*' (May 1760). Five bishops subscribed to the *Sermons* in 1760; one was William Warburton (1698–1779), Bishop of Gloucester, who conspicuously withdrew his patronage shortly afterwards, and who may be Sterne's target in this passage.

p. 72 cf. *Tristram Shandy*, I, xi, where Tristram refers to the mediaeval *Gesta Danorum* of Saxo Grammaticus, in which Horwendillus is identified as the father of Amlethus (Hamlet).

p. 72 cf. *Hamlet*, V.i.191–205 ; 2 Timothy 4 : 14.

p. 73 cf. Virgil, *Aeneid*, VI, lines 450–76, where Aeneas meets Dido in Hades, and VI, 635–6, where he wins entry into the Elysian Fields.

p. 73 cf. Psalm 39 : 7 (Book of Common Prayer).

p. 74 Thomas Killigrew (1612–83).

p. 74 A contested term, as in Fielding's *True Patriot*, No. 2 (12 November 1745), which complains 'that this Word *Patriot* hath of late years been very scandalously abused . . . We have now Men among us, who have stiled themselves Patriots, while they have pushed their own Preferment . . . at the manifest Hazard of the Ruin of their Country'.

p. 74 Johan van Beverwijck (1594–1647), Dutch theologian and physician.

p. 76 'The devil take the serious character of these people ! quoth I – (aside) they understand no more of IRONY than this – ' (*Tristram Shandy*, VII, xxxiv).

p. 79   cf. Psalm 100 : 2 (Book of Common Prayer).

p. 83   To *depart from nobility* (like the 'Chevalier de St. Louis selling *patès*').

p. 83   i.e. West and East, scenes of Anglo-French struggle in the Seven Years War.

p. 83   cf. Daniel 2 : 1–12.

p. 83   After Adonis, the beautiful youth of classical myth.

p. 84   Ironically suggesting the captivity of Israel (Exodus 13 : 3, 13 : 14, etc.).

p. 85   cf. 2 Samuel 9 : 6 ; 2 Kings 16 : 7.

p. 86   François Rabelais (*d.* 1553), Tristram Shandy's 'dear *Rabelais*' (III, xix).

p. 86   Jan Gruytère (1560–1627), Dutch classical scholar; Jacques Spon (1647–85), French antiquary.

p. 87   *Beware water*, euphemistic warning called from windows when emptying slops. In Smollett's *Humphry Clinker* an unlettered servant describes the same practice in Edinburgh, 'and the maid calls *gardy loo* to the passengers, which signifies *Lord have mercy upon you !*' (letter of 18 July).

p. 88   cf. Revelation 20 : 12 ; *Tristram Shandy*, VI, viii.

p. 90   cf. Acts 2 : 9–10 ; *Tristram Shandy*, VI, xxx.

p. 93   The *fermiers généraux* paid the Crown for the right to collect taxes, retaining the profits themselves. Some, like Alexandre-Jean-Joseph Le Riche de la Popelinière (1692–1762), grew immensely wealthy. Writing from Paris in March 1762, Sterne told his wife of 'Monsieur Popelinière, who lives here like a sovereign prince ; keeps a company of musicians always in his house, and a full set of players ; and gives concerts and plays alternately to the grandees of this metropolis ; he is the richest of all the farmer[s general] ; he did me the honour last night to send me an invitation to his house, while I stayed here – that is, to his music and table' (*Letters*, p. 155).

p. 94   *L'Encyclopédie* (1751–80), the great dictionary-in-progress of Enlightenment thought, notorious for the sceptical tendency of many articles. While in Paris in 1762 Sterne grew friendly with its principal editor, Denis Diderot (1713–84), who wrote enthusiastically of *Tristram Shandy* as 'le Rabelais des Anglois' and imitated its methods in *Jacques le fataliste* (1796). The Abbe M*** suggests André Morellet

(1727–1819), who wrote entries on theology and metaphysics for the *Encyclopédie*.

p. 94 Suggesting 'Doolittle' or 'Idler', with a disposition less ready for unperverting than Madame de V∗∗∗'s.

p. 95 cf. *Tristram Shandy*, IX, xxiv.

p. 95 cf. *Don Quixote*, Part I, xix.

p. 96 On Sterne's play here with Andrew Marvell's 'Nymph Complaining for the Death of Her Faun', see above, 'Introduction'.

p. 96 Compare Fielding's play on this word in *Shamela* (1741), esp. the three 'Emotions' felt in Parson Tickletext's opening letter.

p. 97 '*Dieu mesure le froid à la brebis tondue*', proverb recorded by Henri Estienne, *Les Premices* (1593), p. 47; Estienne adds that 'aucuns disent *mesure le vent*, non pas *mesure le froid*'. See also note to p. 149 to the *Fragment*, below.

p. 97 cf. Samuel 12 : 3 ; see also note to p. 98 below.

p. 97 cf. Isaiah 56 : 7 ; Psalms 141 : 2, etc.

p. 98 Unlike the Pharisees of Matthew 23 : 7, Mark 12 : 38, etc.

p. 98 'But the poor man had nothing, save one little ewe lamb, which . . . did eat of his own meat, and drank of his own cup, and lay in his bosom, and was unto him as a daughter' (2 Samuel 12 : 3 ; also cited above, notes to pp. 33 and 97).

p. 98 cf. Luke 10 : 33–4 ; see also first note to p. 16 above.

p. 98 cf. Addison, *Cato* (1713), V.i.5–6.

p. 98 cf. 1 Samuel 14 : 45 and 2 Samuel 14 : 11 ; also Matthew 10 : 29–30 and Luke 12 : 7. See also *Tristram Shandy* on 'the chief sensorium, or head-quarters of the soul' (II, xix).

p. 98 See Eugenius 'drawing *Yorick*'s curtain' in *Tristram Shandy*, I, xii.

p. 101 cf. *Tristram Shandy*, VII, xliii.

p. 102 Adapting, with bawdy hints, a story told Sterne by a young Scot in Italy, John Craufurd of Errol : see Cash, *Later Years*, pp. 230–1.

p. 105 As opposed (the absent full-stop implies) to her hand.

A POLITICAL ROMANCE

p. 107 Horace, *Satires*, I, x, lines 14–15. 'By satire in a pleasant vein, / A weighty point we oft'ner gain, / Than talking in severer strain'

(Christopher Smart, *The Works of Horace, Translated into Verse* (1767), III, 127).

p. 109 Representing the Commissaryship of Pickering and Pocklington, an office in the gift of Dr John Fountayne (1714–1802), Dean of York ('*John*, our Parish-Clerk'), and once sought by the prominent church lawyer Dr Francis Topham (1713–70; represented here as Trim and in *Tristram Shandy* as Didius).

p. 109 The Commissaryship of the Exchequer and Prerogative Court, in the gift of the Archbishop of York ('the Parson of the Parish'). Topham gained this office in 1751, and later sought the right to bequeath it to his son.

p. 112 The churchwardens represent the prebendaries of the minster; the sidesmen represent the Archbishop's officers, among whom Sterne compliments Dr William Herring (1691–1792), Diocesan Chancellor.

p. 112 A new Archbishop, Dr John Gilbert (1693–1761), had been elevated to York in 1757.

p. 114 Topham had recently trumpeted his quarrel in *A Letter Address'd to the Reverend the Dean of York; in which is given a full Detail of some very extraordinary Behaviour of his, in relation to his Denial of a Promise made by him to Dr Topham* (York, 1758).

p. 115 Dr Matthew Hutton, Archbishop of York to 1757, who at Topham's instigation had quarrelled with the Dean over the extent of the latter's powers (the height of '*John*'s Desk').

p. 116 The Commissaryship of the Exchequer and Prerogative Court, secured by Topham in 1751.

p. 116 Dr Mark Braithwaite (*d.* 1750), an impoverished lawyer.

p. 117 The Commissaryship of the Dean and Chapter of York.

p. 117 William Stables, elected Commissary of the Dean and Chapter Court in 1751.

p. 117 Laurence Sterne, who had himself gained the Commissaryship of Pickering and Pocklington in 1751.

p. 118 Alluding to the many other offices held or sought by Topham.

p. 118 Rabbits; also fools, gulls, dupes; also (obscenely) women. *Cony-catching* (or *cunnycatching*) thus hints at both swindling and whoring.

p. 119 Topham's second pamphlet, *A Reply to the Answer to a Letter Lately Addressed to the Dean of York* (York, 1759), which attacked Fountayne's *Answer to a Letter Address'd to the Dean of York* (1758).

p. 119 Associating Trim with the lying bravado of Falstaff, whose report that 'three misbegotten knaves in Kendal green came at my back and let drive at me' is undermined when he adds: 'for it was so dark, Hal, that thou couldst not see thy hand' (*I Henry IV*, II.iv.216–19).

p. 122 Possibly poking fun at a club which met at Sunton's coffee-house in York. Through the club's deliberations, Sterne makes the Scriblerian move of accompanying his satire with an assortment of bogus interpretations.

p. 124 Of 1698 and 1700, relating to the Spanish Succession.

p. 128 *As You Like It*, V.iv.93.

p. 128 Sterne's Rabelaisian source, partly translated by Sir Thomas Urquhart (1653) and completed by Peter Motteux (1693–4).

p. 130 Probably Caesar Ward (1711–59), printer of *A Political Romance*.

p. 130 Monkman reports that Sterne's first intention had been to call this work *The History of a good warm Watch Coat, with which the present Possessor is not content to cover his own shoulders, unless he can cut out of it, a Petticoat for his Wife, and a Pair of Breeches for his Son*. A printer's proof copy now at Texas Christian University reveals another prudent change, cancelling Sterne's original identification of the village in which the satire is set as 'Cocksbull near Canterbury' (E. Simmen, 'Sterne's *A Political Romance*', *Papers of the Bibliographical Society of America*, 64 (1970), 419–29).

p. 130 Topham had alleged the Dean's *Answer* to his first pamphlet to have been '*the Child and Offspring of many Parents*' (*Reply to the Answer*, p. 1), one of whom was probably Sterne.

p. 130 cf. George Villiers, Duke of Buckingham (*et al.*), *The Rehearsal* (1672), III.iv.68–9.

p. 130 Edmund Curll (1675–1747), the notorious literary pirate.

p. 130 Perhaps Ward's cut of two fighting game-cocks, which appears in surviving copies of *A Political Romance* as an ornament on p. 30 (after the Postscript); perhaps the copy on p. 24 (after the Romance).

p. 132 Dr William Herring and William Berdmore, members (with Sterne) of the Dean's party, whose names had appeared in Fountayne's *Answer*. The following paragraphs allude to several passages in the pamphlets of both Fountayne and Topham.

p. 132 Partly quoting a Horatian plea (*De arte poetica*, line 11) for limited poetic licence. Smart translates the whole passage as follows: 'The painters and the bards, 'tis true, / Claim licence as of both their due. / 'Tis a concession that I make, / And hence excuse we give and take : / But not so largely as to coop / The tame and savage in a groupe, / And snakes with turtle-doves to mate, / And lambs with tigers copulate' (*The Works of Horace*, IV, 238).

p. 133 Arthur Ricard, a York attorney quoted in Topham's *Reply*.

p. 134 Pressing to death, a punishment for felons refusing to plead.

p. 135 Juvenal, *Satires*, xiii, line 2, on remorse. Thomas Creech paraphrases the whole passage as follows : 'He that commits a *Sin*, shall quickly find / The pressing *Guilt* lie heavy on his Mind, / Tho' Bribes or Favour shall assert his Cause, / Pronounce him *Guiltless*, and elude the Laws : / None quits himself; his own impartial Thought / Will Damn, and *Conscience* will record the Fault. / This first the Wicked feels : Then publick Hate / Pursues the *Cheat*, and proves the Villain's Fate' (*The Satires of Decimus Junius Juvenalis* (1693), p. 257).

MEMOIRS

p. 139 In fact Hamilton's Regiment, the 34th Foot. The unreliability of the *Memoirs* in many points of detail may be seen by comparison with A. H. Cash, *Laurence Sterne : The Early and Middle Years* (1975), pp. 1–40, and with the extensive notes to Monkman's edition.

p. 139 Sterne's MS reads 'Hobert'.

p. 139 The Gregorian calendar was formally adopted by an Act of 1751, which redefined the day following 2 September 1752 as 14 September 1752 (greatly to the dismay of those who thought their date of death already determined). 'Old Stile' refers to the unreformed calendar.

p. 139 A misspelling (as in Sterne's MS) for Clonmel, Co. Tipperary.

p. 140 Vigo, on the west coast of Spain, was taken by the British in October 1719.

p. 141 Gibraltar was threatened in 1727 by Spanish forces, which withdrew after a few skirmishes. The 34th Foot remained there until sent to Jamaica late in 1730.

p. 142 The surviving MS breaks off at this point. On the previous page, a note reads : 'This I thought fit to set down Sept. 5ᵗʰ 1758 – having in a pensive Moode, run over these Incidents, in my mind I spent half an hour in ~~setting the~~ transmitting them, for my Lydia' (who would then have been nearly eleven). What follows is evidently of much later composition.

p. 142 John Hall-Stevenson (1718–85), Sterne's Eugenius.

p. 142 Lydia, sister of Sterne's future wife Elizabeth Lumley, was married to the Rev. John Botham, of Clifton Campville, Staffordshire.

p. 142 Stephen Croft (1712–98), a member of the wine-importing family, remained Sterne's close friend.

p. 143 Thomas Belasyse (1699–1774), first Earl Fauconberg of Newburgh.

p. 143 The Treaty of Paris (February 1763), concluding the Seven Years War.

AN IMPROMPTU

p. 144 Thomas Becket (*c.* 1722–1813), the bookseller, who published the 1775 edition of Sterne's *Letters* in which the *Memoirs, Impromptu* and *Fragment* were first printed.

p. 144 Sterne's daughter Lydia had run advertisements soliciting items for inclusion in the *Letters*.

p. 144 Playing on 'Defender of the Faith' (a title assumed by Henry VIII and subsequent monarchs), perhaps with a glance at the role of coats in the ecclesiastical allegory of Swift's *Tale of a Tub* (or indeed of Sterne's own *Political Romance*).

p. 145 cf. *King Lear*, III.iv.29 ; III.iv.14.

p. 145 'Illustrious', from *illustrare* to light up, illuminate ; 'splendid', from *splendere* to be bright.

p. 145 'Dark with excessive bright thy skirts appear' (*Paradise Lost*, I, line 380).

p. 146 Playing on the obscenity of John Wilmot, Earl of Rochester's 'Dialogue between Strephon and Daphne', in which Daphne congratulates her lover : 'How shou'd I these show'rs forget, / 'Twas so pleasant to be wet / They kill'd Love, I knew it well, / I dy'd all the while they fell' (lines 41–4).

FRAGMENT

p. 147 Sterne's coinage, suggesting a treatise on the art of sermonizing.

p. 147 Sterne's MS reads 'daintily'.

p. 147 Compare Walter's interruption in *Tristram Shandy*, I, i.

p. 147 A cock and bull story : *OED* cites Philemon Holland's 'Telling tales of a tubbe, or of a roasted horse' from his translation *Plutarch's Morals* (1603) ; the phrase recurs in *Tristram Shandy*, IV, x.

p. 147 MS reads 'than my Arse'.

p. 147 MS reads 'my Little Cods'.

p. 147 MS reads 'as ever piss'd'.

p. 148 MS reads 'Shite! says *Panurge*'.

p. 148 cf. *Tristram Shandy*, IV, xxv, where Homenas (originally a Rabelaisian name, like others in the *Fragment*) 'had to preach at court next Sunday'. In the following chapter (IV, xxvi), Yorick laments his own 'unspeakable torments, in bringing forth this sermon'; see also VI, xi, where Yorick confesses to plagiarism.

p. 148 MS reads 'd – n it'.

p. 148 Dr Samuel Clarke (1675–1725), a divine from whom Sterne's own sermons borrow. In the MS Sterne seems originally to have written, but then cancelled, 'Rogers' (Dr John Rogers (1679–1729), another source of his borrowings); at that point the chapter opened with Homenas 'Rogering it as hard as He could drive'. Smollett went into print with the same innuendo in *Humphry Clinker* (1771), when Tabitha Bramble complains that 'Roger gets this, and Roger gets that; but I'd have you to know, I won't be rogered at this rate by any ragmatical fellow in the kingdom' (letter of 19 May).

p. 148 MS reads '*beshit*'.

p. 149 MS reads 'before G—d, – I may as well shite as shoot'.

p. 149 See above, note to p. 97 to *A Sentimental Journey*, on Maria's '*God tempers the wind*' (a phrase anticipated here).

p. 150 MS reads 'Damn it'.

p. 150 MS reads 'upon his broad Arse'.

GLOSSARY

accommodation compromise
adamant hard mineral
adust dried-up, sallow, gloomy
apostrophe exclamatory address
ambidextrous double-dealing
assay test, experiment
assigne deputy, agent, representative
badinant playful, frolicsome
bag pouch to hold back-hair of a wig
bandoleer soldier's broad belt
beat up to levy or recruit (soldiers)
bidet small horse
billet note
book-sworn sworn on the Bible
broke cashiered, deprived of officer's commission
buckle curl (of hair)
cabal secret meeting of intriguers
cabinet private chamber, centre of fashion or power
call a law invoke, appeal to, a law
career gallop
cast (*sb.*) throw (of dice), fortune ; (*adj.*) cast-off (of clothes)
castor hat of rabbit's (originally beaver's) fur
centinel sentry
chaffer haggle
chaise carriage
clap into enter briskly upon
close-stool chamber-pot
clue thread
cluster bunch (of grapes)
compass the full range of notes of which an instrument is capable (in music)
complexional arising from temperament or constitution
concentre concentrate
conventionist party to a contract
corking pin calkin, large pin
coxcomb fop ; conceited or pretentious fool
croix cross ; insignia of knighthood
cullibility gullibility
declension declined or sunken condition
desobligeant carriage for single occupant
determination decision

diable to exclaim '*Diable*!', i.e. to curse
ductility tractableness, docility
effectually in effect, in fact
eloge eulogy, often of the dead
en conscience in good faith
equipage carriage; also carriage, horses and retinue
esplanade open space
esprit, esprit fort wit, free-thinker
excentrically off centre, askew
farm to lease profits from taxes for a fixed payment
fend and prove to argue, wrangle
fiacre hackney-coach, carriage plying for hire
figure to yourself to imagine
flambeau torch
fob small hidden pocket for watch, etc.
fossè trench, moat
fripier dealer in used clothes
fume one apt to get in a fume or rage (Sterne's coinage)
gage d'amour love-token
gird satirical attack, gibe, hit
gives shackles, fetters
grisset *grisette*, young woman of low status, esp. shopgirl
groat coin worth four pence; trivial sum
gross main body (of an army)
halter noose (for tethering; for hanging)
harquebuss portable gun
hebdomadical weekly
hectic (*sb.*) a hectic flush; (*adj*) feverish
helebore drug for treating madness
heralds officers officers of Heralds' College, regulating the use of armorial bearings
higgling dealing, haggling
hold refuge, stronghold
hôtel town-mansion; also hotel
hussive sewing-case
hydrostatical relating to the equilibrium of liquids
ichnography ground-plan or cross-section (of a fortress)
in verbo sacerdotis on the word of a priest
incontinently immediately
intendment of law construction put upon a thing by the law
investiture right of giving possession
lay out in to spend on
lease and release conveyance of land giving first the possession and afterwards the interest in the estate conveyed
legend text impressed on a coin
livre French unit of currency worth about a shilling
loge box in theatre
louis d'or French gold coin worth about 17 shillings
magazine storehouse
maitre d'hotel steward or butler of a town-mansion; also hotelier

make his market do his dealing, get what he can
mill-race current of water driving a mill-wheel
mounting decorative fitting or setting (of a blade); military apparel or finery; social climbing
nettlesome irritable, restless
nim to take; also to pilfer
orchestra space in front of theatre-stage; its occupants
overset to overcome, overturn
packet packet-boat
pannel rustic saddle
parterre pit of theatre; its occupants
pasquinade lampoon posted in public
patisser *pâtissier*, pastry-seller
pauvre honteux bashful pauper, one ashamed to beg
pavè paved street, pavement
penchant inclination
peregrine travelling abroad; making a pilgrimage
persiflage jest, raillery
pettifogging shifty, quibbling, grasping
pharmacopolist apothecary
pinder officer of a manor charged with impounding stray beasts
planted perdu placed in a hazardous outlying position (in warfare)
plush of shaggy cloth
pontific pertaining to bridges (Sterne's facetious coinage)
potagerie kitchen-garden
pop upon to come on suddenly or unexpectedly
post to travel with speed
prebendary canon or stipendiary of a cathedral
prevenancy prepossessing manner, charm
print moulded pat (of butter)
puissant powerful
quarter sessions criminal and civil court, held quarterly
queue pigtail
racket clamour, fuss
raise a dust throw up a smokescreen
reins seat of the feelings or affections
remise coach-house; also (for *voiture de remise*) hired carriage
riot revel, wild feast
rudiments imperfect beginnings
ruffle ornamental frill worn at the wrist
sabot clog, wooden shoe
sensorium seat of sensation in the brain; percipient centre
sexton church officer charged with ringing bells, digging graves, etc.
shagreen untanned leather
signalize make conspicuous
slop slope (in fortification); legs (of breeches)
solitaire loose necktie
sous one-twentieth of a *livre*
spatterdashes gaiters to protect legs, esp. of riders, from mud and wet
sportability playfulness (Sterne's coinage)

stamina native or congenital elements
stripe weal, mark left by whipping
succours means of assistance or protection; reinforcements
super-induce to introduce over and above something else
sutler victualler (to an army)
take away to depart; to clear away (after a meal)
temperature temperament
thill-horse horse pulling a carriage between thills or shafts
thrum of coarse or wasted thread
tickle it off to do the trick, pull it off, busk it
tourniquet turnstile
traiteur keeper of an eating-house which sends out meals
translation conversion into new language; interpretation; removal, conveyance, carrying (of people)
trimm'd thrashed, trounced
tumble to turn over; to throw about by way of examination
unclasp to open (a book shut with clasps)
vampt-up patched-up
vielle hurdy-gurdy
vis a vis carriage for two persons placed face to face
voiturin carriage; also carriage-driver
watch-coat watchman's coat
whitesmith smith who polishes or finishes metals
wight person (archaic)
wipe satirical stroke or jeer

STERNE AND HIS CRITICS

Elizabeth Carter to Elizabeth Vesey, 19 April 1768, *A Series of Letters between Mrs. Elizabeth Carter and Miss Catherine Talbot*, ed. the Rev. Montagu Pennington (1809), III, 334–6. A formidable woman of letters who in Samuel Johnson's words 'could make a pudding, as well as translate Epictetus', Carter was scathing of the moral pretensions apparent in the *Journey*. Conflating the Yorick of the novel with the Sterne of posthumous gossip, she here alleges hypocritical posturing and self-delusion.

I thought the tone of one paragraph in your Letter did not seem your own, even before you gave me an intimation that it belonged to the Sentimental Traveller, whom I neither have read nor probably ever shall; for indeed there is something shocking in whatever I have heard either of the author, or of his writings. It is the fashion, I find, to extol him for his benevolence, a word so wretchedly misapplied, and so often put as a substitute for virtue, that one is quite sick of hearing it repeated either by those who have no ideas at all, or by those who have none but such as confound all differences of right and wrong. Merely to be struck by a sudden impulse of compassion at the view of an object of distress, is no more benevolence than it is a fit of the gout, and indeed has a nearer relation to the last than the first. Real benevolence would never suffer a husband and a father to neglect and injure those whom the ties of nature, the order of Providence, and the general sense of mankind have entitled to his first regards. Yet this unhappy man, by his carelessness and extravagance, has left a wife and child to starve, or to subsist on the precarious bounty of others. Nor would real benevolence lead a clergyman to ramble about the world after objects with whom he has no particular connexion, when he might exercise the noblest duties of a benevolent heart in a regular discharge of his proper function, instead of neglecting and disgracing it by indecent and buffoon writings.

Editor's Preface to *The Beauties of Sterne; including all his Pathetic Tales, and most distinguished Observations on Life. Selected for the Heart of Sensibility* (1782), pp. vii–viii. This compilation, which had reached its tenth edition by 1787, mediated Sterne's writing to a large public in the form of pure sentiment, though with manifest anxiety.

A selection of the Beauties of *Sterne* is what has been looked for by a number of his admirers for some time ; well knowing they would form such a Volume as perhaps this, nor any other language, could equal. Indeed it was highly necessary on a particular score to make this selection : the *chaste* lovers of literature were not only deprived themselves of the pleasure and instruction so conspicuous in this magnificent assemblage of Genius, but their rising offspring, whose minds it would polish to the highest perfection were prevented from tasting the enjoyment likewise. The *chaste* part of the world complained so loudly of the obscenity which taints the writings of *Sterne*, (and indeed, with some reason), that those readers under their immediate inspection were not suffered to penetrate beyond the title-page of his *Tristram Shandy*; – his *Sentimental Journey*, in some degree, escaped the general censure; though that is not entirely free of the fault compained of.

To accommodate those who are strangers to the first of these works, I have, (I hope with some degree of judgment), extracted the most distinguished passages on which the sun of Genius shines so resplendent, that all his competitors, in his manner of writing, are lost in an eclipse of affectation and unnatural rhapsody. I intended to have arranged them alphabetically, till I found the stories of *Le Fever*, the *Monk*, and *Maria*, would be too closely connected for the *feeling reader*, and would wound the bosom of *sensibility* too deeply : I therefore placed them at a proper distance from each other. – I need not explain my motive for introducing the Sermon on the abuses of Conscience, with the effusions of humanity throughout it ; every parent and governor, I believe, (unless a bigotted Papist), will thank me. – I wish I could infuse the pleasure that attended me in compiling this little work, into the breast of the reader, yet unacquainted with *Sterne* – as it is, I promise him, the hours he may devote to this great master of nature and the passions, will be marked with more felicity, than any, since genius led him to the love of letters.

Vicesimus Knox, *Essays, Moral and Literary* (1778–82), in *Works*, 7 vols (1824), I, 131. Knox was perhaps the severest of Sterne's early critics. Though admiring his 'exquisite touches of the pathetic', Knox castigated the confusion of sentiment and sex that he detected in Sterne's life and writing alike, and pronounced him, 'though many admire him as the first of philosophers, the grand promoter of adultery and every species of illicit commerce'. In *Winter Evenings* (1788–90) he complains (presumably unaware that he had the hint from Sterne himself): 'Mr. Sterne and Mrs. Draper have too many imitators. A goat is a personage of as great sensibility and sentiment as most of them.'

Who has read the exquisite touches of nature and sensibility in Sterne's Sentimental Journey without feeling his nerves vibrate with every tender emotion? Sterne has shown what important effects may be produced by a true simplicity of style, and a faithful adherence to nature. I wish it were possible to give him the praise of morality as well as of genius; but the poison he conveys is subtle, and the more dangerous as it is palatable. I believe no young mind ever perused his books without finding those passions roused and inflamed, which, after all that the novelist can advance in their favour, are copious sources of human misery. Many a connexion, begun with the fine sentimentality which Sterne has recommended and increased, has terminated in disease, infamy, want, madness, suicide, and a gibbet. Every writer, whatever may be the weakness and folly of his own life, should take the side of virtue in his public writings, and endeavour to restrain the irregularity of those affections, which, under every restraint, are still capable of producing more evil than any other cause throughout the whole system of human affairs. It is our reason which wants all the aids which art can bestow. Our passions, without the stimulus of licentious or indulgent principles, will have strength sufficient to produce as much and more than nature has intended.

William Makepeace Thackeray, *The English Humourists of the Eighteenth Century*, 2nd edn (1853), pp. 283–5. Measuring the insincerity and indecency of Sterne's writing against 'the innocent laughter and the sweet and unsullied page which the author of *David Copperfield* gives to my children', Thackeray's celebrated attack set the tone of Victorian criticism.

How much of the paint and emphasis is necessary for the fair business of the stage, and how much of the rant and rouge is put on for the vanity of the actor ? His audience trusts him : can he trust himself ? How much was deliberate calculation and imposture – how much was false sensibility – and how much true feeling – where did the lie begin, and did he know where ? and where did the truth end in the art and scheme of this man of genius, this actor, this quack ? Some time since I was in the company of a French actor, who began after dinner, and at his own request, to sing French songs of the sort called *des chansons grivoises*, and which he performed admirably, and to the dissatisfaction of most persons present. Having finished these, he commenced a sentimental ballad – it was so charmingly sung that it touched all persons present, and especially the singer himself, whose voice trembled, whose eyes filled with emotion, and who was snivelling and weeping quite genuine tears by the time his own ditty was over. I suppose Sterne had this artistical sensibility ; he used to blubber perpetually in his study, and finding his tears infectious, and that they brought him a great popularity, he exercised the lucrative gift of weeping, he utilised it, and cried on every occasion. I own that I don't value or respect much the cheap dribble of those fountains. He fatigues me with his perpetual disquiet and his uneasy appeals to my risible or sentimental faculties. He is always looking in my face, watching his effect, uncertain whether I think him an impostor or not ; posture-making, coaxing, and imploring me. 'See what sensibility I have – own now that I'm very clever – do cry now, you can't resist this.' The humour of Swift and Rabelais, whom he pretended to succeed, poured from them as naturally as song does from a bird ; they lose no manly dignity with it, but laugh their hearty great laugh out of their broad chests as nature bade them. But this man – who can make you laugh, who can make you cry, too – never lets his reader alone, or will permit his audience repose : when you are quiet, he fancies he must rouse you, and turns over head and heels, or sidles up and whispers a nasty story. The man is a great jester, not a great humourist. He goes to work systematically and of cold blood ; paints his face, puts on his ruff and motley clothes, and lays down his carpet and tumbles on it.

Walter Bagehot, 'Sterne and Thackeray', *National Review*, 36 (April 1864), 542–3. Known not only as a lawyer and constitutionalist but also as a literary reviewer, Bagehot was one of Sterne's subtlest Victorian apologists.

In two points the *Sentimental Journey*, viewed with the critic's eye and as a mere work of art, is a great improvement upon *Tristram Shandy*. The style is simpler and better; it is far more connected; it does not jump about, or leave a topic *because* it is interesting; it does not worry the reader with fantastic transitions, with childish contrivances and rhetorical intricacies. Highly elaborate the style certainly is, and in a sense artificial; it is full of nice touches, which must have come only upon reflexion, – a careful polish and judicious enhancement, in which the critic sees many a trace of time and toil. But a style delicately adjusted and exquisitely polished belongs to such a subject. Sterne undertook to write, *not* of the coarse business of life, – very strong common sort of words are best for that, – *not* even of interesting outward realities, which may be best described in a nice and simple style; but of the passing moods of human nature, of the impressions which a sensitive nature receives from the world without; and it is only the nicest art and the most dexterous care which can fit an obtuse language to such fine employment. How language was first invented and made we may not know; but beyond doubt it was shaped and fashioned into its present state by common ordinary men and women using it for common and ordinary purposes. They wanted a carving-knife, not a razor or lancet. And those great artists who have to use language for more exquisite purposes, who employ it to describe changing sentiments and momentary fancies and the fluctuating and indefinite inner world, must use curious nicety and hidden but effectual artifice, else they cannot duly punctuate their thoughts and slice the fine edges of their reflexions. A hair's-breadth is as important to them as a yard's-breadth to a common workman. Sterne's style has been criticised as artificial; but it is justly and rightly artificial, because language used in its natural and common mode was not framed to delineate, cannot delineate, the delicate subjects with which he occupies himself.

Leslie Stephen, *Hours in a Library*, 2nd edn (1892), III, 164–5. Thackeray's son-in-law and the father of Virginia Woolf, this influential critic had a complex response to Sterne: while declaring him 'perhaps the greatest artist in the language', he nevertheless found 'unimpeachable' the overall judgment of Sterne that had been given in Thackeray's essay.

When the moment comes at which he suddenly drops the tear of sensibility, he is almost as likely to provoke sneers as sympathy. There is, for example, the famous donkey, and it is curious to compare the donkey fed with macaroons in the *Tristram Shandy* with the dead donkey of the *Sentimental Journey*, whose weeping master lays a crust of bread on the now vacant bit of his bridle. It is obviously the same donkey, and Sterne has reflected that he can squeeze a little more pathos out of the animal by actually killing him, and providing a sentimental master. It seems to me that, in trying to heighten the effect, he has just crossed the dangerous limit which divides sympathetic from derisive laughter; and whereas the macaroon-fed animal is a possible, straightforward beast, he becomes (as higher beings have done) a humbug in his palpably hypocritical epitaph. Sterne tries his hand in the same way at improving Maria, who is certainly an effective embodiment of the mad young woman who has tried to move us in many forms since the days of Ophelia. In her second appearance, she comes in to utter the famous sentiment about the wind and the shorn lamb. It has become proverbial, and been even credited in the popular mind with a scriptural origin; and considering such a success, one has hardly the right to say that it has gathered a certain sort of banality. Yet it is surely on the extreme verge at which the pathetic melts into the ludicrous.

Virginia Woolf, *The Common Reader*, 2nd series (1932), pp. 79–80. Woolf, who defined her own priorities as a novelist partly in opposition to such recent precursors as Bennett, Galsworthy and Wells, found a more congenial forebear in Sterne.

With the first words – They order, said I, this matter better in France – we are in the world of *Tristram Shandy*. It is a world in which anything may happen. We hardly know what jest, what jibe, what flash of poetry is not going to glance suddenly through the gap which this astonishingly agile pen has cut in the thick-set hedge of English prose. Is Sterne himself responsible? Does he know what he is going to say next for all his resolve to be on his best behaviour this time? The jerky, disconnected sentences are as rapid and it would seem as little under control as the phrases that fall from the lips of a brilliant talker. The very punctuation is that of speech, not writing, and brings the sound and associations of the speaking voice in with it. The order of the ideas, their suddenness and irrelevancy, is more true to life than to literature. There is a privacy in this intercourse which allows things to slip out unreproved that would have been in doubtful taste had they been spoken in public. Under the influence of this extraordinary style the book becomes semi-transparent. The usual ceremonies and conventions which keep reader and writer at arm's length disappear. We are as close to life as we can be.

That Sterne achieved this illusion only by the use of extreme art and extraordinary pains is obvious without going to his manuscript to prove it. For though the writer is always haunted by the belief that somehow it must be possible to brush aside the ceremonies and conventions of writing and to speak to the reader as directly as by word of mouth, anyone who has tried the experiment has either been struck dumb by the difficulty, or waylaid into disorder and diffusity unutterable. Sterne somehow brought off the astonishing combination. No writing seems to flow more exactly into the very folds and creases of the individual mind, to express its changing moods, to answer its lightest whim and impulse, and yet the result is perfectly precise and composed. The utmost fluidity exists with the utmost permanence. It is as if the tide raced over the beach hither and thither and left every ripple and eddy cut on the sand in marble.

Rufus Putney, 'The Evolution of *A Sentimental Journey*', *Philological Quarterly*, 19 (1940), 349–69. In an early reading of the *Journey* as controlled irony, Putney sees its sentimentalism as above all a witty pose. His argument distinguishes the Yoricks of the novels from a Sterne who hides behind them, mocking the extravagance not only of his readers but also of his own recent (though now seemingly discarded) passion for Mrs Draper.

Sterne furthered his mystification of the public by using an old name for a new character. The Yorick who counted grisettes' pulses and flattered impartially coquette, deist, and dévoté in their coteries is not identical with the lousy prebendary of the same name, who could not refuse his neighbors a horse to ride for the midwife. And neither one is quite Sterne, who, if he was never as Shandean as he had made the world think him, was never as sentimental as the new Yorick. Yorick is a Cervantic hero led into ludicrous extravagances by the hyper-sensibility of his heart. Some natural confusion was caused by the use of the first person in the novel which made it easier for Sterne than it had been for Cervantes and Fielding, who often take sides with their quixotic heroes, to step into and out of Yorick's character. Sterne as well as Yorick was moved by the Chevalier de St Louis and by the Marquis de B****'s reassumption of his sword, but Sterne surely laughed when Yorick said :

> It is a miserable picture which I am going to give of the weakness of my heart, by owning, that it suffered a pain, which worthier occasions could not have inflicted. – I was mortified with the loss of her hand, and the manner in which I had lost it carried neither oil nor wine to the wound : I never felt the pain of a sheepish inferiority so miserably in my life.

When all the incidents and characters pass through the distorted prism of Yorick's heart, the inevitable result is comedy. Sterne had passed the spring in a miasma of emotion ; the autumn was occupied with the mockery of it.

The *Sentimental Journey*, then, was a hoax by which Sterne persuaded his contemporaries that the humor he wanted to write was the pathos they wished to read. This theory does not deny Sterne's susceptibility to sentiment or the occasional genuine expression of his feelings in the *Sentimental Journey*. For the most part, however, his sensibility displayed itself in the discovery of situations of true pathos, like the grief of the master for his dead ass, which are carried into sentimental farce by the introduction of an incongruity or exaggeration of feeling, and lifted to the level of high comedy, or dropped into the realms of bathos, by Yorick's sentimental moralizing. This hypothesis does imply that Sterne intended the sentimentality, in the modern sense, of the *Sentimental Journey*, that whomever he gulled he was not his own dupe, and that in those letters where he boasted of his feelings, he was Yoricking now as he had Shandyed before. Far from wantoning with his emotions, Sterne made fun of the man who did.

Arthur Hill Cash, *Sterne's Comedy of Moral Sentiments : The Ethical Dimension of the Journey* (Pittsburgh, 1966), pp. 89–90. Reading

the *Journey* in light of Sterne's sermons, Cash's study defends the
ethical significance of the novel against the allegation of insincerity.

Sterne imparted to Yorick of the *Sentimental Journey* all the
apprehensions of a man suspended between the impending need
to set his house in order and the need to 'exist'. Yorick too is an
'invalid,' so 'pale and sickly' that the Comte de Bissy insists
upon his sitting during their interview. The image of death is
scattered throughout the *Sentimental Journey* – from the opening scene in which Yorick mourns that the French king will take
from his dead body even the picture of Eliza, to the last, when
Yorick, weak and coughing, refuses to sleep in a drafty closet.
We are never far removed from the grave of the Monk, the dead
ass in the road, or the deathbed of the old man in the notary's
story. We cannot mistake the image when Yorick, newly arrived
in Paris, walks 'gravely to the window in my dusty black coat,
and looking through the glass saw all the world in yellow, blue,
and green, running at the ring of pleasure . . . Alas, poor Yorick !
cried I, what art thou doing here ? On the very first onset of all
this glittering clatter, thou art reduced to an atom.' Yorick even
identifies himself to the Comte de Bissy by opening *Hamlet* and
pointing to the grave-digger's scene. 'Now whether the idea of
poor Yorick's skull was put out of the Count's mind, by the
reality of my own, or by what magic he could drop a period of
seven or eight hundred years, makes nothing in this account –
'tis certain the French conceive better than they combine.'
Nevertheless, the Count obtains for Yorick a passport '. . . to let
Mr. Yorick, the king's jester, and his baggage, travel quietly
along.' Thus the English parson acquires the identity of a jester
known to the world only as a skull and a memory.* The hero
of Sterne's sentimental comedy juggles with the most serious
things of life – love and desire and mortality – mere baubles in
his clever hands. Only when we become aware that Yorick
juggles on a tightrope with death below and God above, do we
begin to see the high seriousness of this humor.

---

* Ben Reid, in 'The Sad Hilarity of Sterne,' *Virginia Quarterly Review*, 32 (1956),
107–30, maintains 'that it is not chance, not the need for a simple generic title, but the
tragic sense of life that dictates the choice of Yorick for a name. Surely the nimbus that
endures in our recollection of Yorick is not that he was "a fellow of infinite jest," "wont to
set the table in a roar," but the fact that he *was* : the fact that we meet him as a skull, "quite
chap-fallen," grown plaything of a foolish sententious rustic, "knocked about the mazzard
with a sexton's spade"' (p. 111).

R. F. Brissenden, *Virtue in Distress: Studies in the Novel of Sentiment from Richardson to Sade* (1974), pp. 222–3. Finding the *Journey* 'a much less bawdy work than *Tristram Shandy*, but . . . in some ways much more deliberately and provocatively sexual', Brissenden sets out to explore the work's perplexing blend of 'erotic and moral awareness'.

The key to this aspect of the problem of *A Sentimental Journey* is to be found in the enigmatic statement:

Lamour n'est *rien* sans sentiment.

Et le sentiment est encore *moins* sans amour.

The sentences occur in the letter from the drummer in his regiment which La Fleur produces for Yorick when he is desperately trying to write a note to the beautiful Mme de L∗∗. The first sentence also appears in a letter written in 1765 when Sterne informs John Wodehouse that he carries on his affairs 'quite in the French way, sentimentally – "*l'amour*" (say they) "*n'est rien sans sentiment*" – Now notwithstanding they make such a pother about the *word*, they have no precise idea annex'd to it'.

Despite Sterne's disclaimer the French probably had a number of clear ideas attached to the word 'sentiment' in this context; and by the time he came to write *A Sentimental Journey* Sterne obviously had too. As a preacher he knew the value of a good text, and it would not be altogether inappropriate to see the *Journey* as an extended sermon on this verse out of the Epistle from the Drummer Jacques Roque to the Corporal's Wife. At the simplest level we can take 'L'amour n'est *rien* sans sentiment' to mean that love is nothing unless it has a spiritual, moral or intellectual dimension – and all Yorick's flirtations are certainly sentimental in this sense. But if we extend the signification of 'amour' we can take the statement to mean that spontaneous feelings of benevolence, pity or compassion are not worth much unless they are related to some rationally ordered set of moral ideas, unless they are part of some 'settled principle of humanity and goodness'. This is one of the lessons Yorick learns on his *Journey*; and it is when Yorick merely indulges his tender feelings and fails to act in a consistent and principled way that he becomes one of the objects of Sterne's complex and delicate satire.

But the second sentence needs examination also; and – as the italicised '*moins*' suggests – it is perhaps the more important of

the two : 'Et le sentiment est encore *moins* sans amour.' At the
most obvious erotic level we can take this to mean that spiritual
and lofty feelings between a man and a woman are meaningless
unless they are grounded in genuine sexual desire – it is the
lesson Uncle Toby has to learn when Trim explains to him the
true significance of Widow Wadman's 'humanity'. But there is a
larger interpretation to be placed upon this text. In the widest
sense it means that moral judgments and ideals (settled principles of *humanity* and goodness) are worthless unless they are
motivated by love, by the spontaneous impulses of benevolence
which can arise in man only because he is a physical creature
(albeit with a soul) with physical – and in particular, sexual –
passions and desires. Moral action which comes from the head
and not the heart is cold, empty and inhuman ; and to assume
that sexual feeling does not enter into feelings of benevolence,
compassion and pity, especially (but not only) when these are
directed towards members of the opposite sex, is to indulge in
sentimental self-deception.

Mark Loveridge, *Laurence Sterne and the Argument about Design*
(1982), pp. 172–3. In a study concerned as a whole with pattern,
design and form, Loveridge presents the *Journey* as an elaborate
interpretative game which 'mocks the response Sterne knows it will
create'.

Yorick is a great reader, an inveterate interpreter. His book, the
Journey, is as much about the problems of reading as *Tristram
Shandy* is about those of writing. Yorick rarely presents himself
as the writer or narrator of *A Sentimental Journey* : he provides
a record of his reading of the world – of his interpretation of
events. The reader in turn has to interpret Yorick's text. But this
is an activity fraught with difficulties. Yorick is possessed of a
great confusion between reality and verbality, between things,
events, and things and events as told in words, and this
confusion is preserved everywhere in the text. There is no
viewpoint on Yorick, no second omniscient narrator. The world
is Yorick's text : he feels impelled to provide a 'commentary' on
it, to 'translate', as he puts it, the gestures and actions of men
into phenomena which are comprehensible in terms of his own
system of benevolence. When he goes to the theatre in Paris, he

does not watch the play. The audience, for him, are the actors, the real world aesthetic. All nature becomes his book.

The reader is never told that Yorick's reading of this book is wrong, or even partisan. However most of the scenes in the *Journey* admit of other readings than Yorick's. What the reader makes of the book will depend, of course, on the nature of the reader. He can read one thing into it, or another : but basically the text of the *Journey* is neutral. It says one thing, and at the same time implies satire of it. But at bottom it is neither one thing nor the other. It is about the reader being forced to read, to make his choice.

Q. D. Leavis was probably the first to complain that the history of responses to *A Sentimental Journey* is a history of very partial responses. This is quite true ; I think it is Sterne's intention that it should be true. And Thackeray's complaint about Sterne, that he can always feel him looking in his face to see his reaction . . . is perhaps not so much a complaint as the reaction of an exceptionally shrewd reader.

John Mullan, *Sentiment and Sociability: The Language of Feeling in the Eighteenth Century* (1988), p. 189. Much recent criticism has continued to concern itself with the relationship between the sentimental and the sexual, a relationship Mullan here defines as essentially harmonious.

In *A Sentimental Journey* Sterne . . . conflates the suggestive and the sentimental. The *Sentimental Journey* goes out of its way to find scenes of erotic encounter, and thus seems to risk the production of outrage. It does this by interposing a body – the body of the narrator – whose sentimental whims sanction its erotic encounters. The eroticism of this body is at once innocent and knowing, coy and garrulous. It is a body which gauges sensibility, and whose vibrations register the pleasures of benevolence and of flirtation. Alone in a room with 'the fair *fille de chambre*', Yorick claims to feel 'a sort of a pleasing half guilty blush, where the blood is more in fault than the man', a 'sensation . . . delicious to the nerves' : 'But I'll not describe it. – I felt something at first within me which was not in strict unison with the lesson of virtue I had given her the night before.' Through this body throb the vibrations of a finally conquerable erotic temptation – but also of benevolence, affection, sympathy.

The pleasure of flirtation can be recorded because the body is taken to experience sentiments – fellow-feelings – which transcend 'carnality'. The presentation of each of Yorick's encounters as 'sentimental' renders it innocent, whatever our post-Freudian indictments might be. The *Sentimental Journey* produces its body not as a residue of desires but as a register of 'affections' – of 'feeling' refined by one who is determined to be a specialist in such matters. The contradiction taken to its logical conclusion in *Clarissa* was that the body was both 'sensible' and sexual; Sterne escapes the contradiction by making his narrator confess an utter susceptibility to feeling – by creating a narrator who can interpret every vibration as the symptom of a finally innocent sensibility.

SUGGESTIONS FOR FURTHER READING

The background, composition, and early reception of the works included in this volume are fully detailed in Arthur H. Cash's two-part biography, *Laurence Sterne: The Early and Middle Years* (London: Methuen, 1975) and *Laurence Sterne: The Later Years* (London: Methuen, 1986). Other indispensable sources are *Letters of Laurence Sterne*, edited by Lewis Perry Curtis (Oxford: Clarendon Press, 1935), and *Sterne: The Critical Heritage*, edited by Alan B. Howes (London: RKP, 1974). *The Shandean*, a handsome annual volume published since 1989 by the Laurence Sterne Trust, continues to reprint and describe a wealth of newly excavated primary material, much of it of immediate relevance to the contents of this volume. See, for example, Paul Franssen's account of some fascinating annotations in an early copy of *A Sentimental Journey*, '"Great Lessons of Political Instruction": The Earl of Clonmell Reads Sterne', *The Shandean*, 2 (1990), 152–201.

Critical interest in Sterne remains tied above all to *Tristram Shandy*, but recent years have also seen good studies of *A Sentimental Journey* in various contexts, both historical and theoretical. The following are recommended:

Battestin, Martin C., '*A Sentimental Journey* and the Syntax of Things', in *Augustan Worlds*, edited by J. C. Hilson, M. M. B. Jones and J. R. Watson (Leicester: Leicester University Press, 1978), pp. 223–39

Berthoud, Jacques, 'The Beggar in *A Sentimental Journey*', *The Shandean*, 3 (1991), 37–48

Brissenden, R. F., *Virtue in Distress: Studies in the Novel of Sentiment from Richardson to Sade* (London: Macmillan, 1974), pt. 2, ch. 3

Chadwick, Joseph, 'Infinite Jest: Interpretation in Sterne's *A Sentimental Journey*', *Eighteenth-Century Studies*, 12 (1978–9), 190–205

Dussinger, John A., 'Yorick and the "Eternal Fountain of our Feelings"', in *Psychology and Literature in the Eighteenth Century*, edited by C. Fox (New York: AMS Press, 1987), pp. 259–76

Loveridge, Mark, *Laurence Sterne and the Argument About Design* (London: Macmillan, 1982), ch. 7

McGlynn, Paul D., 'Sterne's Maria: Madness and Sentimentality', *Eighteenth-Century Life*, 3 (1976), 39–43

Markley, Robert, 'Sentimentality as Performance: Shaftesbury, Sterne, and the Theatrics of Virtue', in *The New Eighteenth Century*, edited by F. Nussbaum and L. Brown (London: Methuen, 1987), pp. 210–30

Mullan, John, *Sentiment and Sociability: The Language of Feeling in the Eighteenth Century* (Oxford: Clarendon Press, 1988), ch. 4

New, Melvyn, 'Proust's Influence on Sterne: Remembrance of Things to Come', *Modern Language Notes*, 103 (1988), 1031–55

Seidel, Michael, 'Narrative and Sterne's *A Sentimental Journey*', *Genre*, 18 (1985), 1–22

Todd, Janet, *Sensibility: An Introduction* (London: Methuen, 1986), ch. 6

Van Sant, Ann Jessie, *Eighteenth-Century Sensibility and the Novel: The Senses in Social Context* (Cambridge: Cambridge University Press, 1993), ch. 6

ACKNOWLEDGEMENTS

In preparing this edition, I have been greatly helped by the kind advice of many scholars and friends, among them Geoffrey Day, Cédric Gauthier, Judith Hawley, Ian Jack, John Mullan, Melvyn New, Tim Parnell, Peter Rickard, the Right Honourable Lord St John of Fawsley, Peter de Voogd, and many participants in the Sterne symposium held at the University of York in 1993. My debt to the published work of Arthur H. Cash, Gardner D. Stout, Jr, Kenneth Monkman, and the Florida editors of *Tristram Shandy* will be seen throughout. I am grateful to my colleagues in the Department of English at Royal Holloway, University of London, for making possible a sabbatical term in busy times, and to the Master and Fellows of Emmanuel College, Cambridge, for extending their hospitality throughout it.

TOM KEYMER

The editor and publishers would also like to thank the authors and publishers for permission to quote from the following editions:

Brissenden, R. F., *Virtues in Distress: Studies in the Novel of Sentiment from Richardson to Sade*, Macmillan, 1974

Cash, Arthur Hill, *Sterne's Comedy of Moral Sentiments: The Ethical Dimensions of the Journey*, Duquesne University Press, 1966

Loveridge, Mark, *Laurence Sterne and the Argument about Design*, Macmillan, 1982

Mullan, John, *Sentiment and Sociability: The Language of Feeling in the Eighteenth Century*, Clarendon Press, 1988

Reid, Ben, 'The Sad Hilarity of Sterne', Virginia Quarterly Review, 32, 1956

CLASSIC NOVELS
IN EVERYMAN

A SELECTION

The Way of All Flesh
SAMUEL BUTLER
A savagely funny odyssey from joyless duty to unbridled liberalism **£4.99**

Born in Exile
GEORGE GISSING
A rationalist's progress towards love and compromise in class-ridden Victorian England **£4.99**

David Copperfield
CHARLES DICKENS
One of Dickens' best-loved novels, brimming with humour **£3.99**

The Last Chronicle of Barset
ANTHONY TROLLOPE
Trollope's magnificent conclusion to his Barsetshire novels **£4.99**

He Knew He Was Right
ANTHONY TROLLOPE
Sexual jealousy, money and women's rights within marriage – a novel ahead of its time **£6.99**

Tess of the D'Urbervilles
THOMAS HARDY
The powerful, poetic classic of wronged innocence **£3.99**

Wuthering Heights and Poems
EMILY BRONTE
A powerful work of genius – one of the great masterpieces of literature **£3.50**

Tom Jones
HENRY FIELDING
The wayward adventures of one of literatures most likable heroes **£5.99**

The Master of Ballantrae and Weir of Hermiston
R. L. STEVENSON
Together in one volume, two great novels of high adventure and family conflict **£4.99**

£3.99

£2.99

£3.99

AVAILABILITY
All books are available from your local bookshop or direct from
**Littlehampton Book Services Cash Sales, 14 Eldon Way, LinesideEstate,
Littlehampton, West Sussex BN17 7HE.** PRICES ARE SUBJECT TO CHANGE.

To order any of the books, please enclose a cheque (in £ sterling) made payable to
Littlehampton Book Services, or phone your order through with credit card details (Access,
Visa or Mastercard) on 0903 721596 (24 hour answering service) stating card number and
expiry date. Please add £1.25 for package and postage to the total value of your order.

AMERICAN LITERATURE
IN EVERYMAN

A SELECTION

Selected Poems
HENRY LONGFELLOW
A new selection spanning the whole
of Longfellow's literary career **£7.99**

Typee
HERMAN MELVILLE
Melville's stirring debut, drawing
directly on his own adventures in the
South Sea **£4.99**

Billy Budd
and Other Stories
HERMAN MELVILLE
The compelling parable of
innocence destroyed by a fallen
world **£4.99**

The Scarlet Letter
NATHANIEL HAWTHORNE
The compelling tale of an
independent woman's struggle
against a crushing moral code **£3.99**

The Last of The Mohicans
JAMES FENIMORE COOPER
The classic tale of old America, full
of romantic adventure **£5.99**

The Red Badge of Courage
STEPHEN CRANE
A vivid portrayal of a young
soldier's experience of the
American Civil War **£2.99**

Essays and Poems
RALPH WALDO EMERSON
An indispensable edition celebrating
one of the most influential
American writers **£5.99**

The Federalist
HAMILTON, MADISON, AND JAY
Classics of political science, these
essays helped to found the
American Constitution **£6.99**

Leaves of Grass and
Selected Prose
WALT WHITMAN
The best of Whitman in one volume
£6.99

£5.99

£4.99

£4.99

WOMEN'S WRITING
IN EVERYMAN

A SELECTION

Female Playwrights of the Restoration
FIVE COMEDIES
Rediscovered literary treasures in a unique selection **£5.99**

The Secret Self
SHORT STORIES BY WOMEN
'A superb collection' *Guardian* **£4.99**

Short Stories
KATHERINE MANSFIELD
An excellent selection displaying the remarkable range of Mansfield's talent **£3.99**

Women Romantic Poets 1780-1830: An Anthology
Hidden talent from the Romantic era, rediscovered for the first time **£5.99**

Selected Poems
ELIZABETH BARRETT BROWNING
A major contribution to our appreciation of this inspiring and innovative poet **£5.99**

Frankenstein
MARY SHELLEY
A masterpiece of Gothic terror in its original 1818 version **£3.99**

The Life of Charlotte Brontë
MRS GASKELL
A moving and perceptive tribute by one writer to another **£4.99**

Vindication of the Rights of Woman and The Subjection of Women
MARY WOLLSTONECRAFT
AND J. S. MILL
Two pioneering works of early feminist thought **£4.99**

The Pastor's Wife
ELIZABETH VON ARNIM
A funny and accomplished novel by the author of *Elizabeth and Her German Garden* **£5.99**

£4.99

£2.99

£5.99

AVAILABILITY
All books are available from your local bookshop or direct from
**Littlehampton Book Services Cash Sales, 14 Eldon Way, LinesideEstate,
Littlehampton, West Sussex BN17 7HE.** PRICES ARE SUBJECT TO CHANGE.

To order any of the books, please enclose a cheque (in £ sterling) made payable to
Littlehampton Book Services, or phone your order through with credit card details (Access,
Visa or Mastercard) on 0903 721596 (24 hour answering service) stating card number and
expiry date. Please add £1.25 for package and postage to the total value of your order.

POETRY
IN EVERYMAN

A SELECTION

Silver Poets of the Sixteenth Century

EDITED BY
DOUGLAS BROOKS-DAVIES
A new edition of this famous
Everyman collection **£6.99**

Complete Poems

JOHN DONNE
The father of metaphysical verse in
this highly-acclaimed edition **£4.99**

Complete English Poems, Of Education, Areopagitica

JOHN MILTON
An excellent introduction to
Milton's poetry and prose **£6.99**

Selected Poems

JOHN DRYDEN
A poet's portrait of Restoration
England **£4.99**

Selected Poems

PERCY BYSSHE SHELLEY
'The essential Shelley' in one
volume **£3.50**

Women Romantic Poets 1780-1830: An Anthology

Hidden talent from the Romantic era,
rediscovered for the first time **£5.99**

Poems in Scots and English

ROBERT BURNS
The best of Scotland's greatest lyric
poet **£4.99**

Selected Poems

D. H. LAWRENCE
A newly-edited selection spanning
the whole of Lawrence's literary
career **£4.99**

The Poems

W. B. YEATS
Ireland's greatest lyric poet
surveyed in this ground-breaking
edition **£6.50**

£5.99

£4.99

£3.50

AVAILABILITY

All books are available from your local bookshop or direct from
**Littlehampton Book Services Cash Sales, 14 Eldon Way, LinesideEstate,
Littlehampton, West Sussex BN17 7HE.** PRICES ARE SUBJECT TO CHANGE.

To order any of the books, please enclose a cheque (in £ sterling) made payable to
Littlehampton Book Services, or phone your order through with credit card details (Access,
Visa or Mastercard) on 0903 721596 (24 hour answering service) stating card number and
expiry date. Please add £1.25 for package and postage to the total value of your order.

DRAMA
IN EVERYMAN

A SELECTION

Everyman and Medieval Miracle Plays
EDITED BY A. C. CAWLEY
A selection of the most popular medieval plays **£3.99**

Complete Plays and Poems
CHRISTOPHER MARLOWE
The complete works of this fascinating Elizabethan in one volume **£5.99**

Complete Poems and Plays
ROCHESTER
The most sexually explicit – and strikingly modern – writing of the seventeenth century **£5.99**

Restoration Plays
Five comedies and two tragedies representing the best of the Restoration stage **£7.99**

Female Playwrights of the Restoration: Five Comedies
Rediscovered literary treasures in a unique selection **£5.99**

Poems and Plays
OLIVER GOLDSMITH
The most complete edition of Goldsmith available **£4.99**

Plays, Poems and Prose
J. M. SYNGE
The most complete edition of Synge available **£6.99**

Plays, Prose Writings and Poems
OSCAR WILDE
The full force of Wilde's wit in one volume **£4.99**

A Doll's House/The Lady from the Sea/The Wild Duck
HENRIK IBSEN
A popular selection of Ibsen's major plays **£3.99**

£2.99

£2.99

£2.99

AVAILABILITY

All books are available from your local bookshop or direct from
Littlehampton Book Services Cash Sales, 14 Eldon Way, LinesideEstate, Littlehampton, West Sussex BN17 7HE. PRICES ARE SUBJECT TO CHANGE.

To order any of the books, please enclose a cheque (in £ sterling) made payable to Littlehampton Book Services, or phone your order through with credit card details (Access, Visa or Mastercard) on 0903 721596 (24 hour answering service) stating card number and expiry date. Please add £1.25 for package and postage to the total value of your order.

SHORT STORY COLLECTIONS
IN EVERYMAN

A SELECTION

**The Secret Self
Short Stories by Women**
'A superb collection' *Guardian* **£4.99**

**Selected Short Stories
and Poems**
THOMAS HARDY
The best of Hardy's Wessex in a
unique selection **£4.99**

**The Best of
Sherlock Holmes**
ARTHUR CONAN DOYLE
All the favourite adventures in one
volume **£4.99**

**Great Tales of Detection
Nineteen Stories**
Chosen by Dorothy L. Sayers **£3.99**

Short Stories
KATHERINE MANSFIELD
A selection displaying the
remarkable range of Mansfield's
writing **£3.99**

Selected Stories
RUDYARD KIPLING
Includes stories chosen to reveal the
'other' Kipling **£4.50**

**The Strange Case of
Dr Jekyll and Mr Hyde
and Other Stories**
R. L. STEVENSON
An exciting selection of gripping
tales from a master of suspense **£3.99**

**Modern Short Stories 2:
1940-1980**
Thirty-one stories from the greatest
modern writers **£3.50**

**The Day of Silence and
Other Stories**
GEORGE GISSING
Gissing's finest stories, available for
the first time in one volume **£4.99**

Selected Tales
HENRY JAMES
Stories portraying the tensions
between private life and the outside
world **£5.99**

£4.99

£6.99

AVAILABILITY
All books are available from your local bookshop or direct from
**Littlehampton Book Services Cash Sales, 14 Eldon Way, LinesideEstate,
Littlehampton, West Sussex BN17 7HE.** PRICES ARE SUBJECT TO CHANGE.

To order any of the books, please enclose a cheque (in £ sterling) made payable to
Littlehampton Book Services, or phone your order through with credit card details (Access,
Visa or Mastercard) on 0903 721596 (24 hour answering service) stating card number and
expiry date. Please add £1.25 for package and postage to the total value of your order.